Jackals

By

Stuart R Brogan

Copyright © 2017 Stuart R Brogan

All Artwork Copyright © 2017 Stuart R Brogan

Printed Edition January 2017

All rights reserved. No part of this publication may be reproduced, stored in a retrieval system, or transmitted in any form or by any means without the prior permission of the publisher, nor be otherwise circulated in any form of binding or cover other than that which it has been published and without a similar condition being imposed on the subsequent purchaser.

For all correspondences appertaining to this work please contact the author direct

stuartrbrogan@aol.co.uk

Facebook - Stuart R Brogan Author

ACKNOWLEDGEMENTS

First and foremost I would like to thank you, the reader, for purchasing this book. Without you I wouldn't be doing what I am doing.

To all those who have supported me, reviewed my work, given assistance or just shared a beer with. Thank you.

To my family for their continued support.

To my wife Fiona, the greatest shield maiden a man could have,

I love you.

For my Father, RIP.

ONE

Sunday, 2228 hrs
"Damnit!"

P.C Howard Garrett glared at the crossword puzzle before him and thought to himself that he was getting old and possibly losing his memory. There was no other explanation why he couldn't get this word. After all these years exercising and training his intellectual muscle he was starting to show signs of slowing down. He could feel it, the dulling of his weapon, the blunting of his most prized ability. He sighed and stabbed his biro at the offending clue in the hopes the answer would present itself. It did not; in fact it only seemed to elude him more, to the point of taunting his inner genius. He took a hefty gulp from his coffee cup, wincing as the liquid burned his lips. Glancing up over his glasses he stared at the plain white clock situated on the wall opposite, his academic self-flagellation momentarily giving way to the unbearable fact that it was half-past ten at night and he wouldn't be finishing his shift until seven a.m. His mood was not getting any better and by the looks of it nor was the torrential downpour outside.

Once again Garrett's attention was drawn back to the life and death struggle before him. He smiled as his thoughts wandered back to winning Avon and Somerset's Police Quiz championship three years in a row. His head had swelled with the attention his superiors lavished upon him, his chest fit to burst with pride as he held aloft his prize and the feeling of self-worth when hailed a hero upon his triumphant return to his station. Those cheating Taunton lads had come close but fell at the last hurdle, giving Garrett the title and Wells Station the title of being the "brainy" ones. The local rag had even done a piece on him, topped off with a picture of him in uniform clutching his award. In a bizarre twist of irony, even those Neanderthals in the armed response unit revelled in the kudos and took great delight in rubbing the noses of Bridgwater nick in the fact that this "little" station outperformed the big boys. Some might have thought this a small victory but amongst a non-descript and uneventful police career with nothing of real accolade or accomplishment to brag about, it was the best he could hope for. In truth, it had been the pinnacle of his crime-fighting career. Of course he was secretly annoyed with himself for failing the detective exam twice in a row, and for the time he got reprimanded for forgetting his sergeant's exam date, but after thirty years as a copper and at the ripe old age of fifty-three, Howard Garrett was officially ready to retire. He'd live out his twilight years tending to his garden in the company of his trusted companion, Tess the Labrador. He subconsciously puffed out his chest, his inner voice heroically stating that they could take his badge and uniform but could never take the pride he felt, for not only serving his community, but of beating those city lads in Bristol at Scrabble.

The sudden gust of wind and mournful creak of the station door opening snapped Garrett back to his late night reality. He raised his head to greet the new arrival but before he could speak he felt the cold, razor-sharp blade pressed to his throat. He stared, paralysed with fear at the figure before him, his mind racing at the unfolding events. He could see two other figures dressed in black slowly enter the small station foyer behind the main assailant, their mere presence commanding attention, inducing fear. The figures stood motionless, staring unflinchingly at the policeman.

"What do you ..." Garrett didn't get to finish the sentence. The swiftness of the slash was so quick he didn't feel the knife sever his carotid artery. A fountain of blood erupted from the policeman's throat, showering the desk and walls with the crimson fluid. Stumbling backwards he clasped his throat, slipping on the spreading puddle on the floor beneath him. He reached out with one hand in an attempt to steady himself but missed the desk, knocking his coffee cup and sending it tumbling to the floor, shattering amongst the carnage and maelstrom. All the while the three figures stood motionless, their gaze fixed upon him. He tumbled to the floor, landing on his back, blood soaking into his shirt and trousers, his mind racing, trying to remember his first aid training. He could feel himself slipping away; he had to act fast, no time to delay. His eyes started to weep and myopically he stared to the ceiling as he began to drift into unconsciousness.

Through his tears and blurred vision he could see his attacker leaning over him, smiling. His companions flanked him, all of whom looked upon the gruesome scene with delight, relishing the final moments before the life force was extinguished. As Garrett descended into the dark oblivion he heard his attacker speak.

"I want you to suffer."

TWO

2236 hrs

The three figures stood in silence, gazing proudly at the body of the gore-covered policeman. Their eyes were transfixed at the lifeless corpse which only moments before had been a living, breathing human but now had been reduced to nothing more than a slab of butchered meat. The knifeman wiped the blood from the blade on his dark shirt, staring at the shiny metal, admiring the elegant lines and forged workmanship, a thing of true beauty. An artist must look after his tools. After a minute of admiration he slowly turned to his companions. At 6'2" he was imposing. He always had been. His taut muscular frame was disguised under his loose fitting clothes. His short, swept-back, dark brown hair trimmed and tidy. He commanded respect. All his life he had been a leader—never a follower—and always knew he was destined for greatness. But unlike those who struggled and toiled amidst the ruins of the fake world with its superficial distractions, craving adulation and public approval from their peers, his work was to be carried out in the shadows away from the prying eyes of the everyday man and woman. Its final momentous results however were meant to be shared, to be marvelled at, designed to be a spotlight thrust upon the dark recesses of the sheep that stumbled through a mediocre and pointless life. He knew only the elite few would truly understand the message he was bestowing upon the world and this was only right, for not everyone should be allowed to comprehend fully the magnitude of his actions and to attain the ultimate knowledge. Only the pure of heart and those that possessed clarity of vision could see the mastery in his art.

He locked stares with one of his silent companions, a female. The girl shifted uncomfortably under his piercing gaze.

The leader spoke, his voice low and articulate, "Be swift. Be silent and bring me his head. Kill everyone you encounter, for they are carrion and deserve no mercy."

All three smiled in mutual agreement at the thought of what was about to begin. The girl reached under her black parka jacket and retrieved a small axe, running her finger along the blade. She winced as it cut her digit; lost in her own world she intently watched as a trickle of blood flowed down her hand. The other male, silent, also momentarily lost in his own thoughts stood motionless clutching a baseball bat with nails protruding along the end. He closed his eyes and began to hum to himself, stretching his neck and lifting his head to the skies, tightening his grip on the handle until his hands ached. At an unspoken command the girl and second attacker leapt over the counter and pushed through the double doors leading into the inner confines of the police station. The Alpha stood astride the body and dipped his fingers into the congealing pool of blood, then set to work. He had a message to send.

2239 hrs

WPC Kenning hefted the freshly boiled kettle and carefully poured the steaming liquid into her Bristol FC coffee mug. She was looking forward to this. It had been a busy shift so far and she desperately needed the caffeine to refuel her flagging enthusiasm. Three shouts regarding domestic abuse and a crazy cat lady who had locked herself out of her flat all before eleven and she still had the joy of the local pubs and clubs calling last orders, followed by the raucous exodus of vomit and alcohol-drenched patrons into the streets. She was only half-way through her graveyard shift and could already feel her body ache and muscles throb from the weight of her belt and body armour. It wasn't shaping up to be the career for which she had hoped. Her mind wandered back to watching *The Bill* in her younger years. She had decided that this was what she wanted to do with her life, reminiscing she especially had been impressed by the fact that they could solve a murder in half an hour. She sighed as she gently stirred her coffee. Being stationed at Wells wasn't going to be the thrill ride she was hoping for when she joined the force a year ago. She had wanted to be based in Bristol, the big city with constant action and the hub for front line police work. When she learned of her first posting she had gone out that night and gotten wasted with her friends, some of which had laughed at her, telling her that the farmer's tractors and Somerset sheep would sleep easy knowing she was on patrol. It had taken a full year for her to be able to smile, let alone laugh at that remark. Her ego was a slow healer.

She finished stirring her coffee, placed the spoon on the counter then turned to walk over to the table where she could enjoy her ham salad sandwich in peace. The force of the axe embedding into her forehead stopped her instantly, its momentum crushing the front of her skull and slicing into her brain. Her body shook in shock and convulsed as the axe was tugged free and rained down for another blow. Blood cascaded down her face and across her crisp white shirt, her bowels opening as she fell. She was dead before she hit the floor. Her female attacker whooped with excitement as her nostrils filled with the odour of excrement and blood. She closed her eyes and began to touch herself, breathing in the fumes of her kill, her long sandy blonde hair dripping with blood and sweat clinging to her forehead like crimson tentacles. How she loved this part. She especially revelled in the way they seemed so surprised that a girl of 5'4" and of slim build could kill so easily regardless of the physical size of her victim. Rosie had always been underestimated even when she used to attend anti-hunt protests. She would stand her ground against the huntsman's thugs and vicious farmers who thought that killing animals for sport was fun and that these stinking vegetarian hippies wouldn't fight back. Of course this was not the case, for Rosie did fight back and had enjoyed watching the hunters' expressions when she embedded her axe firstly in their groins, then their faces. She had enjoyed watching them bleed out, their bright red tunics soaking up their own blood as opposed to the blood of an innocent animal. She started to get mad. How could anyone kill a defenceless animal for sport? What kind of sick bastard gets a kick out of acts of unimaginable cruelty? Rosie shook herself in an attempt to dislodge these horrible thoughts; there was work to be done. She stood on the WPC's head and tugged at the axe that was firmly wedged in the policewoman's skull. With a little effort and snapping of bone it came free. Rosie turned and headed for the canteen door. She was happy again and wanted to find more people to play with.

2243 hrs

PC Turner remained silent straining his ear towards the door, convinced he had heard something strange outside of the interview room.

"There's nothing there, Steve," said Detective Constable Carl Devlin, sitting next to the tense PC.

"Sorry Sir. I thought I heard a scream," Devlin chuckled, rubbing his forehead. "It's just the telly in the staff canteen. Bloody idiots must be watching a horror movie or some useless talent show."

PC Turner turned to face the DC. "I'm sure your right, Sir." He cracked a smile at the DC's retort regarding the state of weekend night TV in the UK.

"Right then, where were we?" Devlin looked up, directing his question to the figure sat opposite who stared back at the two police officers, unblinking and silent. His scruffy jeans were dirty and well worn, his torso clad in a tatty Iron Maiden t-shirt, his long straggly hair grimy and sweaty. Dark rings under his eyes and a pale, gaunt face gave the impression of an illness or dependency. The DC studied the interviewee. He looked a mess mused Devlin, a bloody smack-head for sure, a useless dole-grabbing waste of space that did nothing but create paperwork and run rings around the judicial system. That being said he didn't recognise him. Wells was a small place and the DC had never had anything to do with this man. It was probable that this guy was from Bristol but yet even though he looked like a prime candidate for *Crime Watch* there had been no hits on the PNC which, considering his appearance was rather puzzling. Granted, they didn't have a name and when arrested he had no form of ID on him but nothing popped up regarding finger prints; in fact it appeared he had no finger prints at all. After three hours of questioning he was no further forward in their investigation. To others less enlightened it might have seemed to be a straightforward case of theft—that, and him being a first-rate social fuck-up— but Devlin couldn't shake the feeling that there was something peculiar about this prisoner and after all his years on the force he had learned to trust his gut instinct. To DC Devlin this was indeed a mystery, a mystery he was determined to unravel not just because it bugged him but also because his shift was ending soon and he just wanted to get to his bed.

"Okay mystery man; let's go through it once again. Who are you?"

The gaunt man remained stoic in his refusal to talk. Devlin grimaced, his annoyance starting to show, "Listen funny man, it's late and I'm tired." He glanced towards his colleague who was intently staring at their guest, unaware of the DC's growing frustration.

"I am no one of importance, not at least to you, Mr Policeman."

Devlin held his gaze and slowly and deliberately delivered his response to the cryptic statement. "Is that so, mystery man? Is this the part when you inform me that you are Christ resurrected and that earthly laws need not apply to you, or more likely, you're a raving smack-head who's taken too much Bolivian marching powder and you are, in fact, a raving nut job?"

Gaunt Man smirked, "You think you are safe tucked up in your castle, Mr Policeman? You think that badge gives you the power to wield your world view upon me?" With a sudden movement he stretched open his arms and gestured the expanse of the room. "You think *this* room will save you from what's coming?" Slowly he lowered his arms and placed them on the table, once again returning to silence.

DC Devlin remained calm, slowly started to smile, finally breaking into a hearty laugh, clapping his hands in mock applause.

"Did you hear that, PC Turner? We are all doomed and will die a horrible death at the hands of the rapture that is soon to be upon us, for the Lord has spoken unto us and we must repent or suffer the consequences." Devlin glared at Gaunt Man. "Your idle threats don't scare me, little man," he rasped.

If the interviewee was fazed by the DC's aggressive tone he didn't show it. He stared unflinchingly at the DC. It was Devlin who broke first, his scowl slipping slightly, his tone slowly descending into cynical yet somewhat nervous laughter. Gaunt Man grinned, knowing full well he had unnerved the policeman. Psychological warfare and the power it commanded had captivated him from an early age. It had become his addiction, his weapon of choice. He enjoyed inflicting its virtues upon his enemies, watching them crumble from within and finally bending to his will. Physically he may not be able to win a battle or confrontation but through patience and practice he had developed a natural ability to get inside his opponent's head and bring even the strongest of them to their knees. It just so happened it was working faster on the victim who now sat before him and in truth he was enjoying tormenting this particular victim more than usual.

Across from him PC Turner was stunned by his superior's flippant tone and couldn't believe his response to the interviewee's threats. He smiled, shifting uncomfortably, all the while referring to the official rule book regarding the ethical treatment of those in custody. Somehow this seemed like a major deviation from official protocol. But then again, who was he to second-guess his superior's interview technique? He decided to remain silent and not share his thoughts. Once the laughter had subsided Devlin returned his attention to Gaunt Man, this time in a less threatening manner.

"Enough of the games. You've had your fun, now it's time to get with the program and come back to the real world. If you won't tell us your name, tell us why you were stealing fuel from Morrison's garage and who were your friends in the car that fled the scene."

Gaunt Man chortled under his breath, "You will meet my friends soon enough, in fact sooner than you think, Mr Policeman."

Devlin was starting to lose his temper again and all three men knew it. The DC was just about to fire back when a knock at the door interrupted the escalating exchange.

Devlin glared at the door, shouting his reply, "What!" No answer. Devlin growled under his breath, his annoyance steadily growing, "Turner, go see who the hell that is."

PC Turner immediately jumped to his feet and headed for the exit, snatching at the handle, yanking the door inwards to confront the person whose timing was somewhat impeccable, albeit a welcome respite from the interview. The sight of an empty hallway stopped Turner in his tracks and for a split second the policeman started to panic. A feeling of impending doom swept over him like a tidal wave of negativity.

"Well, who the hell is it?" snapped Devlin from inside the interview room.

PC Turner turned to face his superior "Nobody, Sir. There's no one here." As Turner returned his gaze to the corridor the force of the nail-infused baseball bat caught him square in the face, the nails puncturing his right eye, left cheek and forehead. His body trembled with the impact of the colossal weapon; his legs buckled, sending him crashing to the floor. The last thing he saw was a stocky looking male dressed in black smiling at him, reaching down to retrieve his face-embedded weapon. DC Devlin spun around, facing the bloody conflict at the doorway. A rough looking man dressed in black stepped over the threshold calmly clutching his weapon and smiling, eyes fixed on the DC, the battered body of the PC at his feet. Devlin started to back away, conscious of the other occupant in the room but not wanting to tackle the killer who was now inside the room, blocking the doorway. He heard a female's voice, "Coo wee" then giggling. A young girl slowly appeared from behind the baseball bat wielding man, a bloodied axe in her right hand.

"Hello, Mr Copper," she sneered, waving the axe at him. Devlin was in the corner now, the interviewee to his right. He glanced at him. He was grinning at the terrified DC.

"Warned you about meeting my friends didn't I, Mr Policeman?"

Devlin's mind was a swirling mass of hysteria. Who the hell were these people and what did they want? He was rooted to the spot, he eyes bulging with terror at the sight of what was unfolding. He heard footsteps in the corridor and as one Mr Baseball Bat and Axe Girl parted to allow a third person to enter the room. Devlin stared at the tall, well-built stranger, a knife clasped in one hand. He was obviously the leader but not like the other three. He seemed educated and full of purpose, a sense of calculated menace emanating from his very pores.

He slowly turned to face Devlin's prisoner, "Hello, Brother. Are you ready?"

Gaunt Man smiled, "Yes, Brother. I am ready."

Devlin looked on, unable to neither speak nor move. He knew he was going to die. There was no way out of this.

In unison all three assailants lifted their arms and said as one, "It is time."

Without warning the three armed intruders rushed towards Gaunt Man, who was standing with his eyes closed, arms outstretched, a look of acceptance and resignation on his face, but there was something else. Devlin could swear there was a smile and a look of absolute serenity. He thought about making a run for the door but couldn't get his limbs to move. In a flurry of a nails, axe and knife the three killers decimated Gaunt Man. Blood sprayed around the walls, floor and ceiling whilst brains and internal organs spilled to the floor as blow after blow ripped the victim's body apart. They laughed hysterically as flesh was torn from bone and eyeballs ripped from their sockets. Only when his head finally came free did they slow the ferocity of their attack. Devlin looked on in horror as they turned their attention to him. All of them were grinning, their clothes saturated in blood and sweat, the smell of euphoric bloodlust permeating the confines of the small interview room. The DC soiled himself at the anticipation of the imminent onslaught. They moved forward together as one, raised their weapons, and then they were upon him.

THREE

Sunday, 2215 hrs

"Are you actually listening to me, Jesse?"

The statement stunned her. In fact, the conversation had been a whirlwind of emotions ranging from disbelief to downright anger. Unfortunately Jesse Reid had become accustomed to this kind of conversation and sadly it was not uncommon these days. She secretly harboured resentment when this side of him would rear its ugly head. Being protective was one thing but this was starting to grate on her nerves. She thought it best not to rise to the question and remained silent, instead returning to the important task of poking her salad with her fork, aimlessly pushing it around her plate in an attempt to deescalate the brewing argument. They had been in the Black Swan for two hours and had arrived in good spirits, eager to celebrate their wedding anniversary but as they ate it was apparent that her husband was in one of "those" moods. After sixteen years of marriage she had learned when to stay quiet and when to speak her mind. This wasn't because he was violent or controlling, far from it. Damien had been the first nice, straight down the line normal man to show her any attention without the prerequisite of expecting something in return. He had been kind and patient when she had been at her most vulnerable and insecure, unlike her previous forays into the turbulent world of relationships. She knew he loved her with all his heart and would do anything for her; however, he got jealous easily and hated any other man lavishing her with unsolicited attention or even paying her the slightest compliment.

To make matters worse, despite all his qualities he was easily intimidated and loathed confrontation. In fact she got the feeling that every other man around could sense it like an alpha wolf senses a subordinate, one growl and he would retreat, his tail between his legs. Jesse had her own reasons for avoiding confrontation but as the man in the relationship she was under the impression that he should be the strong one. Alas, it was not to be. To add insult to injury was the fact that Damien wouldn't say anything to the male in question but would stay silent and approach the subject once they were alone. He aimed his pent-up frustration at her, hence the current conversation which had commenced at least an hour after the young barman had paid her a little too much attention when serving their meal.

"You're not seeing this from my perspective, are you babe?" he asked. "I know you think I'm over-protective, maybe even possessive but it's just that I love you so much and hate other men drooling over you." He paused for a second, awaiting a response. There was none. "I know you think I have a problem with my jealousy but I am trying,

Love…" he let the sentence trail off, paused then spoke again, this time in a subdued tone, "I'm sorry, Love."

Jesse looked up at her husband and with a soft sigh placed her fork on her plate. "Why do you have to spoil a perfectly pleasant evening with these pointless arguments? You know damn well I only have eyes for you." She reached across the table and took his left hand in hers and gave a little squeeze, their own private way of telling each other of their love.

He smiled, acknowledging the signal given. He lifted his pint of real ale in his right hand. "Here's to us then, my love" taking a swig of brown liquid.

She let go, retracting her own hand to her glass of white wine to reciprocate the gesture. "To us. Now and forever." She took a gulp sensing the argument had been diffused, and an inward sigh of relief engulfed her. The conversation had come full circle as per normal and now they were free to enjoy their evening once again. Maybe she was being too harsh in her feelings towards her husband. Maybe it was in fact her fault that this conversation was doomed to repeat itself. A sudden cheer erupted from across the pub, shaking her from her musings. A darts team hollered and cheered as their team were victorious over the visiting side. Jesse and Damien glanced at each other and in unison chuckled at the timing of the celebration, once again helping the tension to subside.

"Do you think they were cheering for us?" asked Damien.

"Let's pretend they were, shall we?"

They laughed together. These were the moments Jesse loved the most. The little nuances, secret little whims and codes that couples share when they are alone. Some of her friends were envious of their relationship as were some of his. They belonged together and despite the fact that he wasn't exactly a knight in shining armour she would always look upon him as her hero and as such had to put aside the little things that irritated her. Nobody was perfect, after all. Jesse glanced to the window. The rain was relentless, heavy droplets bouncing off the glass before ricocheting into the night. They both loved this pub. It was homely and inviting, a place where a weary traveller could enter and feel well-received. A hearty meal, warm log fire and a range of real ales were offered in an Old English pub complete with wooden beams and Elizabethan booths. They had visited this pub for the last ten years and looked upon it as their second home. In fact Jesse had regularly fantasised about leaving her career as a dental receptionist to become a landlady of such an establishment. They had both come to look upon the Black Swan as a tranquil oasis amongst the droves of theme bars and trendy lounges dominating every town and city. She smiled to herself. The best part of living in Somerset was the traditional English Pub and the best part of living in Wells was they knew they would always be welcome at this particular watering hole. Another cheer erupted from the darts team, disrupting her nostalgia.

"Sounds like they are having a good time." Damien offered.

"So are we, aren't we?" retorted Jesse.

"We are indeed, and I get to go home with the most beautiful woman in here."

She blushed, basking in the compliment.

He glanced at his watch. "It's half-ten; I reckon it's time to make a move. You finished?"

She downed the remnants of her wine, tugged on her woolly hat and gathered her coat. "I presume you are settling the bill, kind Sir."

He smirked, then stuck out his tongue in playful rebuke.

"I'm glad you are not a high maintenance kind of girl, I might have forgotten my wallet."

She too stuck out her tongue, copying the playful banter. "Oh really?" she quipped. "I don't want to fleece you just yet." She got up, glancing back as she did, "That comes later if you are a bad boy." Winking, she headed for the door. "Don't forget to pay," she said without turning.

Damien laughed and was overwhelmed by how much he loved her. He gathered his jacket, pulled out his wallet and headed for the bar to pay the bill.

Jesse pulled up her collar and tugged on her woolly hat so that it was covering her forehead, her long black hair pulled tightly in a ponytail. For thirty-six years old she looked good, hence the attention from men, especially younger lads who fancied their luck with an older woman. Her frame was athletic and taut despite the fact she detested sports of any kind and at 5'10" gave the impression of a strong woman, but she felt like a fraud. When her friends tried Yoga she had declined; in fact she declined every invitation regarding physical exertion thrown at her. It seemed to be a running joke amongst her friends that she could remain skinny and fit without lifting a finger. Of course if they knew the truth they would be less than impressed. The secret of her perceived success was that she suffered from severe depression; in fact she had suffered in silence since her early years. Four psychologists and umpteen tests had revealed a plethora of triggers for her self-loathing. Bullying, low self-esteem, feelings of worthlessness all played a part in her daily battle. Of course no one would ever give a definitive answer. It was only now that she had come to terms with the fact that it all stemmed from her relationship with her father, or lack thereof. Every day was a fight to stay positive, every night a prerequisite for another day. She smiled, musing on the old adage, 'that which doesn't kill you makes you stronger'. Outwardly she projected confidence and but deep inside she was still the scared little girl she had always been—she had just become better at hiding it.

Bathed in the dull neon light she stood under the smoking shelter outside the front door of the Black Swan, urgently rummaging in her pockets to find the small pouch of rolling tobacco and a lighter. She chortled to herself when she realised that as a grown woman of thirty-six years she was trying to have a sneaky cigarette before her husband came out and caught her red-handed. She rolled the cigarette, popped it into her mouth and with one hand shielding the flame lit it, inhaling a hefty amount of smoke. She gave a little cough, then exhaled the excess. She had been trying to give up for years but had never been able to break the one-month barrier. Of course Damien hated it and was always nagging at her to give up but for Jesse it wasn't just an act of rebellion against political correctness and the nanny state, it was one of life's little pleasures that distracted her mind from wandering into the dark abyss of her mental illness. She stretched out her arm, holding the offending item aloft.

"And so the rebellion continues," she announced to the empty carpark. Giggling, she took another drag then quickly tossed it to the ground, grinding it underfoot as to discard completely the evidence of her socially unacceptable crime. The rain was showing no signs of easing, large puddles of water littered the pub carpark amongst the swath of luxury cars that had chauffeured the clientele to their evening's frivolities. Money talked in Wells. It was famed for being the smallest city in England as well as a hotbed of Masonic activity. Not that she was bothered by this nor for that matter involved with such organisations, but she did harbour a secret suspicion that her boss was a closet Mason partial to dodgy handshakes and clandestine meetings. She sniggered, amused by her own dramatic imagination. A wave of laughter and music swept across the quiet carpark as Damien exited the pub, immediately diminishing as the heavy door closed behind him. Pulling up his collar he ran across the tarmac, desperately jumping puddles while doing so, eager to limit the amount of water splashing up his legs. Jesse giggled, watching him failing miserably.

"What's so funny?" he asked as he shook himself off, happy that he was under shelter. "Nothing," she said, fighting back her stifled giggling.
"Right then little lady, let's get you back home before you turn into some sort of pumpkin..." He shook himself once again, "Or some sort of drowned mammal."

Jesse took his hand and stared up the quiet street.

"Remind me again why you parked the car a mile away?"

Damien let out an exaggerated sigh. "Thought you could do with the exercise," he quipped. Jesse playfully punched him on the arm. Feigning injury he started to walk, pulling her along behind him.

"Come on woman, it's dark and I need you to protect me." Hand in hand they left the confines of the smoking shed, determined not to let the unrelenting barrage of rain and cold night air dampen their spirits. It had been a good evening after all despite the rehashing of old issues. Contented, they made their way up the dark, lightless street towards the centre of the city.

"At least it's eased off," said Jesse, squeezing her husband's arm as she and Damien strolled across the small park. Sporadically placed iron lamps cast islands of light amongst the wet grass and walkways. The park was surrounded by domineering period houses and lay in the shadow of the city's cathedral. Jesse had always thought it seemed different at night, like a scene from a Dickensian play or Hollywood movie—by day a busy thoroughfare but by night a picturesque scene of architecture and affluence.

Only the wealthy could afford to dwell in such a location but a girl could dream.

Damien smiled, pulling her close and whispering in her ear, "Sods law really, eh babe? Just as we get near the car and already soaking wet."

She laughed, inwardly happy that the night really was ending on a high note.

"What time are you working tomorrow?" Damien asked.

"Jenny swapped shifts. I don't have to be in until midday, so I get to have a lie in."

"All right for some," he quipped, secretly annoyed that he had to get up at 6 a.m. to travel to London for a business meeting.

"Don't worry; I'll have your dinner on the table for when you get home like the dutiful wife I am."

"As well you should," he retorted. "Remember, I'm not a fan of high-maintenance women."

As they left the park they headed down Cullcott Road, left at Madison Terrace then down the final stretch towards Morrison's carpark were they had left the car. The carpark was empty, bar three other vehicles and their modest Ford Mondeo. Damien fumbled in his pockets for his keys while Jesse checked her mobile phone, the cold harsh glow illuminating her face and upper torso. The sudden female voice took them both by surprise. They turned to face their visitor and immediately wished they hadn't.

FOUR

2249 hrs

He grinned, nodding slowly in agreement with his inner voice as he admired his artistic endeavour freshly painted upon the foyer wall; the heavy smell of iron clung to the air, his hands crimson. He enjoyed this part. The comedown after the hunt and the serene calmness he felt after the adrenaline had dispersed. Silently and discreetly he reached into his trouser pocket with one hand and started gently nudging his swollen member through the soft material. Eyes closed, he rubbed himself out of sight of his subordinates, recalling the look on the policeman's face as he sliced his throat. He ejaculated at the point when the policeman died. It excited him and he wanted more—more carrion to send on their way to the Void.

When he had finished and gained his composure he slowly looked around the room at his team, each submerged in their own ritualistic intoxications. Rosie stood close by, cleaning her axe with a scrap of material, diligently rubbing the blade to make sure it was spotless after the night's activities.

"You've been quiet tonight Denny, what's the matter, not having fun?" she said without looking up. Denny was sat perched on the front desk, his fingers rubbing the blood-encrusted nails protruding from his baseball bat. He remained silent, choosing not to engage with Rosie or her stupid banter.

"For a man with your propensity for violence you sure are a miserable git," she quipped. He ignored her. She decided to turn her attention to the leader, annoyed that Denny wasn't playing or taking the bait. "What do you reckon, Felix?"

Felix paused, then turned to face her, "I think we did well. I think we should be proud of tonight's performance for it was magnificent, a true work of art and I am eager for the world to see what we have done here. Well done, my friends. I am proud of you."

Both Denny and Rosie listened intently to their leader, longing for his words of praise, hypnotically staring at him, awaiting his next commands. He gently nodded, acknowledging their devotion, then returned his attention to the wall and his artwork. This was the most crucial part of the evening's festivities, nothing less than perfection would be tolerated. He gazed lovingly at the red triangle smeared in blood, three vertical lines running through it with one horizontal line across the middle, his calling card to the world. His sigil. To some it may seem like a mere ploy to gain attention from the world's media, those paparazzi parasites hungry to feed on the misfortune of the slain, but to the select few it was an awakening, an acknowledgement of a higher power. Visual confirmation that the word was spreading and a new age beckoned.

"Well at least the rain has stopped. I hate the bloody rain."

Rosie looked up, shocked that Denny had spoken, and in her mind about something so trivial. Denny remained engrossed in cleaning his weapon, unaware that Rosie was staring at him.

"After two weeks of saying nothing and all that has transpired this evening the first thing you want to talk about is the bloody weather?" She slowly shook her head in sarcastic disappointment. "That's all you got to say, eh Denny? That's the apex of your intellectual conversational skills?" she sniggered "You are one strange bloke. I don't know what scares me more, the fact that you are a raging head case or that you have the brain capacity of a cabbage," she started to laugh.

Denny raised his head, glaring at his female companion, unimpressed by her patronising barrage. He despised her. In fact he despised them all, not just those in the immediate vicinity but the whole human race. They were nothing more than cattle to him. All those years working on building sites and having to interact with them on a daily basis made him feel physically sick. The torment of his imagination regarding the ways he would kill them and make them suffer yet unable to act out his true desires had been unbearable. Every day he ached to reveal his true self upon the drones that surrounded him. He would sit alone in the canteen watching his work colleagues tell obscene jokes, talk about football and letch over scantily-clad celebrities. They had tried to include him but he politely declined. Luckily being six feet tall and eighteen stone had helped dissuade the inevitable workshop banter. He had a presence and even though he was quiet, he gave off the impression that he could handle himself. And so it went on year after year, the banality of life surrounded by soulless meat. For so long he had kept his inner cravings secret. He didn't drink nor seek out the affections of the opposite sex. He had dedicated himself to the ideal of being absolutely single-minded and now it was time to release all those years' worth of repression and claim his rewards for his abstinence and no one was going to stand in his way, especially a stupid little bitch and her toy axe.

He slowly rose to his feet, as did Rosie, locking stares and hefting their weapons, neither one looking to back down or show any weakness in the presence of their leader. Despite his personal feelings Denny understood that Felix was the only one that could be useful with regards to attaining his immortality. Felix had recruited him six months ago and had saved him from the drudgery of his ordinary life and as such Denny owed him a little in the way of mercy. That's why he had decided to kill him last when the time came, but until then he would play the part of dutiful follower. The girl, however, was a different matter. He was willing to mutilate that goby little whore right now. Felix looked on like a proud parent secretly wondering who would win such an altercation. Rosie was young, agile, quick and utterly ruthless. Denny on the other hand was strong, powerful and a sheer mass of brutality. Whomever the victor, the battle would indeed be bloody. He raised his hand. They both looked his way and immediately both understood the command. Weapons were lowered and once again they went about their own business, attending the cleaning of blades and metal.

The silence was broken by Felix, "We have much work ahead of us, we must not turn on each other for we are family and even though we may argue and disagree we must all remember the greater service to which we have pledged ourselves."

All three nodded in agreement. Rosie glanced up, a look of excitement on her face, "Who is next? Is it my turn, Felix?"

"I think I should choose," retorted Denny before Felix could reply, knowing full well his remark would wind up the already volatile Rosie.

She shot him a scathing glare. He giggled. Felix also laughed, as a father would laugh at his offspring's amusing remark.

"Of course Rosie, it's your turn now, so choose wisely."

She jumped up, waving her axe around her head, cheering like an excited child. Pointing at Denny she stuck her tongue out.

"Did you hear that, Mr Cabbage? It's my turn to choose!" She spun around on the spot, dancing for joy at her good fortune.

Denny returned to his weapon, imagining the day

he would kill her, slowly. Felix glanced at the clock on the wall. 11 p.m. It was time to leave this place for their work was complete and there may be many miles to travel before they found suitable candidates for the next hunt. He slammed his fist on the counter as to gather attention from his followers.

"It's time to leave, friends."

Both Rosie and Denny gathered their weapons and jackets, then followed Felix to the main entrance. Felix opened the door and let them pass. He slowly gazed lovingly around the room one final time. He closed his eyes and inhaled deeply the stench of his evening's work. Smiling, he turned quickly and walked out into the night air.

Rosie stood on the front stonework steps rolling a cigarette whilst Denny looked to the heavens, pleased it had ceased raining. Felix stood admiring the calmness of the evening and the smell of petrichor. It had been warm lately and the heavy downpour had been a welcome relief to the plants and trees. He had always been a keen gardener and as a child loved the great outdoors. It was always after a large storm that he felt the most alive.

"Where to now then, Felix?" asked Rosie.

"Where do you think we should go, little sister?" he replied.

She blushed under the responsibility of making such a monumental decision. She took a drag on her cigarette and let her mind wander to find a suitable answer. Her ears perked up as she heard voices. She glanced at her companions; they too had heard the same. She smiled and ran down the steps towards the road. She stopped, cocking her head to one side to determine where the voices were coming from. They were close. She crouched behind a thick bush and slowly parted the branches to get a good view of what lay beyond. Illuminated under a street lamp she could see two people, one male and one female, slowly walking to a car. Her view was abetted by the large Morrison's sign illuminating the puddles in the carpark. She turned to see Felix and Denny behind her. She gazed at Felix, grinning with childlike eyes, nodding, pleading for his blessing. Felix gently smiled and returned the nod, giving her permission to proceed. Denny tightened his grip on his baseball bat; he could feel his heart rate starting to speed up, adrenaline beginning to pump around his body. Rosie pushed through the hedge and silently crept up on her prey, crouching as she expertly stalked her quarry. When she was within ten feet of the couple she slowly raised her axe, its metal work gleaming from the neon shop sign and scattered water.

"I hope you had a lovely evening because it's over now. In fact, everything is over for you now."

The man and woman spun around to face the unexpected voice. The female's eyes were drawn to the axe first and she started to shake; the man stood silently, unable to comprehend the situation that was unfolding in front of them. Behind the axe-wielding female two other, bigger figures emerged out of the shadows, both males dressed in black clothes, one carrying a spiked baseball bat, the other a large knife. All three were smiling. Jesse and Damien Reid looked at each other and started to panic.

FIVE

2307 hrs

There was no warning of the attack. No preamble, no reason. Both Jesse and Damien knew this wasn't just a weekend punch up, nor was it an opportunistic robbery. This was something else entirely. The weapons they carried, the menace portrayed—Damien knew they had to act, there was no talking themselves out of this. He shot an urgent look at Jesse.

"Get in the car!" he bellowed.

She froze, splitting her gaze between her husband and their attackers. The sudden movement from the female jolted her back into action. Jesse spun around and grabbed the door handle, flinging the door open with jarring force. Rosie sprinted at her, her axe arm pulled back ready to strike; she swung with all her force, the axe crashing into the door frame, the screech of metal on metal resonating from the impact. Jesse clung on to the door with all her strength, pulled it towards her then slammed it back towards her attacker, the impact colliding into Rosie, sending her sprawling to the floor, her axe skidding across the wet tarmac out of her reach.

Damien bolted for the driver's side door; Denny was right behind him hefting the baseball bat for an attack. Damien stumbled but managed to keep his balance, he glanced behind and to his horror saw Denny was nearly upon him. Acting on instinct he suddenly stopped, slightly turned his body and launched a vicious side kick into Denny's exposed stomach. The killer crumpled under the impact and fell to his knees, gasping for breath. Damien gripped the car door and flung it open, smashing the edge into Denny's face who then stumbled backwards, blood gushing from a deep laceration to his forehead. Damien didn't hesitate and hit him again, this time knocking Denny to the floor clutching his blood-soaked face, screaming in agony.

Rosie scrambled for her axe, leapt to her feet and once more threw herself into the fray, her face contorted with rage at the sight of Denny being taken down. She charged towards the passenger side, her axe raised high once again. Jesse and Damien slammed the car doors and locked them. Damien frantically tried to put the keys in the ignition barrel, his hands slipping on the key fob. He looked to his left. Jesse was crying, tears streaming, her make up smeared across her face. She glanced up and saw the blade coming towards her. Closing her eyes in terror, Jesse covered her head in an attempt to protect herself from the incoming blow. The colossal impact of the axe shattered Jesse's window, the implosion showering both her and Damien with broken glass. Jesse clenched her fist and instinctively threw a punch out of the window towards her attacker. The blow caught Rosie on the side of her head but caused no damage as it slid harmlessly off of her. Unfazed by her victim's poor attempt at self-defence, Rosie immediately responded with another slash, this time catching Jesse's arm and opening up a large wound. Jesse winced in pain and retracted her arm into the car just as Rosie took another swing, but this time she had adjusted her position so that the angle of attack was into the car itself. Jesse pre-empted the attack and flung her upper torso down across Damien's lap just as the vicious axe blade swung through the open window, slamming into the head rest of the passenger seat. She rolled onto her back and threw a brutal kick out of the window just as Rosie reached in. There was a deafening crack as Jesse's foot collided with Rosie's jaw. Rosie reeled backwards dropping her axe; clutching her face she bent over and spat out a mouthful of blood, complete with three teeth. She stared at Jesse, her eyes savage and grinned maniacally.

"Is that all you got, bitch?" she hissed scathingly.

The car suddenly roared into life. Damien let out an audible sigh of relief as he slammed it into reverse; he put the pedal to the floor and strained to look over his left shoulder, his eyes blurred from the attack, his retinas trying to focus out of the rain-splattered rear window. The car wheels spun under the sudden acceleration, the screech on the wet tarmac deafening as it shattered the late night ambience. Damien and Jesse were thrown forward as the tyres suddenly gained purchase, propelling the car backwards away from the attack. Jesse looked on as her husband struggled to keep control of the vehicle, adrenalin and fear causing him to weave from side to side. Damien kept going regardless, his mind racing, the wet conditions making their escape more hazardous. He buried the rev needle in the red and gunned the accelerator even harder, his limbs aching from the exertion, his head still swimming from the ferocity of the brutal assault, every few seconds returning his attention to the progress of their attackers.

In the passenger seat Jesse was clinging on to the dash board, her eyes fixated on the windscreen and the perusing attackers. She roared at her husband to go faster as their assailants' unrelenting violence showed no signs of abating or ceasing. Jesse felt something wet on her arm. She glanced down to see it covered in blood then caught her reflection in the wing mirror, her face peppered from the broken glass. She touched her wound as if to ease it somehow. Suddenly there was a massive crash. Damien and Jesse's heads were violently thrown forward into the dash board from the immense collision as the car slammed into a security post situated in front of the super store's cash machine, the impact forcing the rear of the car into the air, wedging the back axel on the twisted hunk of metal. The car stalled. Damien rubbed his face trying to will back his senses and reached out to his wife. She moaned quietly as she started to come to. Through the cracked windscreen Damien could see the killers closing in on the stricken vehicle; he furiously tried to restart it but was unsuccessful. He shook Jesse violently on the arm, rousing her from her daze.

"We aren't moving anywhere...get out and run!" he roared.

She faced him, tears flowing freely. "I won't leave you!" she yelled, grabbing hold of his arm.

"Go. Now!" he retorted with greater urgency, pushing her towards the door in an attempt to get her moving.

Reluctantly she swung the door open, jumped out and ran. She briefly looked back, expecting to see Damien heroically standing his ground against their attackers. To her relief he wasn't, in fact he was only a short distance behind, running after her and screaming at her to keep moving. Behind him Jesse could see Felix, Denny and Rosie, their pursuit relentless. Jesse powered forward; she sprinted across the carpark, over a bedding area and through a small hedge, only stopping when she reached the road. She slid to a standstill, her lungs burning from breathing so hard, her body doubled over, gasping for air. Jesse wiped her hair from her face and frantically scanned her surroundings, searching for any sign of activity or better yet, a safe place of refuge. Through tear-filled eyes and residual concussion she caught sight of the blue neon Avon and Somerset Constabulary sign hanging like a beacon above the police station entrance and for a split second it gave Jesse a surge of relief and hope. She turned screaming at Damien, her outstretched hand pointing to the police station. He understood, signalling her to keep going. She took off as fast as she could, fearing to turn around. Behind her she could hear Damien's footsteps gaining ground. Her muscles screamed in agony but she kept going, her determination and will to survive driving her to keep moving. She leapt up the steps two at a time and slammed through the front doors into the station's foyer, skidding into the front desk with the momentum. Seconds later Damien burst through the door clutching his side and breathing heavily. She screamed for help but no one answered.

"Go!" Damien yelled.

Without hesitating she vaulted the desk, landing with a heavy thud and immediately slipped on the pool of blood surrounding the officer's body, sending her crashing into the wall. Momentarily dazed, Jesse dragged herself to her feet. She screamed just as the outer doors burst open and their assailants rushed in, their weapons at the ready. Damien spun around to face them as they entered. In a desperate act of survival he recoiled and launched himself head first over the counter, just as Denny swung the baseball bat, a nail slicing into Damien's leg then embedding into the wall. Denny rasped as he tried to tug the weapon free and glared at his intended victim.

"You are fucking dead family man!" he bellowed, then started to laugh hysterically.

Damien crashed to the floor, his body sprawling over the policeman's corpse, the momentum causing him to roll head first into the wall. He couldn't focus, his brain rattled from the impact, blood flowing from his vicious leg wound. He tried to stand but his legs gave way. Suddenly, out of the maelstrom he felt Jesse's hands grab his arms, violently dragging him to his feet then yanking him through the double doors into the station itself. Rosie and

Felix silently watched on then slowly started to giggle, all the while Denny laughed uncontrollably, delighted with the evening's hunt.

"We are coming for you, piggies!" shouted Felix as his quarry disappeared through the double doors and out of sight.

On the other side of the doors Jesse limped down the corridor, buckling under her husband's weight. She wrapped her arm around him, helping him to stand. Damien was unable to run due to the leg wound that was now continually pumping out blood, leaving a trail of crimson along the corridor's polished floor. Behind them they could hear their pursuers laughing and taunting.

"Nowhere to go little piggies, nowhere to hide!"

They kept pushing forward, determined to find someone to help them. It was a police station after all, there had to be someone here. Jesse hoped those bastards had slowed their attack because of their location but something didn't sit right with her. She had the sense they were playing games with them and couldn't shake the feeling they had them exactly where they wanted them.

She glanced at her husband; his head was sagging and ashen-white, his face pasty through blood loss. He was cold and drifting in and out of conciseness. The severity of the situation hit her hard, the adrenaline flowing into every pore. The realisation was that he was dying; if there was any chance of him surviving, and her for that matter, they had to find help sooner rather than later or at the very least find a first aid kit and put her two-day training course to good use. She couldn't believe how brave Damien had been; in fact she couldn't believe how she herself had reacted.

She paused, standing motionless and processed her surroundings, her attention drawn to a double set of doors a few meters to her left. Those are as good as any, she reasoned. Jesse kicked open the doors leading off of the main corridor and stumbled in. She found herself in a kitchen. Bright metal work tops and sinks lined the walls. It looked unused and brand new. With her free hand she hit the light switch; the room was immediately engulfed with bright florescent light and she winced as her eyes acclimatised to her new surroundings. Propping Damien up against a counter she set to work searching the heavy metal drawers for anything of use. She didn't find a first aid kit but couldn't help but smile when she found something else she was looking for, a twelve-inch kitchen blade. She had watched enough horror films to know that you have to find a weapon or was that extreme paranoia? Did she really expect to get out of this alive? She started to doubt herself. The darkness inside her mind distorted and played tricks on her. She shook her head and counted to five, breathing out heavily to steady herself once again. She tucked the blade into her belt and made her way back to her husband. She took off her black t-shirt and ripped it in two. Using one half she lashed it around Damien's leg and repeated the procedure around her own wounded arm.

"You still with me babe?" she whispered in her husband's ear, trying to sound composed and under control.

He raised his head and tried to smile.

"Ain't going anywhere, love," he croaked.

It was her turn to smile. "We are getting out of this Damien, just hang on a bit longer...do it for me," she said.

He chortled, his breathing laboured. She heard something outside in the corridor. Slowly and gently she left Damien propped against the work top, pulled her blade from her belt and made her way stealthily to the door. Opening it slightly she strained to listen for any movement. There was none forthcoming; in the distance she could still hear their pursuers somewhere in the building. They weren't shouting anymore but something else—it sounded like they were singing. Jesse closed her eyes and strained to hear what they were saying. She shivered when she realised what was being said, a single phrase repeated over and over again, "Pork is on the menu, pork is on the menu."

Jesse gently eased the door shut and cautiously made her way back to her injured husband. She paused to gather her thoughts, took in a deep breath and tried to focus. They needed a way out. Calm down and think, she told herself. Her mind swirling and tumbling into that dark place she tried so hard to avoid, she couldn't afford to lose herself now. She pinched herself, a technique she had used to snap her wandering thoughts back to the present many times before but never in a situation as life-threatening as this. Her eyes scanned the room searching for inspiration. She reasoned that they would have the front and the back doors covered for their escape so she had to think of an alternative plan. In the far corner was another door. She cursed herself for not noticing it before. She put her arm under her husband's and hoisted him to his feet; he mumbled in pain but remained silent.

"Let's go," she said as much to herself as to him and together they staggered towards their possible escape route. She steadied her husband and with her free hand pulled the blade from her trousers, her grip tight in anticipation then slowly pushed the door open just enough for her to see into the next room. It was a brightly lit canteen with tables and chairs; a small kitchen was on the other side of the room. She could hear the faint sound of music from a radio at low volume but no other sounds of movement. From her vantage point she could see approximately a third of the room and on the far side what looked like blood splattered over the worktop and cupboards. She grimaced at the thought of having no choice, she would have to take the risk, and unsure if it was clear to proceed Jesse decided to push forward and slowly edged herself into the room.

Once inside she was relieved to see that it was empty. Sitting Damien down she decided once again to have a look around for anything useful, her mind acutely aware that their pursuers were nearby and could find them at any moment. Jesse glanced up at the brightly coloured bunting hanging from the ceiling. "Happy Retirement," it stated. In the corner was an old school guillotine and reams of flyers advertising an upcoming party and party hats and balloons littered a makeshift workbench, blissfully unaware of the horror taking place. Jesse huffed to herself, hard to imagine good times in their current predicament she mused. There was no time for reflection or self-pity; she would have to move fast.

As she manoeuvred her way to the work counter she momentarily slipped but managed to steady herself. She cursed and looked down. The body of the WPC lay at her feet, the floor around her awash with a pool of blood and brains. Jesse pressed her hand to her mouth, stifling a scream. Frantically she scanned the room, her mind racing. The sudden sound of the door smashing off of the wall as it was kicked open galvanised Jesse into action; she spun around facing the doorway and to her horror saw Rosie charging at her, her axe raised and ready to strike. The killer bypassed her husband, her eyes hate-filled and focused on her target, she had chosen her victim; she was making a bee line for Jesse. Rosie threw a colossal swing aimed at Jesses head. Jesse stepped back out of the path of the attack but tripped on the dead WPC sending her tumbling backwards, landing on her back, the axe's blade missing her face by inches. Rosie roared in frustration, her miscalculation costing her the advantage but immediately recovered and followed up with a back swing angled slightly downwards in the hopes of catching Jesse in the forehead. She missed; the axe head slammed into the heavy tiled floor scattering fragments of crimson-soaked travertine into the air. Jesse started to hyperventilate as she scrambled to get up, her hands sliding in the putrid organic mess spreading across the floor around her, broken tile fragments ripping at her palms. Once again she lost her footing and slipped back down, unable to get up in time to escape the relentless onslaught.

Rosie was looming over her now, hefting her weapon, grinning and lining up for the final blow. Jesse desperately scanned the gore-saturated floor searching for her knife in a final act of survival. She couldn't see it. She looked up at Rosie in defeat, resigning herself to the final incoming death blow. The impact of bone being splintered was jarring. The top of Rosie's head suddenly exploded as the heavy guillotine blade carved its way into the top of her skull and came to a stop just to the left of her nose. A stunned and confused Jesse looked on as her head split open; blood erupted from her face, the flow cascading down her body and washing over Jesse, filling her nostrils and mouth. She started to choke and threw herself to one side, her arms covering her head and face, her legs pulled up into a foetal position. She gripped on tight; her limbs throbbing from adrenalin, her eyes screwed closed, not wanting to face her end. Somewhere close by she heard the thud as Rosie's lifeless body hit the floor, swiftly followed by the metallic crash as the blade found its way free from her cadaver. Jesse gripped on tighter, unable to move, still paralysed with fear. Then there was silence.

Cautiously Jesse opened her eyes and found herself face to face with her female attacker, her head effortlessly carved in two by the catastrophic blow. Trembling, she looked around, unable to comprehend what had transpired. Through blood and tears she could see a silhouette backlit in florescent light. She squinted trying to focus, wiping bodily fluids from her eyes. Damien reached down, offering his hand to help her to her feet. He was smiling.

"Let's get the fuck out of here, eh?" he stated calmly.

Jesse stared myopically back at him, her relief obvious. She grabbed his hand and staggered to her feet, immediately throwing her arms around her injured husband and pulling him tight.

"Oh my god Damien, I thought you were dead..." She hesitated. "I thought I was dead," she added, squeezing him tighter. He gave out a little squeak and cringed at the pain.

"I'm okay, babe. Just a flesh wound."

Jesse released him and kissed him on the lips. "What the hell did you do?" she asked. He shifted on his injured leg and rebalanced himself.

"Saw you were in trouble and used the guillotine blade from the desk."

She glanced at the gore-soaked body of Rosie, then at the razor-sharp blade lying menacingly on the blood-washed floor.

"Jesus Christ babe, could you have found anything bigger?" she found herself asking. He started to grin.

"Always said I should have gone into art design," he quipped.

She laughed and cried at the same time, her emotions pushing to the surface. He pulled her close.

"Come on, let's go," he said reassuringly.

They made their way to a second doorway--the doorway they hoped would lead them to safety.

Jesse held the door ajar and listened intently—nothing. Arm in arm Jesse and Damien tentatively maneuvered themselves into the corridor and were confronted with yet more doors, both to their left and right. Jesse paused, unable to clear her head enough to make a rational decision, her psyche still reeling from the brutal confrontation. Damien gently nudged her and nodded towards a sign hanging to their left. Jesse smiled at the emergency exit sign and nodded to Damien, embarrassed by her momentary lapse. Cautiously they made their way towards the set of heavy double doors, relieved to see the thick metal bar unchained.

"They might be alarmed," Damien offered in a subdued whisper.

Jesse grimaced at him then returned her attention to the doors, studying the door frame for any sign of alarm wiring.

"We have no choice babe, they could be anywhere in the building," she replied sedately.

Damien slowly nodded in agreement.

"When we do it we have to move fast. Are you okay to run if need be?" she enquired imploringly.

He glanced down at his crudely bandaged leg and started to feel the prong of pain once again. He stared at his wife, a look of defiance on his face.

"Damn right, love!" he exclaimed.

She smiled and once again returned her attention to the doorway. "We will go after three. One…two…" They braced themselves, staring at the exit, "…three!" Jesse slammed the security bar and as one they both rushed out into the unknown.

They found themselves in a dimly lit alleyway running the length of the station. Frantically, Jesse surveyed left and right for immediate threats and let out a sigh of relief when there was none forthcoming. Damien steadied himself and scanned the floor around them. Jesse looked on, puzzled.

"What are you doing?" she whispered. Damien remained stoic.

"Looking for a weapon, went and left the bloody guillotine inside."

Jesse couldn't help but let out a nervous laugh, the horror of Rosie's demise still fresh.

"Forget it, let's go!" she insisted, tugging at his arm. Once again Jesse stabilised her wounded husband and they made their way to their right, heading towards the front of the police station. Jesse reasoned they would stand a better chance finding help on the main road situated at the front as opposed to the quieter streets at the rear. Also the fact that there was an industrial estate located behind the station might make the attackers think they would go there for a place to hide, rather than make another attempt to locate help in an area in which they had already been unsuccessful. Jesse started to doubt her decision-making skills. She shook her head dismissively. Either way they had to do something; any action was better than non-action, at least that's what her psychologist had always drummed home to her. At the end of the alleyway Jesse cautiously peered around the corner, mentally aware not to expose herself for too long.

When satisfied the area was secure she turned to her husband, "I reckon it's as good as its going to get, love. I think this is our best chance to make a break for it."

Damien starred at Jesse blankly. "Then what?" he asked abruptly.

Jesse was taken back by both the question and his tone. "What do you mean by that?" her voice tinged with genuine confusion.

Damien pulled himself up straighter and leaned himself against the wall facing her. "If we manage to make it, what do we do then? We know we can't phone the local police, they are all dead. If we call the main police in Bristol, do you really think they are going to believe us? We will be their number one suspects in the murder of, Christ knows how many cops. We only saw two in there but I bet you there's a damn sight more."

Jesse remained silent. In truth she hadn't given it any thought, she had presumed that the police would rescue them and that would be it, all over once they caught and arrested the murderers. Not for a second did she even contemplate any other scenario, especially one that involved her and her husband being suspects, their names splashed across every newspaper and website. She shivered, her body numb at the thought of them spending the rest of their lives in prison over crimes they hadn't committed. As much as she hated to admit it, Damien had a valid point.

"What do you suggest then?" she snapped, a little

too forthright for Damien's taste.

"I say we get home and forget all about it...," he paused, "they don't know who we are. They would have gotten rid of the CCTV inside the station to cover their escape and conceal their own identities," he added. Jesse once again remained silent. "We just forget about the whole thing, babe and get on with our lives....they won't be able to find us and we are no threat to them because we have no bloody idea who they are."

Jesse was thinking about Damien's plan. Could they really get away with it?

"What about the car? That cash machine would have CCTV," she retorted.

Damien lent forward as to put emphasis on his reasoning. "I don't know, maybe we could say the car was stolen, deny all knowledge ...we will think of something," he offered, his eyes imploring her to agree yet not saying as much.

In reflection Jesse was struggling with what he was suggesting; it was totally absurd to think that they would get away Scot-free without police involvement but yet all she longed for was a return to normality and to forget the whole affair. Before she realised it she had nodded and agreed to Damien's plan. Despite her acquiescence and lack of objection she somehow hated herself for it and had a deep-rooted feeling that this wasn't going to be the end; in fact her instinct screamed at her that it was going to get worse. Or was that just her mental health issues rearing their ugly head? She wasn't sure and once again her inability to make a decision annoyed her.

For a second time Jesse covertly scanned the area directly in front of the steps and entrance. Satisfied it was clear she and Damien made their way across the street towards the supermarket carpark. Halfway across the road Damien suddenly stopped, his eyes wide, his gaze fixated on something back towards the police station entrance. Jesse paused and slowly turned to see what had captured Damien's attention and froze, unable to speak. At the top of the front steps stood Felix and Denny. Denny was motionless, his gaze predatory, his posture like that of a wolf ready to attack when commanded, whilst Felix appeared calm and relaxed, his left hand in the air gently waving it backwards and forwards at Jesse and Damien as if to wish them a safe trip. Jesse grabbed her husband tighter and moved forward, all the while expecting their pursuers to launch a second attack. To her surprise they didn't; instead they remained stationary at the entrance, looking on. Jesse and Damien moved quickly and cautiously across the car park and finally out of sight. With their paranoia heightened, one of them constantly kept on guard watching their rear should a second attack come. As they hobbled down the street arm in arm both Damien and Jesse were breathing heavily, their bodies battered and bruised, both blooded and concussed yet somehow they were smiling. They had survived. Neither knew why their pursuers had let them go nor for that matter why they had targeted them in the first instance. All they knew was that they were going home and still had each other. Jesse lowered Damien onto a low level wall and started to cry.

"You okay, love?" Damien asked, his concern evident. She smiled, wiping the tears and some dried blood from her eyes.

"I'm okay," she replied softly. Damien strained his neck to look to his right and saw the familiar sight of a taxi slowly coming up the road towards them, its roof light on, indicating its availability. Damien let out a hearty chortle and glanced at Jesse.

"Just like a scene out of a movie. I would suggest we get this taxi but I left my wallet in the car," he quipped. Jesse smiled and nodded.

"That's the least of my worries. I left my baccy in my jacket and I'm gasping for a fag," she joked nervously; this time they both started to laugh. Damien stood up groaning, sticking out his arm in an effort to flag the taxi down. It slowed to a stop.

"Let's go home, love," he said. Jesse nodded and got into the taxi. Damien took one last look around, was convinced they were safe then followed suit. The taxi driver turned off his roof light and slowly pulled away, happy he had another fare that night. Not once did he question the state of his new arrivals. Just another weekend night, he mused.

From his vantage point Denny silently watched on as the taxi pulled away, its lights disappearing around a corner. He sighed and slowly made his way back across the rain washed carpark returning to Felix who was still casually standing on the stone steps.

"They have gone," he grumbled disappointedly, secretly wondering why Felix had let them escape. The Alpha grinned and gently touched Denny on the shoulder.

"Patience my friend. I know it bothers you. You are wondering why I would let such mere creatures elude us this fine evening, aren't you?"

Denny remained silent. He knew some bullshit arty excuse or rhetoric was coming so decided it was best just to keep his mouth shut.

"The hunt has only just begun my friend," he added. Felix reached into his jacket pocket and retrieved a mobile phone. He punched in a number, held it to his ear and awaited a response. Once he was connected he started to speak. "It's me…I need replacements." He was nodding, "Tomorrow morning will be fine; we'll await location and exact time. I understand. Thank you." He finished the call and replaced the phone in his jacket pocket.

Denny had often wondered whom he had been talking to after such calls but was wise enough to know their leader would never divulge such information and that it would be unwise to ask such a question. Denny smirked to himself. One day when he was in charge he would surround himself with only the most worthy to assist him in his work and he sure as hell wouldn't leave any witnesses. This evening had its highs and lows—the best part had been when he hid and watched Rosie get that blade in her head. Oh, how he laughed! Of course he could have saved her but where was the fun in that?

"Denny, go and get us a vehicle, please."

Felix's order snapped Denny back into check and he dutifully wandered off to find transport, all the while grinning at the thought of that smug little whore getting her head caved in. Felix was left alone on the steps breathing in deeply the cool night air. It had been a good night, he mused silently. It started to rain again, tiny droplets at first but then slowly getting heavier. Felix reached into his jacket pocket once again but this time retrieved a wallet. He flipped it open, scanning the credit cards and thumbing the notes stuffed inside. He found what he was looking for and smiled. Damien Reid's driver's licence gave him all the information he required.

SIX

~~~~

Monday, 0230 hrs

Lewis grabbed the bottle of Jack Daniels and popped off the lid. With one hand he poured the amber liquid into the tumbler, filling it halfway. *Fuck it* he thought and filled it to the brim. Replacing the lid, he pushed the bottle to one side and returned his attention to the small bag of weed and rolling papers. Diligently he rolled a joint, lit the end and inhaled a heavy breath. He held it in his throat, tilted his head back and slowly exhaled, smiling as he watched a plume of smoke gently rise to the ceiling, the sweet aroma of lemon filling his nostrils. He sighed as the familiar wave of relaxation cascaded through his body, his senses dulling, his body relaxing back into his armchair. He reached for the tumbler and downed half of the bourbon, his throat recognising the fiery liquid. With one hand he wiped his mouth and returned his attention to the laptop screen in front of him—so much porn to choose from, he mused. He grinned, eager to relax even further. It had been a shit day after all and it was his time now. He needed to switch off and chill.

It always impressed him how much porn was on the

internet. He had come to the conclusion that one person could surf the net all day, every day and never watch the same clip twice. He chuckled at his philosophical meanderings and took another long draw on the joint, once again embracing the blissful oblivion. He decided that tonight he fancied some good old fashioned girl-on-girl action. Sometimes his tastes wandered into the fetish side of things but tonight he was having a normal evening. He didn't discriminate; everyone had their kinks and quirks—to be honest there wasn't much out there he hadn't tried or wouldn't try, given half the chance. He wasn't ashamed of his vices, even his dependency on whiskey was deemed acceptable these days and he couldn't care less that he was a trustee of modern chemistry.

At 46 years old some would say Lewis was overweight, despite being six feet tall and big-boned. He was going grey and had a touch of arthritis but inside still felt he was in his twenties. Of course his body had other ideas. He wasn't married and had no kids so in his mind he could do what he damn well wanted. Who was he kidding he reminded himself. Basically his life was shit, even his career was shit—in fact he hated his job. In truth, he had never really been any good at it. These days he was just going through the motions. He often thought there was something more out there for him but in all honesty he was lazy and he knew it, happy to let whatever it was come to him but not being overly bothered if it didn't.

He chortled and took another hefty swig followed by another long drag. He glanced at the screen. The clip he had chosen was still buffering, the frame frozen on a girl named Courtney pouting at the camera, her tight ass clad in French knickers, her legs encased in black stockings, eagerly awaiting her girlfriend to arrive. He adjusted his seating position, wanting to get started.

His phone started to ring, vibrating on the desk in front of his keyboard. He glared at it, willing it to switch off. It stopped. He relaxed once again. Glancing at his glass he was perturbed it was empty and immediately re-filled it. His mood darkened as the phone rang again.

"Bollox!" he rasped as he stabbed at the green 'accept' button. "What?" he snapped. He listened to the voice on the line and started to nod. "I understand. See you in a bit," he finished the call and tossed the phone on his desk, annoyed that his well-deserved evening off had come to an abrupt end. Lewis gazed longingly at the pouting Courtney. "Sorry love, going to have to take a rain check," he said, blowing her a kiss then slamming the lid of the computer shut.

He got up and made his way to the bathroom, catching his reflection in the mirror, his stubbly unshaven face stared back at him, dark rings under his eyes. He splashed his face with water, urinated, and then made his way back to his living room. Looking out of his tenth-storey window he was actually glad he lived in Bristol, and especially his flat. He loved the hustle and bustle of the big city, the anonymity it bestowed. He couldn't understand why anyone wanted to live in the country where it was full of Tory supporters and smelt of cow shit. He tugged at the top drawer in his unit and retrieved his car keys, wallet and a small bag of cocaine. He rummaged for his credit card, emptied a large mound of white powder on the table and began to chop it up into equal lines. Once finished he rolled a twenty pound note and with one hand snorted each in turn. His brain was electrified with the chemical, the euphoria sweeping through him. He grinned, pleased with the quality of his purchase. He grabbed his keys, threw on his jacket and headed for the door. At the last moment he paused to check if he had his wallet. He did. He flipped it open and gazed at the picture of his younger self, happily smiling back at him.

"Fuck you," he said under his breath. The photo ID of Detective Inspector Lewis Class remained sickeningly cheerful. Grimacing he left his flat, slamming the door behind him.

SEVEN

Monday, 0343 hrs

"Morning, Sir."

The PC seemed awfully chipper for this time in the morning, that and the fact he was stood amongst a horrific crime scene, the victims of which were fellow coppers made the DI somewhat uneasy. Class had an ingrained cynical distrust for anyone that was overly happy, especially at times such as these. He remained silent and looked at his watch, 3:45 a.m. It had taken him less than an hour to get to Wells; the traffic had been light this time in the morning, the journey made more bearable by the high given from the cocaine. He stroked his chin, his stubble rough on his fingers. The station was awash with activity. Uniformed members of Avon and Somerset's finest busily scurried around going about their superiors' orders, the building cordoned off, the wet pavements a sea of blue-flashing neon. Class had witnessed more than ten people dressed in white forensic suits collecting evidence from all around the station. The crime boys were going to have their work cut out on this one he mused. The powers that be would want a quick result and heads would most certainly roll if they were denied it. When he arrived he had walked around the entire building taking time to study each of the six bodies, four of which were officers and the other two as yet unidentified. He liked to gather his first impressions; some might call it running on intuition, for in his experience your first assumptions were normally correct, well that was what all the decent coppers had told him. Class stood motionless, his eyes scanning the sigil painted on the wall of the foyer. You didn't need to be a scientist to know it was drawn in blood, he presumed from the dead PC behind the counter. Class had always had a vague interest in the occult; he wouldn't call himself an expert but liked to think he knew more than the average copper. He tilted his head trying to see any hidden message within the glyph but any answers eluded him.

"What do you think it means, Sir?" the cheerful PC asked inquisitively. Class shrugged. "Not entirely sure. Never seen anything like this before," he replied, his eyes never leaving the wall. The young PC coughed to clear his throat.

"I've been assigned to assist you in your investigation, Sir." Class glanced at him, his expression stoic.

"By whom?" he asked. The PC shifted uncomfortably under his superior gaze.

"The Chief Super, Sir. He is on his way down now, should be arriving in the next half an hour or so," he stated a little too smugly for his superior's tastes.

Class smirked, reminiscing how much of a fan the Super was of him, how much he was impressed by his glittering career not to mention his insubordination, and of course especially the time Class dumped his daughter on their wedding day. Class quietly groaned to himself, the spectre of the Chief Superintendent looming ever closer. He knew he had been stitched up and was in all likelihood going to be the sacrificial lamb should the case fall apart. If on the other hand he was successful, the Super would swing in and snatch the win from under him, knowing full well he wouldn't be able to complain. It was a win-win for the Super regardless of the outcome. He had waited a long time for some proper payback and it would seem his time had now arrived. Class found himself wondering how he could get out of running this case but seeing as it was of such high value he very much doubted it. Once again the DI sighed, he had been right royally fucked over and there nothing he could do about it.

"Go get me a coffee will you, black no sugar," he barked at the PC, determined to vent some frustration. "What the hell is your name anyway?" he asked after him as the PC went to leave. The chipper PC turned to face his superior.

"Collins, Sir" he stated proudly.

Class smirked and stifled a giggle, "Your first name isn't Phil, is it?"

PC Collins looked unimpressed; he had obviously heard the joke before but was secretly glad the DI was acting a little less irritated towards him.

"No Sir. It's Nigel," and with that he turned and strolled off in search of his superior's coffee. Class sniggered and rubbed his eyes.

"Jesus Christ, I'm working with someone named Nigel," he said to himself, amused by his own wit. The sudden gust of wind made the DI look up, his face contorted as the front door swung open and an entourage of suits walked in. At the head of the group was Chief Superintendent Sir Harris Walcott, his face stern, his walk imposing and he was heading for Class. Class sighed deeply and muttered under his breath. He turned to face his boss and with a well-practiced fake smile engaged in conversation.

"Morning, Sir," he stated with more than a striking resemblance to the greeting he himself received from his subordinate.

"What the hell is going on, Class?" Walcott's tone was abrasive boarding on accusative. Class was just about to respond when the Chief carried on. "I want a media blackout on this, do you understand, Class? I don't want any of the officers' families informed or tipped off before we have any information on the sickos that were responsible. Do I make myself understood?" He glared at Class as if to hammer the point home.

Class could only shrug. "I will endeavour to do my best, Sir." He paused then added, "Am I to take it that I am the lead on this case, Sir?"

Walcott intensified his glare, obviously unimpressed by the DI's question.

"What the hell do you think, Class?" he snapped then turned and started to walk away but paused and turned to face Class once again. "In truth Class, I would rather a more moralistic and reputable officer take point but you are all I have right now. I don't like you and I don't care for your cavalier attitude towards police work. Just keep your head down and get me a fucking result. When this breaks the whole country will have their eyes focused on this force and if we can't even solve the murders of some of our own what kind of message will that send to the public? I don't need that kind of scrutiny, Class. The police bashers will have a field day; hell, they might even start to throw parties celebrating our monumental fuck-ups." He momentarily paused to catch a breath. "I want a daily brief first thing on my desk typed up by you giving me all the information you have and how the investigation is proceeding. No excuses, no waffle, just facts. I want this case closed ASAP. Forget everything else you are working on." He paused once again, his face beginning to turn scarlet. "…just do your fucking job Class and do it quickly," he growled and stomped off, his entourage in hot pursuit.

Class tutted under his breath and fumbled in his pockets for his cigarettes and Zippo. He popped one in his mouth and made his way outside. The DI stood on the stone steps and took a long deep drag aimlessly looking around at the cacophony of emergency service vehicles and staff rushing to and fro.

"Here you go, Guv."

PC Collins appeared clutching two cups of steaming coffee. Class smirked and took one of the cups from him. Collins was the first to speak.

"What now then, Sir?" he asked sedately. Class shrugged and turned to face the young PC taking a sip of the hot beverage.

"Honestly Nigel, I have no fucking idea," the DI retorted, his answer genuine.

"Excuse me, Sir."

The voice startled Class who had been focused on his coffee and PC Collins. He turned to face the new arrival. WPC Lowe stood just a few steps down, facing Class. Her blonde hair was swept back and pinned under her hat. Class looked her up and down; under the uniform she looked like she had a great body. He inwardly smiled but revealed nothing on the outside.

"What can I do for you, Constable," he asked, taking a final drag on his cigarette then flicking it to the ground. The WPC smiled at him warmly.

"Just thought you might want to know that we have a crashed and abandoned car in the carpark across the road, it's banged up pretty bad. There seems to be signs of a violent struggle, blood splatter. Forensics is heading over there now, Guv."

Class grinned. Holy fucking shit he thought, maybe there is a God after all. He cleared his throat.

"I presume you think it is related to our investigation?"

He already knew the answer of course but enjoyed giving a little kudos to newbies, especially when they were blonde and extremely attractive.

"Yes Sir, in my opinion they are connected," she replied confidently.

Class finished the final dregs of his coffee and handed his empty cup to Collins.

"Be a good chap and go get another one, will you? I will meet you at this car this nice officer is on about..." He gestured to his female officer. "Please lead the way, my good lady," he said as smoothly as he could.

WPC Lowe blushed but was unimpressed by her superior's blundering attempts at flirting. She walked away with Class walking closely behind her. PC Collins sighed, he couldn't make out whether he liked Class or not. Part of him admired the DI whilst the other part thought he was an arrogant prick. He walked off in search of more coffee all the while wondering if the rumours he had heard about Class were true.

EIGHT

Monday, 0217 hrs

Jesse stepped out of the shower and wrapped the towel around her torso, dabbing dry her body as she did so. Resting on the side of the bath she gently scrutinised the wound on her arm. Satisfied it had stopped bleeding and was clean she applied a new bandage, gently tucking the end into the wrapped material. She reached for a second towel and wrapped her long black hair in a bundle. Wiping the steam from the mirror she gazed at her reflection. She looked tired, battered and bruised. She was pretty sure that she was still in shock and had been replaying the night's events over and over again in the hopes of finding some semblance of reason behind her and her husband's ordeal. There was none. No version of the event could carry forth any reason why they had been targeted and with such vehemence. To Jesse this was even more terrifying than any meaning posed. The fact that these people could carry out such cruelty against total strangers and with such little regard froze her very core; it truly was beyond all reason. You only hear of this sort of thing happening to other people but never expect to be the one on the receiving end.

She shuddered, recalling their lucky escape.

Upon returning home they hadn't really spoken to each other, just a handful of small talk but mostly awkward silences. Damien had refused to talk about what happened; the only thing Jesse prised from him was that they would never talk of it again. Jesse was confused; on the one hand her husband had shown immense bravery fighting off their attackers and defending her yet now was acting like a scared child unwilling to face his fears or accept what had happened. His polar opposite character traits were once again causing Jesse to harbour resentment. This conflicting behaviour wasn't helping her own fragile state of mind and she started to doubt if it had really happened. Of course her wounds spoke of a different story.

In the shower Jesse had time to reflect on their decision regarding the police and had become resolute in phoning Bristol HQ in the morning. She had faith that the truth would be uncovered and that they would see that she and her husband were victims in this case, not the perpetrators. She had to believe that the law would be on their side. Damien used to say that the law and justice were two separate things entirely but Jesse had always clung to the hope that he was just cynical, therefore mistaken. A lot of people these days had lost faith in the police but Jesse was one of the few who still believed that they stood for truth and honesty and were not just the corrupt government-employed Stormtroopers of capitalism as Damien continually stated. To this end she had also decided not to tell Damien of her plans to inform the police. He wouldn't understand but she was sure he would come around eventually, especially after it was all done and dusted and life had returned to normal.

Despite this, there was one major fact that was playing on her mind. The really strange thing about the whole ordeal was that there was nothing on the news about the attack, considering it happened in a police station, of all places. Jesse thought that it would have been all over the news by now; it should have been a major story replayed and rerun over and over again, but it wasn't. The fact that police officers had been murdered was too big a story to hide. This strange turn of events wasn't exactly helping her rationalise what had happened and once again she found herself questioning her mental state of mind. She had even seriously asked herself if she had suffered some sort of catastrophic breakdown; were her hallucinations so vivid and real that she actually confused it for reality? She glared at herself in the mirror in an attempt to shake herself loose of this self-harming spiral of confusion. She had to get a grip. It really did happen and in the morning after some well-needed sleep she was going to visit the police in Bristol and explain what had transpired.

Jesse dried herself, slipped on a pair of pyjama bottoms and vest then padded her way to the bedroom. Damien was already in bed, asleep. She slipped herself in and pulled the duvet up to her chin as if it were a shield, her mind a cacophony of static. Jesse rolled over to face her bedside table. Situated between a small lamp and her mobile phone sat a small tub of anti-depressants, or more specifically Valium, strategically placed by a glass of water. She eyed them cautiously; they seemed to be calling her name. She closed her eyes but struggled to ignore the temptation to down a couple. She screwed her eyes tight, an attempt to hasten sleep. It was not forthcoming. In one swift movement Jesse swung herself out of bed and popped the lid off the container. She tipped two white tablets into her hand and immediately placed them in her mouth followed by a hefty gulp of water. She closed her eyes and swallowed, the acidic bitter taste tumbling down her throat and into her stomach. She was anxious; she knew in a matter of minutes she would feel that all too familiar sensation, like being wrapped in a soft blanket of cotton wool. She ached for the peace it bestowed but was equally disgusted with herself regarding her lack of inner strength—the strength normal people have to face life without the need for a chemical crutch. She gave out a long sigh of disapproval and secretly vowed that once this was all over she would start afresh. She would throw those damn pills down the toilet and face the world head on, armed with a renewed vigour. She was determined no longer to be one of life's victims. She was tired of being afraid and it was time for the whole world to witness the phoenix-like rebirth of Jesse Reid. She grinned. Happy with her newfound resolve she once again retreated under her duvet and within a couple of minutes she was asleep.

Monday, 0347 hrs

The figure in black had been watching intently and waiting patiently across the road for over an hour. The figure had witnessed Jesse's lights go out ten minutes earlier but had remained as one with the darkness, his surveillance covert and undisturbed. The cul de sac was quiet and lined with heavy tree cover, the mix of semidetached and detached houses evenly spread. No one in the road had seen the figure arrive, nor had they witnessed him conceal himself between two large bushes directly opposite the Reid residence. The watcher had stealthily used a derelict property and building site to gain entrance to the perfect observation post, keeping low as not to be sky-lined against the surroundings. The figure smiled at his good fortune regarding tonight's location, his subjects of enquiry unaware they were under close observation. The watcher had studied the dwelling with expert eyes and upon arrival had carried out real time reconnaissance regarding exit points, lines of sight and escape routes should the order to terminate come from those in command. A dog barked in the distance, no doubt as a result of a late night animal foraging for food. The watcher remained still and glanced at his back-lit tactical watch, its dull red glow giving off no external light but informing the watcher of the time. No order to proceed had been communicated at the pre-arranged time. The figure slowly rose to his feet and once again paused, tuning his senses into his surroundings. After a few more minutes he slowly melted back into the shadows, retracing his steps to a waiting vehicle.

Monday, 0745 hrs

Jesse's alarm went off and jolted her from the depths of her drug-induced slumber.

With one hand she switched it off, never one for snoozing. She gazed myopically at the digital display, trying to focus on the time. Rubbing her eyes she rolled over to find the bed empty. Damien had already left. She presumed he had travelled to London as planned and felt a strange surge of relief as this meant she didn't have to explain her plans for the day. Jesse flung the duvet back and manoeuvred herself out of bed and headed to the bathroom. After a quick shower she headed for the kitchen to make herself a coffee, making a point of switching the television on before starting the brew. As Jesse cupped her hand around the steaming mug she flicked through the news channels, silently hoping for any indication that the story had broken. Once again she felt the deflation when nothing was mentioned. In a momentary fit of anger she threw the remote across the room. It landed on the floor with a thump, narrowly missing the glass TV unit.

Jesse sank back into the safety of the sofa's comfy embrace and started to plan the day ahead. Early morning traffic would be heavy heading in to Bristol so she decided that it would be better to leave Wells after 9 a.m., thus missing the mad Monday rush into the city centre. Obviously she would call in sick today— the thought of having to interact with people made her feel sick. She also toyed with the idea of an early morning visit into the town first, maybe grab a bite for breakfast and treat herself to a nice posh coffee at one of the many coffee houses; a slice of normality might do her good. Jesse didn't know what time Damien would be back that day and as far as she could tell he didn't leave a note. Chances are he would take his time and may even stay overnight in London once his business meeting had concluded. In truth Jesse thought that maybe it was for the best—a little personal space for each of them after what had happened. They had polar opposite views regarding how to handle the aftermath but she had eventually decided not to share with her husband her plan to visit the police. Part of her felt like she was betraying his trust but Jesse really couldn't see any other way around the situation. A little white lie was okay if it served the greater good, Jesse reasoned.

Dusting off her apathy, she got up and quickly dressed, grabbed her handbag and mobile phone, snatched up her car keys and headed towards the door, only stopping briefly to catch sight of her reflection in the hallway mirror where she paused. She looked good, considering. Her hair was pulled back in a loose ponytail and paired with blue jeans and trainers, a lightweight hiking jacket draped over her arm. Jesse smiled a weary smile; years of hiding inner torment had become second nature to her, a little bit more wouldn't hurt. She glanced down to find Damien's car keys missing, Nice of him to say goodbye she mused, slightly miffed by his lack of empathy. She paused, suddenly remembering the car crash, her guilt starting to well up. Jesse was starting to have second thoughts regarding the path she was about to walk—once she contacted the police there was no going back. She stared at her reflection and sighed.

"Get a grip, woman," she told herself. "You are doing the right thing. Damien will understand," she added, trying to convince herself her actions were morally justified. The fragile Mrs Reid exited the house and made her way to her modest little Corsa on the drive, all the while her mind second-guessing her true motives. She sighed, unlocked her vehicle and after a quick reassuring glance in the mirror started it up and drove off, blissfully unaware of the black BMW watching her from across the road.

NINE

Monday, 0906 hrs

The services on the M5 were shabby and heaving with people. Hordes of termites stopped off mid-journey to consume vast amounts of highly-priced food and rest their weary eyes from the drudgery of motorway driving—a short-lived rest before continuing on their way to whatever sad excuse passed for their lives and mundane jobs at which they were forced to slave. Felix stared blankly at the people swarming around the restaurant and despised them. Men, women, children—it mattered not. He hated these places, always had. If he had his way he would kill them all. None of them deserved to be here and the fact they were breathing the same air as he made him feel physically sick.

He sat at a small table near the window as far from other people as possible, anxious not to be in close proximity with his prey unless it was for the hunt. The appearance of Denny slumping himself down in the chair opposite snapped Felix out of his daydream. Denny smiled and tossed a boxed ham sandwich across the table at Felix who poked at it with disgust whilst watching Denny devour his own. Felix pushed the pack to one side and took a swig from his coffee cup.

"What's the plan?" asked Denny, stuffing the last few remnants of sandwich into his mouth.

Felix sighed deeply and gazed out of the window.

"Now my friend, we wait here until we have replenished our numbers. Rest assured our patience will pay off and make it all the better when we recommence. But for now we must bide our time and use our cunning."

Denny grinned. "Then we get back to that shit husband and his bitch wife?" he asked, excited at the prospect at taking care of their unfinished business. Felix gave the briefest of smiles.

"Yes Denny, our new colleagues shouldn't be long arriving, two new friends to join us on our next hunt, like-minded kin to join our cause. And yes, the husband and wife are to be the carrion, so rest while you can, Denny and prepare yourself for what needs to be done. No mistakes will be tolerated, you know what the Order expects of us and that's what we must do, there are no half-measures in this life we have chosen. We are blessed—you and I, Denny—for not everyone is granted access to the secret knowledge of our ancestors…" Felix paused, casting his gaze around the bustling restaurant, "…These people are nothing but cattle and we are the jackals feeding upon their carcasses. They serve no other purpose than to give our lives meaning. They give us the opportunity to reach the Primitive, the pinnacle of mankind's true nature, free from servitude, remorse and greed. Darwin was just the tip of the iceberg Denny; weakness is a plague that spreads like a virus and only the very few are immune to its effects. Like nature, there is no good or evil, just "what is". This is what we must achieve, that is what the Primitive is Denny—true freedom, our utopia created through our own personal will. To kill is to live. This is the way it has always been. Its man's arrogance and morality that has enslaved us and blinded most to the truth." Felix paused, realising his voice was raising in volume; he composed himself and continued, this time in a more sedate tone, "I had the pleasure of speaking to one of our new friends this morning and he has information for us. I'm sure you will approve." He sipped his coffee, his expression stern and emotionless.

Denny turned away from his glare. It unnerved him. He was secretly annoyed that Felix had been in contact with others and had not made Denny aware of it. What possible information could this new member have and in such a short space of time, he wondered. After a brief silence Denny spoke.

"Why did you let them go, Felix?" murmured Denny, his head low, averting eye contact. Felix let out a slight chortle.

"I let them go because I wanted to. Simple as that. It is not your place to question my motives Denny, all you need to know is that they are the carrion. They were chosen by Rosie and in her name we shall finish them and send them screaming, covered in blood, into the Void. Remember Denny, we would be doing the same if it were you lying dead on the floor." Felix jabbed an angry finger at Denny,

"We would avenge you. Do you not think it right that we should honour Rosie, in fact, all our brothers and sisters in our actions? Do you not think I may have some sort of reasoning behind my decisions or do you think me weak for adding a little spice to our game?"

Denny started to shrink under Felix's tirade. He felt like a chastised child, willing the ground to open up and swallow him. He shrugged.

"No Felix, I don't think you are weak," he said quietly.

"Good," Felix said, his face beaming with joy, again back to his normally composed self. Felix glanced to his left, his eyes drawn to two men entering the restaurant. One was approximately 6'6", heavy-set and muscly with short, cropped hair, dressed in jeans and a Harley Davidson t-shirt. The other was 5'11" with shoulder-length, black hair swept back into a tight ponytail, a thick heavy beard with specks of grey down to his chest and was also dressed in jeans with a dark green t shirt, a picture of a v-twin engine on it. They made eye contact and manoeuvred their way to Felix's table.

"Be a good chap and sit next to me, Denny." Denny dutifully obeyed and eyed the newcomers as they sat themselves down.

"Jasper and Dave, I presume," Felix said, more of a statement than a question. Both men nodded. Jasper, the bearded one, reached out a hand to Felix.

"I'm Jasper. Good to meet you. We have been looking forward to working with you. Your reputation precedes you."

Denny scowled. "What kind of fucking name is Jasper?" he rasped, his tone full of venom.

Jasper shot him a scathing glare and was immediate in his response.

"The kind that will bury you in the fucking ground if you ever speak to me like that again," he growled threateningly. They locked glares. Felix smiled. These men are going to prove most useful, he mused. Denny rose to the challenge.

"Is that so, little man?" he turned his attention to the larger man. "…and you are Dave, are ya?" again his tone aggressive.

Dave smirked and slowly leaned forward, "That's right and I'm the one you really don't want to fuck with. I think you look like a little girl. What's your name?"

Denny felt somewhat uncomfortable, his bravado starting to wain in the big man's presence. "Denny," he stated, not wanting to show any fear or weakness.

Dave grinned, "Not anymore. I'm gonna call you 'Daisy' from now on. You can be my bitch." He threw his head back in raucous laughter, as did Felix and Jasper.

Denny could feel his temper start to rise but this was neither the time nor place. He also started to laugh but inside was already planning the best way to kill his new team members. Felix broke the tension.

"What have you got for us then, gentlemen?"

Jasper reached into his back pocket and retrieved a small envelope and tossed it across the table to Felix, who opened it and examined the contents.

"I did a recce at their home address this morning," Jasper stated. Felix looked at the information regarding Jesse and Damien Reid. Jasper continued, "She is a dental receptionist in Wells and he is an accountant. He works from home mainly but his company is based in London. Seems he deals with clients in the West Country. Been married for sixteen years." Jasper grinned, "In fact, it was their anniversary yesterday." Once again all four men laughed.

"It would appear Rosie choose well and her timing was impeccable," Felix said, amused by the serendipity of the latest hunt. "What else?" Felix asked. This time it was Dave's turn to answer.

"No children. She has an estranged father, some rich businessman who made his money from textiles down this neck of the woods. They don't speak anymore and she hasn't seen him in years. Looks like she has been seeing shrinks for years too, we reckon because of her relationship with her father."

Denny chortled, "Aaawwwww the bitch has daddy issues." They laughed again. "What about the husband?" asked Denny.

"Both parents died in a car crash about ten years ago, neither siblings nor close family members to speak of. He was left a little money in the will, that's how they managed to buy their house in a nice part of Wells. We have both their mobile phone records and numbers, too."

Denny was impressed but didn't show it. How the hell did they manage to get this information? Just who the hell were these guys? Felix folded the paper and tucked it in his jacket. He clasped his hands together on the table.

"Right then Gents, I think it's time we got underway."

They joined hands and in a quiet tone as to not rouse questioning looks they said as one, "Embrace the Primitive." After a silent pause all four got up to leave.

Felix turned to Jasper, "I trust you have a vehicle?"

Jasper nodded, "As you requested, it's parked outside."

The four killers made their way out into the service station carpark and Jasper led them to a tatty white transit van parked amongst the swathe of vehicles.

Felix grinned, "Who would suspect just another white transit van on Britain's roads?"

Jasper puffed his chest out, pleased to get praise from such a revered man. Dave ignored their conversation and hefted himself into the back through the side door, his large frame stepping over a cable-bound body lying semi-unconscious amongst the debris on the grubby floor, its mouth wrapped in industrial tape. He leaned forward and with his left hand, grabbed the body by his throat and with utter brutality punched his victim square in the face twice, the force of the blows sending his head slamming into the metal work. The body groaned and went limp. Dave smirked and let it crumple to the floor, blood gushing from a broken nose. Jasper giggled at his friend's onslaught and pulled himself into the driver's seat whilst Denny and Felix clambered onto the front passenger bench. Denny glanced into the rear of the van, intrigued by Dave's plaything. Dave caught his gaze.

"Hey Daisy, this is for you," he gleefully announced then returned his attention to his victim. He picked up a rusty screwdriver and proceeded slowly and methodically to insert it into the body's thigh, the immense pain temporally rousing the body out of his slumber, his stifled screams muffled by the tape around his mouth. Dave pushed the implement in further, twisting as he did so, his gaze not for a second leaving the tear-filled eyes of his victim. Once again the body passed out. Dave smiled at Denny, then sardonically blew him a kiss.

Denny once again could feel his temper rise. He looked away, angered by his colleague's lack of respect. His time will come, he thought. Jasper handed Felix a mobile phone.

"It's ready to go, just hit the green button."

Felix jabbed at it and it began to ring. A voice came on the line.

"Hello?" Felix smiled and stared lovingly into the rear of the van at Dave's plaything.

"Good morning, Jesse. We have your husband."

TEN

Monday, 0932 hrs

Jesse froze, her mind tumbling into emotional freefall at the horrific statement. How the hell did they get this number, let alone know whom they were? She looked around the coffee shop frantically scanning the area for anyone suspicious, anyone that may be watching her and reporting her movements. Were they watching her now? Did they know where she lived? Did they really have Damien or was it a bluff? The voice on the phone spoke again, its calmness unsettling.

"I know Jesse; it's a lot to take in, isn't it? One minute poor old Damien is leaving for work, the next minute he's got a hammer wrapped around his head and is bundled into a van." Jesse let out a muffled gasp, trying to remain calm. "It's not a bluff Jesse, we really do have him, I would love for you to talk to him but my colleague has just beaten him half to death and stabbed him in the thigh with a screwdriver. As you can imagine Damien is a little worse for wear and as such I don't want to disturb the poor bloke from his little nap. Sleep is such a welcome release for those in severe pain, wouldn't you agree?"

Jesse could feel the tears welling up in her eyes.

"What do you want from us?" she struggled to get the words out. Jesse could hear the subdued sound of laughter at the end of the line.

"We want you to try and survive Jesse, we want you to run from us and hide, beat us at our own game, teach us naughty people what's what and that good always prevails over darkness. After all, that's what you think we are, don't you—evil? But that couldn't be further from the truth. We are purists Jesse; we are here to help." There was a slight pause.

"What have you done to Damien?" she asked, her voice beginning to crack.

"Don't worry Jesse, as long as you play by the rules Damien will be fine. What happens here on in is down to you, and you must follow our instructions if you want to see your beloved again."

Jesse felt sick, her stomach summersaulting. She paused, unsure how to proceed. Attentively she began to speak, "What are the rules?" There was a deep exhalation of air on the line, then the voice issued their demands.

"Good girl Jesse, I'm glad you understand the futility of your position and have agreed to play with us. Here are the rules…" Jesse gripped the mobile phone tight in anticipation, her temples pulsing with the embryonic stages of a migraine. "Of course it stands to reason that if you go to the police, Damien is dead. Likewise, if you seek out help from any friends or relatives not only will we kill you and Damien, we will visit those who helped you and using Stanley knives chop them into little pieces. Hell, we will even kill their children, pets and their neighbours for good measure." The voice continued without waiting for a response, "It's simple Jesse, you must run and evade us for as long as you can, we will come for you and when we do you must stop us, that's the only way you survive. Could you take another's life to save your own? Personally I think you stand a good chance. You did rather well last night, you even managed to kill one of us, and I for one applaud you for that. Very impressive, I tip my hat to you, my dear girl. For us to die doing what we were born to do is the highest honour. There are, however, just a few more details I need to impress upon you. No guns are too be used. We have very strict rules regarding weapons and it's only fair that these rules extend to you. You are only allowed to use those deemed as primitive weapons—hammers, knives, axes and such-like; you can even use your bare hands should the mood take you. I have to make you aware that if you break any of these rules the consequences will prove drastic for your husband. We will flay Damien alive and mail his skin to the tabloids."

It was Jesse's turn to speak, her voice monotone and even. "How do I know you will keep your end of the agreement? How do I know you will play by your own rules?"

The voice started to laugh. "Now you are getting into the spirit. You don't know, but I assure you that the rules that govern us are sacrosanct, the penalty should any one of us break them would be more severe than anything we could ever do unto you, my dear."

Jesse probed further. "And who would do these things to you? Who is pulling your strings?"

Felix could feel his temper starting to surface, how carrion dare demand such answers. "That is knowledge beyond your comprehension, little girl," he seethed. "The game starts at 10 a.m. I suggest you get yourself ready Jesse, because we are coming for you." And as quickly as the conversation started, the line went dead.

Jesse shuddered and placed the phone on the table. She glanced up at the wall clock. 0940 hrs. Jesse sat motionless, trying to think of what to do. She knew she couldn't risk going to the police and to be honest none of their small circle of friends would help in such a dangerous situation. There was no way she could lie and keep the stark truth away from them, anyway. For a split second she thought about seeking help from her father but immediately discarded the idea, angry she had even contemplated it. She had no choice but to go it alone. She had to run for her life.

She grabbed her handbag and studied the contents as to make an inventory of what she had, should she be unable to return to the house. She figured her credit cards would be useless in about twenty minutes so it would be wise to draw out as much cash as possible, as quickly as possible. It appeared these people had access to vast swathes of intelligence and might be able to track her through the use of her credit card. As paranoid as it sounded, Jesse didn't want to take the chance. In her purse she had roughly two hundred pounds; luckily she had drawn the cash out before entering the coffee shop with the intention of treating herself in Bristol market, where cold hard cash meant better deals. Her rolling tobacco and lighter were also present. Thank God for small mercies, she mused. Other than that, she was traveling light.

"Damn!" she said out loud, raising a few questioning looks from other patrons. She had to go home and get more; maybe she should get her passport and try to get out of the country. She stopped herself. No, they might expect that. She had to get moving as soon as possible and create distance between them and her. Jesse jumped up, grabbed her bag and headed for the door. She had to go home, and quickly.

ELEVEN

Monday, 0910 hrs

Detective Inspector Lewis Class looked up as young WPC Lowe knocked and immediately entered his office without waiting to be summoned. She looked chuffed and eager to speak to him.

"Got a hit on that crashed car, Guv," she said enthusiastically.

Lewis dropped his pen and casually leaned back in his chair, arms behind his head. "Pray tell then, my pretty young thing," he said and she blushed.

"Car belongs to a Mr Damien Reid, 13 Oak Mount, Wells. SOCO found traces of three types of blood in the car, one of which belongs to the dead unknown female in the station. We presume that the other two will match Mr and Mrs Reid, although they have no criminal records so matching DNA is a no-goer until we catch up with them and get a sample."

Lewis grinned in response, "Why do we assume the other two samples belong to the Reid's? Could they not belong to whomever stole the car, if in fact it was stolen?"

WPC Lowe walked to his desk and dropped some

photos next to his coffee mug.

"These were taken from the CCTV camera located in the cash point machine at the supermarket last night. We can't be one hundred percent sure but we reckon that this is both Jesse and Damien Reid running away from the crashed vehicle."

Lewis studied the photos before him. It did show what looked like one male and one female fleeing the scene but in all honesty he couldn't be sure who he was looking at.

"Did you pull their driving licences to get photo IDs for a cross-match?"

Lowes smiled, "Yes, Sir."

She placed two more photos on his desk. Lewis once again studied the photos. Damien Reid was rather non-descript; in truth looked like a bore and in Lewis's opinion had victim written all over him. Jesse Reid, however, was a different matter; he paused, running appraising eyes over her photo. Very attractive, he thought—nice facial features.

He tossed them down and looked up at Lowe, "Anything else show up on that CCTV footage?"

Lowe carried on, "No Sir, just the two figures seen running away."

Lewis stood up, flicked his desk drawer open and retrieved a packet of cigarettes and Zippo lighter. He popped one in his mouth and lit it. WPC Lowe coughed loudly, a sign to show her disproval and hint to her superior that he wasn't allowed to smoke. Lewis didn't acknowledge her subtle rebuke, instead he opened the window and blew out a steady stream of smoke.

"What are forensics saying about the bodies in the station, any news there?" he said without turning. WPC Lowe moved slightly forward.

"As requested, we have checked the service records of all the officers and found nothing untoward regarding conduct. A few minor issues or reprimands but nothing that would indicate anything worthy of investigation within this case, Sir."

Lewis took one last drag of his cigarette and tossed it out of the window. He turned to face Lowe.

"What else do we know about the two other bodies found in the station? Have we managed to ID them yet?"

Lowe looked somewhat sheepish. "No Sir. It would seem getting a positive ID on them is proving tricky to say the least."

Lewis looked puzzled. "How so?" he retorted.

"Well Sir, SOCO are saying that neither of the victims have any fingerprints. They have been removed by some sort of acid and their DNA isn't on file, plus they weren't carrying any ID," she paused. "In fact it appears one of them was already in custody. We found some notes that suggest that the officer in charge of that investigation had hit a dead end and was going to bounce it up to us this morning."

Lewis grimaced at the lack of tangible evidence, the Chief Super's threat echoing in his head.

"What about clothing?" Lewis was grasping at straws, his annoyance obvious to his subordinate.

Lowes cleared her throat, "Nothing Sir, no labels or any other distinguishing marks, all traces of manufacture had been erased."

Lewis dropped his head and sighed. "So we have got fuck all, then," he stated, more to himself than to the WPC. "What kind of people go to all this trouble to hide their identity and why hit a police station? There has to be a reason, even hard-core career criminals don't do this sort of thing in this country; they know it's bad for business and brings a hell of a lot of heat. It just makes absolutely no sense." Lowe shrugged at the proposed questions. Lewis closed his eyes.

"Tell me we have some CCTV from inside the station at least," he said in a slow and methodical way.

"Nothing Sir, all CCTV was taken or erased." Lewis opened his eyes and stared at Lowe.

"Tell me that the CCTV was backed up on the force's cloud system. What kind of station in this day and age uses tape or onsite standalone systems?"

She squirmed under his questioning. "I believe this station was due for closure Sir. It wasn't deemed cost effective to link it up to the cloud system."

The DI scratched his head in disbelief, "What about that mark painted on the wall?" The WPC shook her head.

"Another dead end so far, Guv. We have consulted the UK's leading authorities on ritualistic murders and cult iconography but nothing has been forthcoming, at least nothing on the PNC so far, but the data base is huge. It could be cross-referencing for weeks before we get a hit.

None of the experts we talked to have ever seen this symbol before. If it is some sort of devil-worshipping sign then it's a new one. The only thing we know for sure at this point is that it was painted in blood and the blood belonged to PC Garrett, the deceased officer that was murdered at the front desk. But like I said the system works slowly so we might get lucky over the next few days."

He hesitated before he retorted, then posed a question to the young WPC.

"Why leave such a calling card if no one was ever going to see it? Surely the whole point of leaving such a mark is to have the whole world recognise your signature, yet you tell me our experts are not aware of this particular symbol." Lewis slumped back down into his chair and once again reached for his cigarettes. This time the WPC spoke up.

"Sorry Sir, but you do realise you can't smoke in here?"

Lewis glared at her, his features softening as he lit another cancer stick, "To tell the truth, sweetheart, I really couldn't give a fuck right now. I'm in charge of a dynamite case with the whole force watching me. The Super is breathing down my neck and has painted a bullseye on my back and to top it off I have some satanic fucking nutter running around topping coppers like it was partridge season," he paused to catch his breath. "I think being caught having a fag is the least of my fucking worries, love."

She lowered her head. "Sorry, Sir," she said quietly then quickly turned and left the room, closing the door behind her.

Lewis rubbed his eyes. He was tired; he hadn't been to sleep and had come straight into the office from the crime scene full of enthusiasm and eager to get a flying crack at the case. Alas, it wasn't going according to plan. In truth he had nothing but a planned visit to Mr and Mrs fucking normal to look forward to and he didn't expect much to come from that meeting. At the very least they would deny all knowledge and say their car was stolen. At worst they would crack and would admit to drink driving then deny all knowledge of the incident in the station. Either way, at this moment Lewis didn't have any concrete evidence to link the Reid's to anything regarding his case or to place them anywhere near his crime scene. It would take days for SOCO to go through all the evidence and analyse blood found at the station and even if they did by some miracle find Damien's or Jesse's blood he needed a sample from them to compare and get a match. Even then with such a scene and so many victims it would take months of investigation. By then who's to know what might happen to the evidence, possible cross-contamination was always an issue—one slip up and everyone walks.

"Bollocks," he muttered under his breath and drained the cold remnants of his coffee mug. He stood up and reached for his jacket. Glancing at his watch he decided to get the pointless meeting out of the way first then hopefully put his effort into something more productive. He wouldn't bother phoning but instead decided just to turn up unannounced. Who knows, maybe he would catch them unawares and off guard; after all they didn't strike him as the master criminal types with planned alibis and rehearsed stories. Once again he checked his watch. 0920 hrs. He could get to the Reid residence for just after ten he surmised, have the meeting then head to the pub for a quick JD and Coke and maybe sneak in a few lines of Charlie to clear his head. Class let out a wheezy sigh. He was out of his depth and he knew it. There was no chance he was going to solve this case; it was a screw up from the start. He smiled to himself at the realisation that he was now entering the final days of his career and in truth he really didn't care, he just wished it would hurry the hell up. He was wasting valuable drinking time.

Lewis grabbed his car keys and stoically plodded to the door. He paused and took a look around. Somehow he sensed this could be one of the last times he spent time in this office. Without saying a word he left, slamming the door behind him.

Monday, 0950 hrs

Jesse pulled the car onto her driveway and switched off the ignition. Cautiously she exited the vehicle and took in her surroundings, visually scanning the quiet cul de sac for any signs of things out of place. She scrutinised every parked car and stared intently at every possible hiding place, convinced that someone was watching her. Her heart was racing, her mind running over every possible scenario. Who were these people who had wreaked havoc upon her and her husband? She shivered involuntarily at the thought of Damien being mercilessly tortured, held captive by forces unknown. Satisfied she wasn't being followed she made her way to the front door, rummaging in her handbag for her keys. As she put the key in the lock her fear started to gain momentum. What if they were already in the house waiting for her? She froze, unable to proceed but too terrified to turn back. What if that's what they wanted her to think so she would turn and run right into their waiting trap?

"Calm down," she whispered to herself. "Get a grip. Get in and out as fast as you can." She turned the key and slowly opened the door. The hallway was clear, no signs of a disturbance. She tentatively made her way inside, half-expecting someone to jump out at her from some dark, unchecked corner. No one did. Cautiously she moved through the downstairs, systematically checking for intruders. The lounge and kitchen were clear; nothing had been touched or moved out of place. Jesse grabbed a kitchen knife and made her way to the stairs. She paused at the bottom, her gaze focused up the stairwell. If anyone was left hiding in the house they would be up there, she thought. Gingerly she started her ascent into the upper levels. Jesse reached the top and glanced to her left. Two bedrooms lay with doors closed, in front of her lay the bathroom; she decided to check there first. Jesse worked the handle then kicked out at the door, sending it flying back into the bath and shower screen. It stopped with a loud bang as it hit metal and glass. Jesse ran in and was confronted with an empty room. She let out an audible sigh of relief and made her way to the first bedroom.

She repeated the same procedure but also checked the built-in cupboards; again she found nothing. Jesse stood on the landing, staring at the remaining door; she grasped the knife tightly in her right hand and with the left turned the brass knob that led into her and Damien's bedroom. She ran in, her heart racing at the impending confrontation. It too was empty. Her whole body convulsed with the adrenalin.

She sat on the edge of her bed and started to sob uncontrollably, the knife falling harmlessly to the soft, carpeted floor. Jesse clasped her head in her hands and started to shake it from side to side in an attempt to make it all go away. It didn't work. After a few minutes Jesse shook herself back to normality and got up, retrieving the knife as she did so. Jesse gathered her thoughts and moved with purpose. She grabbed a hold-all from the closet and gathered up a few clothes--knickers, bras and some socks, and stuffed them in the bag. She raced to her chest of drawers, her actions becoming increasingly urgent, the need to run starting to take hold.

She gathered up her meagre savings of two hundred pounds cash from a tin and snatched up a torch with spare batteries. Satisfied she had gotten what she needed, she headed downstairs to collect other supplies. Jesse flung open the under stairs cupboard door and retrieved a backpack that contained their camping equipment. Ever since the heavy snow two years ago and they found themselves stranded, Damien had said they should keep an emergency bag packed and ready to go should they ever find themselves snowed in or in an emergency situation. The pack contained MREs, a tent, two sleeping bags, a water-carrying sack, cooking equipment, a survival blanket, a medium-sized survival kit and a small folding blade. Jesse snarled, thinking about the UK's archaic laws regarding self-defence and knives. She would happily trade all of these items for a pistol and some ammunition right now. Jesse grabbed the rucksack and together with her small backpack threw them in the hall and once again headed for the kitchen. She looked around. She selected another two kitchen blades and placed them on the work counter, then headed for the garage via the back door.

Jesse flicked the light switch and saw what she was looking for. At the back of the sparse garage were three small plastic jerry cans of fuel, another blessing in disguise courtesy of Damien's overactive imagination and disaster preparedness. She was starting to regret all the times she had made fun of Damien and his sudden interest in prepping. Sure, he wasn't a full-on survival nut like you see on those documentaries but she had thought that "us British" have no need for such hoarding of goods and the chances of society collapsing into lawless chaos in their lifetime was pretty remote. For once she was glad to be wrong. Jesse eyed the fuel. She figured she would take them as to eliminate the need for stopping; this she reasoned would limit her exposure to CCTV or any other surveillance system at their disposal. Jesse felt like some sort of conspiracy nut, her own paranoia saturating her every thought process. Ordinarily she would dismiss such notions and scoff but the events of the last few hours had triggered something inside of her, something primordial. She scanned the garage for any last minute items. She smiled when she caught sight of the large wood axe hanging on the wall. She snatched it up and with her free hand scooped up the jerry cans and made her way back into the house. It was at the back door when she heard the voice calling her name.

TWELVE

Monday, 1010 hrs

Without making a sound, Jesse carefully put down the jerry cans and axe and sprinted through the back door of the house, scooping up one of the kitchen knives still sitting on the worktop. She pressed herself up behind the kitchen door listening, for the source of the visitor. Her breathing was heavy, her heart pounding; she could feel the liquid fear coursing through her body, making her head thump and her senses magnified.

Once again they called out, "Hello, Jesse?"

A woman's voice. She couldn't think who the voice belonged to, her survival instinct smothering all rationality. Jesse remained silent and heard muffled footsteps coming down the hallway towards the kitchen door. Jesse's body tensed; she gripped the knife handle forcing her knuckles to turn white. Cautiously she raised the blade ready to swing down at her would-be attacker. She took in a deep breath, held it for a second then slowly and silently let the breath out, calming her nerves and loosening her reactions. A figure walked into her view. Jesse didn't hesitate. She screamed in rage and struck out with the blade with savage intent. The figure turned to face her, also screaming, surprised by the ferocity of the attack. At the last second Jesse recognised the intruder and pulled the blade to one side, just catching the female on her right shoulder. The female jumped back in horror at the sight of Jesse lunging at her with the razor-sharp blade.

"Bloody hell, Jesse! What the hell are you doing!" she screamed, tumbling back into some units.

Jesse let the blade drop to the floor and threw her arms tightly around her best friend and next door neighbour, Chloe. Chloe was crying. They embraced tightly, both relieved they were still alive.

"I'm so sorry Chloe, I…," she let the sentence trail off, unable to control her emotions. Chloe took a second to calm down, then gently placed her hands on Jesse's shoulders and eased her back, all the while keeping eye contact.

"What's going on Jesse? I just came home and saw your front door open, then you go all *Halloween* on me and come at me with a carving knife," she paused , the relief tangible. "A little extreme even if I were a burglar!"

They both giggled, the tension starting to ease. Jesse wiped her eyes, pulled her hair straight and backed away towards the kettle, flicking it on.

"Want a coffee?" she asked as normally as possible.

Chloe smiled, "Wow, a free stabbing and a cup of coffee, I am a lucky girl!"

Both women smirked at the witty diversion. Jesse liked Chloe; she always had a wicked sense of humour and would always see the good in any situation. However, Jesse doubted even Chloe's ability to joke her way out of the current situation. She decided to play it down, not wanting to get Chloe involved. As a single mum with three kids Jesse couldn't risk Chloe becoming a target, the threat of repercussions still fresh in her mind. Jesse glanced at the kettle, watching its blue glow as the water boiled, then slowly turned to face her friend.

"I'm sorry Chloe, just got a little scared and freaked out." Jesse tried to sound as sincere as possible, unsure if Chloe would buy into her lie.

Chloe gestured to the hallway, "Saw your bags packed, going anywhere nice?"

Jesse hesitated, "Nah, just a few days camping down in Cornwall. Some quality me and Damien time." Chloe simply nodded, unconvinced.

Jesse quickly changed the subject, "I'm really sorry, Chloe."

Chloe gave a beaming smile, "Don't be daft, girl. I know you are a bit mental but I'm here for you, you know that. That's what best friends do."

They both moved towards each other and embraced, pulling each other close to reaffirm the unbreakable bond that existed between them. Jesse hugged her tightly. She felt somewhat better, if not a little embarrassed. Wiping her tears with one hand she pulled away to continue the conversation. She glanced to her left just as the hammer smashed into the right-hand side of Chloe's face, the force of the blow shattering her jawbone, her cheek imploding with the impact. Her head jolted under the ferocity, causing her neck to snap. She tried to scream but was unsuccessful. The second blow collided with her gaping mouth, ripping out her teeth in a shower of blood and saliva. Her legs crumpled as she crashed to the floor, her face impacting off of the tiles. Jesse stumbled back into the work counter, her eyes transfixed on the menacing figure of Dave as he rained down blow after blow on Chloe's head and face. Jesse screamed as her friend's features were reduced to crimson pulp. Dave slowed his attack, raised his head and focused on Jesse then calmly made his way towards her, his hammer at the ready to inflict more carnage. Jesse glanced at the knife that was out of reach, Dave noticed it, too. He started to shake his head slowly from side to side.

"Sorry baby girl, you ain't gonna need that," he roared in triumph as he leapt towards her, his hammer raised.

Jesse spun to her right and grabbed the newly boiled kettle; she popped the lid and swung with all her strength towards Dave's face. Dave was stopped in his tracks, screaming as the torrent of boiling water exploded across his head. He dropped the hammer throwing both hands to his face, his skin melting into his palms. He was screaming in agony. Jesse didn't waste time; she punched him in the face with the kettle, forcing him to stumble back across the kitchen. She reached for one of the knives and using both hands plunged it behind his knee, severing ligaments, the tip erupting out the front of his leg just below the kneecap, causing the big man to fall to his knees. Dave pulled his hands away from his face, his skin peeling in clumps, flesh falling to the floor like melting wax, the deep muscle burnt.

Through bloodied and scalded eyes he scanned the floor for his weapon; he noticed it across the other side of the kitchen, out of reach. He looked up and could just make out the figure of Jesse standing before him. She smiled down at him.

"Sorry babe, you ain't gonna need that," she said as she swung the kitchen knife up under his chin, the blade puncturing the bottom of his jaw, severing his tongue and finally into the roof of his mouth. His eyes rolled back into his head and his body started to sway. Jesse causally walked across the kitchen and picked up his hammer then slowly made her way back to Dave, who was still alive but unable to move. Jesse stared emotionlessly at the hulking killer before her, then without another word swung the hammer down on his head. The kitchen was momentarily filled with the sound of breaking bone as the heavy hammer decimated his skull. Dave's lifeless body slumped to the floor, resting in a puddle of his own melted flesh. Jesse subconsciously dropped the hammer.

She slowly took in the carnage before her—the floor and walls splashed with blood and gore. She felt nothing. No fear, no guilt, nothing.

"What the fuck…" the voice stunned Jesse; she looked up, ready for another confrontation. The male stranger stood in the kitchen doorway; Jesse didn't recognise him.

"Who the hell are you?" she growled under her breath, her adrenaline still surging from the confrontation.

Detective Inspector Lewis Class smiled and reached

for his police ID. "I'm the police and I think we need to have a little chat Mrs Reid, don't you?"

Jesse backed off slowly, unsure whether to believe this new arrival. If he was one of her attackers he would have started by now, but if this guy really was the police why had he turned up here? A thought suddenly occurred to Jesse. What if her husband's abductors saw this policeman arrive and assumed Jesse had called them, then Damien would be killed over a misunderstanding. She had to get rid of him. She certainly couldn't kill him and there was no way in hell she was going to the station now.

"You need to leave," she said fiercely holding his gaze. Class looked around the room, then straight back at Jesse. He smiled.

"I don't think you understand how this works, Mrs Reid. You are standing in your kitchen with two dead bodies and I presume your DNA all over the murder weapons, not to mention the small case of six murders at the police station and a serious RTA," he grinned. "I really don't think you are in any position to make demands. Now come with me and you can tell me what happened here." Jesse shifted uncomfortably.

"You don't understand what is happening to me and I don't have time to explain. All you need to know is that I have to go and if you get involved you are placing yourself in grave danger. Do you understand, Detective Inspector?" She took a step towards him. "These people are everywhere, they know everything and the only thing they understand is violence. You can't stop them or arrest them, they are above the law."

Class reached into his jacket pocket and retrieved his cigarettes.

"Mind if I smoke?" he asked, casually lighting one before getting permission. He took a drag and offered one to Jesse. She smiled.

"No thanks, I'm trying to quit," she quipped.

"Come on Jesse, cut the bullshit, let's get down to the station and you can tell me your story."

Jesse let out a guffaw, "You wouldn't believe me, Detective Inspector....?" He grinned.

"Class, Detective Inspector Lewis Class, Bristol CID, pleased to meet you."

Jesse was just about to reply when she froze, noticing the figure behind the policeman. Class saw the look on Jesse's face, and feeling something behind him he spun around to face the new arrival. He didn't even see what hit him. The blow across the forehead knocked him unconscious before he hit the ground. Jesse looked on in horror as the all-too familiar figure of Felix entered the kitchen.

"Hello Jesse, how are you this fine morning?" he asked politely. He was grinning. She couldn't move, paralysed by terror. Felix studied the room and started to laugh, "My word, you have been a busy little girl." He turned, bent down and grabbed Class by the collar, lifting him off the ground. "Wow, he's out cold," he jested. With his free hand Felix reached into his jacket and pulled out a scalpel. He smiled as he held it to the unconscious policeman's throat. "What do you reckon Jesse, shall I end it now?"

"No!" Jesse screamed.

Felix shrugged and gently rested Class' head back on the floor and tapped his cheek.

"Maybe next time, Mr Policeman." He sprung up to his feet, staring at Jesse. She was shaking.

"I didn't call them, I swear."

Felix nodded slowly in agreement, "I know Jesse, that's why you are still alive." He moved to one side and gestured her to the door, "What do you say Jesse, one last try?" He started to laugh, "Come on baby girl, I'm giving you another head start. Go now."

Jesse didn't move, her eyes trained on the kitchen knife embedded in Dave's chin.

Felix followed her gaze and grinned, "Reckon you could make it before I killed you Jesse? Do you think you are fast enough?" His sarcastic tone was starting to irritate her, his over-confidence saturating her.

"How do I know you won't kill me before I leave?" she asked, a little more grit in her tone.

Felix sighed, "You are becoming tougher Jesse. I can see it in you."

Jesse huffed, "I don't care about gaining your approval. You are nothing but a fucking maniac and I swear to God if you hurt Damien I'm going to kill you."

Felix moved towards her, his gaze predatory. "You wouldn't be the first to try Jesse and I wish you luck but you are trying my patience. I don't normally play with my prey but I have made an exception in your case." He paused and turned his back on her, "I suggest you go now before

I change my mind. My friends are on their way and they don't play as civilly as I do."

Jesse suddenly sprinted for the hallway. As she ran she grabbed the rucksack and holdall and headed for the car. She threw the bags in the back seat, jumped in the car, started it and slammed it into reverse, the vehicle screeching as the tyres spun on the road surface. Jesse accelerated out of her street all the while checking the rear-view mirror for signs of them giving chase.

Felix casually bent down and dipped his fingers in the blood surrounding Chloe's head. This new element of the hunt was pleasing to him. He knew his superiors wouldn't be amused with him changing the rules but Felix was sure he could talk his way out of any reprimand they deemed fit to issue him. It was exciting to be so close to the prey and to give them a head start. Normally he would just kill them but Jesse was different; there was something special about her and he wanted to know what it was that intrigued him so. He smiled as he began to draw his mark on the kitchen wall. Once he had finished he stepped over Class and made his way out of the house. He intended to get a few hours' rest then commence the hunt. Maybe Dave wasn't going to be as useful as he first thought, he mused.

THIRTEEN

Monday, 1030 hrs

"Sir, Sir, can you hear me?"

The voice sounded like it was floating in the ether. Class struggled to open his eyes, his head swimming from the concussion. Mournfully he propped himself up on one elbow, rubbing his forehead. His vision started to clear and he looked about his surroundings.

"What the hell happened?" he said, his voice rough and gravelly.

"You were attacked Sir, took one hell of a smack but the medics say you are going to be okay."

Class focused on the voice, "Is that you, Nigel?"

PC Nigel Collins reached down to help up his superior. "Yes, Sir. We got a 999 call and responded. We found you lying here with two other bodies." Class staggered to his feet, clinging onto the door for support.

"Where's Jesse Reid?" he barked. PC Collins appeared subdued.

"She wasn't here, Sir. No one else in the house."

Class punched the door in anger. "Fuck!" he rasped. "She was here goddamnit; I was bloody talking to her."

Collins looked confused.

"You were talking to her, Sir? But she is the primary suspect."

Class glared at his subordinate. "I know that. I got here to find her caving in that one's head," he pointed to the body of Dave. Class glanced at the wall, noticing the same sigil as in the police station.

He sighed, "Well that wasn't here when I arrived. It must have been drawn by the one that clocked me."

Collins seemed agitated, "Excuse me Sir, but who did hit you?"

Class scowled at the young PC, "If I knew that, smart arse, we would be out there hunting them down, wouldn't we?" Class reached for his cigarettes. The packet was empty. "Bollocks!" he hissed and tossed the empty packet to one side.

"What the hell is going on, Sir?" Collins enquired.

Class rubbed his head. "I have a funny feeling Mrs Reid and her husband are involved with something a lot more sinister than drink driving." He paused and looked at Collins. "In fact, Nigel, I think Mr and Mrs Reid are the victims in this and that the one who done me is the same one who is behind the attacks at the station." He walked over to get a closer look at the sigil painted on the wall. "This is his mark, Collins. I think Mr and Mrs Reid stumbled upon them somehow and are now the targets."

Collins interrupted Class' flow. "Maybe they witnessed the murders and are on the run," he offered.

Class shook his head, "If that were the case he would

have done me, then killed her. You would have found her body here." Class started to pace, his mind racing, trying to connect the dots of the case. "She told me that these people were above the law and that we couldn't protect her," he stopped and looked at Collins, a look of realisation upon his face. "Jesus Christ Collins, she has met them, she has talked to them. There is more than one, possible a handful. Somehow she knows what they are capable of. We haven't seen hide nor hair of Damien Reid and his work said he didn't turn up for a business meeting. I'm willing to bet they have Reid hostage and are using him to control Jesse." He was excited. For the first time in his career he had passion for solving a case. He let out a stifled giggle. "We have to find her. Wherever she is they are going to be right behind her."

Collins spoke up, a look of confusion on his face, "But to what end, Sir? If they have Mr Reid what do they want Mrs Reid to do that warrants keeping him hostage?"

Class shook his head slowly. "I don't know Collins…" he replied. "…but they must want something important because if not then they would have left one more corpse here this morning." Collins looked bemused regarding his superior's new-found vigour, especially after receiving a severe clout to the head.

Class moved closer to Collins. "I want you to put out an all-points call. I want Jesse Reid's description across every law enforcement, port and airport desk. I even want the bloody parking wardens out looking for her. I want her photo, her car details, everything out there. She's on the run with limited resources...," he paused, scratching his head. "Cut off her bank accounts and credit cards. Let's give her no option but to come in to us."

PC Collins nodded, "Yes, Sir," then turned and headed off.

"But I still want a media blackout!" he shouted as an afterthought.

Class slowly looked around the room, staring at the two bodies on the floor. He crouched next to the impressive carcass of Dave. "Jesus mate, I bet you didn't expect to get done in by a woman, did you?" He stood up, his head still pulsing from the blindside attack. Who the hell hit him, he wondered, and what the hell were the Reids mixed up in? The appearance of three SOCO members entering the kitchen stirred Class from his reflections.

"Everything okay, Sir?" the first remarked.

Class nodded. "Yeah, just my ego took a bruising," he retorted, smirking.

They didn't reply but began to set up their testing equipment. Class made his way out of the kitchen and headed down the hallway towards the front door. He paused, then casually took in the scene. He suddenly remembered the backpack and rucksack that he had passed when entering, yet were not there now. He smiled to himself.

"You clever girl," he said out loud, heading for the door.

"Collins!" he shouted. PC Collins came rushing up the driveway.

"Yes, Sir?" he asked.

Class was grinning. "When I came in there were two backpacks in the hallway. I think they contained supplies and camping gear. I think Jesse Reid isn't as stupid as we think. I think she's preparing to go off-grid." Class started to laugh. "Expand the search to cover campsites and known wild camping areas. Check her computer search history for any favourite camping forums and such-like. I think she is going to disappear, Collins, and if that happens we are not going to get a second chance."

Collins nodded and once again ran off to carry out his superior's orders. The DI's head was pounding and he needed a cigarette. He also needed a stiff drink and possibly some coke to sort himself out. Class stretched and scanned the cul de sac. Three police cars, a van and an ambulance were parked outside the Reid's residence. Class sniggered at the thought of the neighbours hiding behind their net curtains, intently watching the neon circus in their otherwise quiet road. Class didn't really pay much attention to the black BMW slowly driving past and quietly leaving the scene.

Monday, 1157 hrs

On the journey back to Bristol station Class had been deep in thought, trying to figure out why they had Damien Reid. Class determined the most probable and therefore most obvious reason had to be that using his accountancy credentials he had embezzled money from some very dangerous and nefarious types who took exception to his sticky fingers. However this didn't stand up to serious scrutiny because if they wanted their money back they would have snatched the wife in an effort to force Damien's hand. Class half-heartedly thumped the steering wheel in frustration. Once again he was back to square one, his only tangible lead being Jesse Reid, who was currently on the run and as yet leaving no clues to her whereabouts or intentions.

Class pulled the car into the station carpark, switched off the engine and sighed. Rummaging in his pocket he found the bag of what was left of his cocaine and proceeded to finish it off. Once again the feeling was familiarly sublime. His headache was slightly improving yet he still craved a drink. He made a mental note to pick up another bottle later, or maybe two, he mused. He checked himself in the rear-view mirror to make sure there were no remnants on his face and exited the car, heading for the station entrance.

"Excuse me, Detective Inspector Class?"

Class turned around to face the unexpected voice.

"Yes?" he replied. The old man in his late seventies stood before him, his neatly-trimmed beard and flat cap giving the impression of subtle refinement, his grey coat covering a dark brown three-piece suit, a loose wool tie around his neck. Class didn't recognise him and wasn't in the mood for reporters or people in general for that matter.

Class spoke in a rehearsed and monotone voice, "If you want to make an appointment just call the office and…"

The old man moved closer, as if not wanting anyone

else to hear their conversation.

"My name is Professor Michael Stokes. I was a Professor of Humanities and Religious Studies at Bristol University and I need to speak to you most urgently." Class sighed, his indifference obvious.

"I'm sorry but I'm a very busy man at the moment. I'm sure any officer will be able to help you, if you would just like…" Stokes looked agitated, shifting from one foot to another, constantly looking around.

"I'm afraid I must insist, Detective Inspector." Class was starting to lose patience with his unwanted guest.

"Mr Stokes," he said firmly, "I just haven't got the time for this; please direct any enquires to the front desk and…" Stokes once again took another step forward, this time entering Class' personal space. The DI stood his ground.

"Mr Class, I really don't think you understand the magnitude of the information I possess, if I could just have a few minutes of your time." Class grimaced and looked at his watch, then to the building. He sighed.

"Okay, you have until I nip 'round the shop to get some fags. Let's walk and talk."

Stokes smiled, then nodded. Class led the way out of the carpark and turned the corner towards the main road.

"Start talking then, Mr Stokes," he said begrudgingly.

Stokes was eager to get started. Class decided to listen but had no doubt this man was a nutter. One of those educated but barking mad types that have loads of bits of paper stating how clever they are but possess no real world intelligence.

"Back in the early 60's I was a young upstart wanting to make a name for myself within my chosen field. I had just gotten my doctorate and was one of the youngest ever to receive it. As such, I was gaining a lot of attention by those who work behind the scenes regarding education and the government." Class was feigning interest, looking forward to a cigarette. The professor carried on, oblivious to the DI's wandering attention.

"I was approached one day by a group of enlightened individuals with the purpose of recruiting me into their highly-secretive and extremely well-funded think tank whose manifesto was the expansion of Darwin's human evolution theory and the creation of a new classification regarding a religion-free society." Class entered the little shop, ordered then paid for his cigarettes. Opening them he turned to Stokes.

"I'm sorry Mr Stokes, it's all very impressive but what exactly are you going on about and what the hell has it got to do with me?"

Stokes smirked, "Everything Mr Class, if you would just bear with me. I went along to an initial meeting at a very expensive private estate on the outskirts of Hampshire and there I sat before a council of thirteen men, some of whom I didn't recognise but some I did." He was starting to get animated. Class lit a cigarette and started to walk back towards the station.

"Time's running out Mr Stokes, I suggest you get to the point and quickly." Stokes nodded.

"Some of these men were prominent judges, others were top-class psychologists, I mean, the best in their field, men who are regarded as gods within the medical profession. Some were neurosurgeons specialising in human motivation and decision-making rationale and at least three were high-ranking cabinet ministers. One I recognised as a serving police commissioner. They knew everything about me, my family and my career. They said they had been watching me and felt that I would be beneficial to their agenda. I was sworn to secrecy."

Class stopped as they reached the entrance to the carpark. He turned to face Stokes.

"It's all rather fascinating but it has nothing to do with me. A bunch of toffs meeting up for clandestine meetings, giving dodgy handshakes and shagging each other's wives is an everyday occurrence these days, thanks to the Tories, and it's not news anymore. Everybody in the country knows and doesn't care. Thanks for dropping by and I hope you have a nice evening." He turned and started to walk away, heading for the station door.

"They had a symbol!" Stokes called after him. Class kept walking. Stokes shouted louder, "A triangle with three vertical lines and one horizontal!"

FOURTEEN

Monday, 1205 hrs

Class froze and then turned slowly to face Stokes. By his expression Stokes knew he had his attention.

"What did you just say?" he asked slowly, his face starting to contort, a slight snarl at the corner of his mouth. He paced towards Stokes, his posture aggressive and meaningful. He stopped within only inches of the slightly worried Professor. "How do you know of this sign, who have you been talking to?" his tone heavy with suspicion.

Stokes shuffled backwards a couple of steps, not wanting to be within striking distance should the DI lose his composure. Stokes struggled to get his words out.

"No one, Mr Class. I told you, I met with this group back in my younger years and I'm sure they are still at work in the shadows but I fear their influence has spread and their power increased."

Class' mind was racing. Only a few people knew of the sigil and the man in front of him was certainly not in the loop regarding the specifics of the investigation, yet he knew the sign left at the crime scene. Class scrutinised the

Professor, watching his posture, gauging for any tells that he was lying. He saw none. The DI started to relax.

"I think we should get a drink. What's your poison, Professor?" he asked.

Stokes smiled. "I'm quite partial to brandy," he replied.

Class chuckled, "Then let's go forth and partake."

Stokes was relived. Class led the way out of the carpark and down the street to the nearest pub. The black BMW in the carpark started its engine and began to follow.

Monday, 1210 hrs

Class watched as Stokes downed his brandy and reordered another. Inwardly he smiled. At least the man has good taste in alcohol, he thought. Class picked up his tumbler and swirled the glass, watching the ice cubes bob to and fro within the amber liquid. He lifted the glass and downed it in one. He too ordered another.

"Okay, you've got my attention. Tell me more about these men, Professor." Class stared intently at the old man who was halfway through another brandy. Stokes shifted under his gaze.

"I never truly knew who all the members were. They encourage you to use an alias, something innocuous boarding on bland," he started. "The group itself have no official name. They used the term, 'the Order' but it was never their true name. Some suggested that to have a name limited their existence, that they would forever be bound by the confines of that name. But it amused them to think some referred to them as such. You see Mr Class, they are smoke and mirrors, and you learn what they allow you. The thirteen members control vast resources throughout the world although their seat of power is very much UK-based." Class sipped his drink, listening intently. "The thirteen are the ruling council and below them they have generals whom they refer to as 'The Selected'. These in turn are responsible for recruiting teams containing three members as well as themselves for the purpose of carrying out horrific acts of violence. These teams of four people are collectively known as 'Jackals'." He paused, nervously looking around the sparsely populated pub. Satisfied they were not being overheard he carried on, "Nobody really knows how many teams of Jackals are out there, at least I was never given access to such information but rest assured they are everywhere and are utterly ruthless."

Inwardly Class was stunned by the professor's story but his face remained expressionless.

"What does this Order want?" he asked, probingly.

Stokes shifted in his seat and leaned in closer, "They agree that Darwin was ninety percent correct in his theory of evolution but believe that only a few within the population would transform into a higher form of human. By this I don't mean like super heroes flying around and having special powers but in the sense that the select few could transcend the morality placed upon our species by our emotions and socially programmed dogma. They believe this limits us from reaching our full potential and what they see as total freedom. They call this perfect state, 'the Primitive'." The DI inwardly sighed. If this old man was telling the truth he was out of his depth and he knew it. "The Primitive is a concept taken from nature itself. When we look at nature we see neither good nor evil. What is chaos for the fly is normality for the spider. There are no emotional attachments made with regards to killing in nature. Animal behaviour denotes that there is no good or bad choice just the choice to act or not to act; it is hard wired into every fabric of being." Stokes was beginning to get excited. He downed his drink and ordered a third. "The Order believe that killing brings them closer to the Primitive and that their victim is sent to a place they call 'the Void'; however when they kill it must be indiscriminate and without malice. They look upon their victim as a kind of sacrifice, not to a god but to the Primitive essence itself. They believe they are feeding off them, hence why they name them 'carrion'. The act of killing is totally sublime; it's a kind of Zen moment for them, a place of utter fulfilment." He paused then carried on, this time a little more subdued, "You must understand that in the beginning it was about the greatest minds coming together to predict how mankind would evolve and in what form. That's why they had people from every discipline so they could work out a blueprint for the future; however, as they delved deeper into the unconscious human mind they found that we as a species are destined to revert back to our animal instincts. There will come a time when our technology will cease to be important and we will cry out for devolution, we won't be able to stop it because it is our own DNA that craves it. As a group they just wanted to be ahead of the curve."

Class downed his third whiskey and stared at Stokes. "Carry on," he stated blankly.

"The sigil I mentioned, and by your reaction the very same of which you are aware, is the sign of the Jackals. It represents a kill or kills in the name of the Primitive. Sometimes the media may catch a glimpse inadvertently but more often than not, nothing is mentioned. Rest assured the Council always finds out even if it isn't documented. They have very effective methods and tried and tested ways of flooding or manipulating media sources, including the internet, with disinformation, should anyone stray too close to their agenda. Because in their eyes, it should only be the elite who can truly comprehend their intentions and motivations. Most of the western world is too consumed by celebrity dating and quasi-geo politics to see what is happening, even the more enlightened conspiracy buffs are too engrossed with who killed JFK or who's hiding UFOs to put it together. That's why there is so little evidence or information about them in the public domain. A secret society that truly is secret." It was Class' turn to lean forward. "What about the police? Why haven't we heard of this group before? Surely if they have been going around killing innocent people and leaving bloody signs everywhere we would know about it?" his tone was abrupt and abrasive.

Stokes winced. "That's the point; they have members everywhere, Mr Class. There is no specific criteria on who they recruit into the Jackals. The Selected are exactly that but the Jackals themselves can be from any religion, faith, colour, creed and sex. They can be from a wealthy background or from a rundown council estate in Manchester, it doesn't matter. The Selected are experts and have been trained since young children in spotting something within people that they themselves may not even know exists."

Class rubbed his head. The headache was coming back with a vengeance, or was it the whiskey, he pondered.

"So you reckon they could have members even in the police force?" Stokes sat back in his chair.

"I'm not suggesting Detective Inspector, I'm stating categorically that they have hundreds and I think some of them work at your station, some you may even call friends."

Class tugged a cigarette out of the packet and lit it. He sat back in his chair and let out a steady plume of smoke. "Fuck," he said, under his breath.

Stokes carried on, encouraged by the policeman's openness to listen.

"The sigil itself is broken down into three elements. Firstly the three triangle sides represent the three words EMBRACE – THE – PRIMITIVE, the words they live by and their mantra. The second element is the three vertical lines; these represent the three members of the Jackal team. The third is the horizontal line going across; this represents the selected leader of that group."

Class was stunned. How could such a group exist virtually unknown in today's computer age where information could be hacked, stolen and bought on the black market? He stared blankly at Stokes, assessing how to use this information.

"I realise that this must seem like a storyline from some Hollywood movie Detective Inspector, but I assure you it is very real."

Class paused then issued his response, "If these people are the all-powerful bunch of ruthless killers you claim, how come they haven't killed you for leaving their ranks or are you still part of them?"

Stokes looked down sheepishly. He looked weary and afraid, "I'm ashamed to admit that for the first few years I agreed with the principles and agenda of the Order. I was instrumental in constructing simulations and formulating hypophyses regarding the effect of such devolution within the general populace and how religion would play a part."

Class smirked, "So they are a bunch of religious loonies then, a cult?"

Stokes let out a subdued gasp, "Absolutely not. Religion or faith has nothing to do with it; in fact they have come to despise religion. They see it as a control mechanism for the masses. Saying they are a cult would be a serious mistake Mr Class; they see themselves as transcending organised faiths and to be honest, I agreed with them." He paused, avoiding eye contact with the suspicious DI. "However, over time I realised what extremes they would go to in order to bring about a faster conclusion. You must understand Mr Class, it was purely academic at first but the more they uncovered the more radical the objective became. They started to expand their influence, their tentacles reaching into the highest echelons of our society, more and more people were being seduced by what they saw as the inevitable progress and as such wanted to be part of it."

Class lit another cigarette. "Didn't these people realise that they would lose all their wealth should mankind revert back to this Primitive state? Surely it wasn't in their best interests if and when this change took place."

Stokes smiled, "That's the point. The Thirteen knew full well that when the change came they would be dead and gone and it wouldn't happen for possibly centuries but were enjoying the power and influence it had in their present. Some members have died over the years but have been replaced; the Thirteen still exist. Those who joined them witnessed first-hand what they could do and had decided that it was better to be with them than against them. Be it fear or greed, these people sold their souls, Mr Class." Class scowled at the old man.

"That still doesn't explain you, Mr Stokes," he said, jabbing a finger in his direction.

"Like I said Mr Class, I left them and they let me go unobstructed at first, then after a few months I started seeing people following me. My house and phone were tapped. Then one day I revived a letter saying I was being investigated for alleged offences against children whilst I was at university." He looked away, seemingly embarrassed. "I can assure you, Mr Class that the allegations were utterly false but it was apparent that The Order had decided that instead of killing me they would character assassinate me, so in the event I talked, no one would believe me."

Class called the bartender over and ordered another round of drinks, his head throbbing from the ever-increasing headache and the information overload.

"If that's true, what have you been doing all these years?"

Stokes adjusted his seating position; he sat up straight.

"I have been writing articles under a false name for graduates and those studying from home. I'm also an online tutor. I have been carrying on my research into The Order and have been keeping tabs on them and their progress, collating any available snippets of information I may find, which to be honest isn't much."

Their drinks arrived. Class thanked the bartender and handed him a ten pound note. The bartender smiled gratuitously and left.

"How did you know of this investigation? There has been a media blackout." he said.

Stokes grinned. "One of my few remaining colleagues was asked about the sigil but had no idea what he was looking at so in turn he approached me. He told me that the young policewoman who asked him mentioned your name, so here I am."

Class took a hefty swig from his drink and briefly closed his eyes in an attempt to rationalise the conversation.

"What do you want, Stokes?" he asked, a twang of

sarcasm audible.

"To put it bluntly Mr Class, I want justice. I want the world to see what they are doing, and I want to expose them." The Detective Inspector smirked.

"And you expect me to stop them, eh? I'm your white knight, the lone policeman who single-handedly brings down the evil secret organisation?" He laughed, amused by his own satirical wit.

Stokes sighed, "No Mr Class. In all honesty I don't think you stand a chance. I am merely warning you about the danger you are in. For want of a better description the Order are a worldwide social club for serial killers and they will let nobody stand in their way."

Class was shocked. It wasn't the response he expected; in truth it pissed him off. "Thanks for the vote of confidence, Professor" he said gruffly. He finished his drink then scratched his stubble. "Any other pearls of wisdom you want to give me?" he asked, aggravated by the old man's blasé comment.

"There are some other bits of information that may prove useful in the short term, Mr Class."

Class huffed a sneaky retort. "Like what?" he enquired abruptly.

"The Jackals are bound by a certain amount of rules that are considered sacrosanct within The Order. To disobey them would be met with unbelievable reciprocity," he paused to catch his breath, his excitement growing. "For a starter they are forbidden to use firearms. All murders have to be carried out with primitive weapons—knives, clubs, bare hands and such-like. They must also leave their sigil at the site of each murder and each member must take turns in choosing the next victim or victims. There are no limits on how many they kill but all must be primitively killed. Should one of their team be captured the remaining Jackals must kill that member regardless of their location or die in the process. They are then replaced by a new member chosen by the Thirteen."

The realisation hit Class like a hammer. He smiled and slammed his fist on the table.

"That's why the fuckers went into the station!" he exclaimed. "One of their own was in custody over some stupid little theft charge and they were duty-bound to kill him. They took out four coppers to get to him!" he flung himself back into his chair, his arms outstretched. "It was an assassination," he said to no one in particular but ecstatic with his reasoning.

Stokes looked on with a bewildered look on his face; he stared at the DI who was chuckling to himself.

"May I ask what is so funny, Mr Class?"

The DI stood up, his eyes never leaving Stokes. "Thank you, Mr Stokes. You have been most useful." He gathered up his lighter and cigarettes and started to leave.

Stokes eyed him nervously, "Where are you going? After all I have explained you are just leaving?"

Class laughed. "Mr Stokes, you have told me who they are without giving me any real actionable intelligence to work with, then you proceed to tell me that I stand no chance in stopping them. The way I see it, at worst I'm going to get brutally murdered. At best I get fired, my reputation dragged through the mud, thus being unable to even get a job working security at a supermarket."

He turned and walked towards the door. Stokes jumped up and followed him.

"I truly wish there was something I could share with you that would help you defeat them, Mr Class, but I honestly don't know where they are nor do I know how to contact them."

Class was walking at quite a pace now, eager to distance himself from the professor. Stokes slowed, unable to keep up with the anxious DI.

He shouted after him, "I doubt you will see me again, Mr Class. I wish you all the best. They know about you now, they will be watching you!"

Class reached the carpark and swiftly made his way to the station entrance. Behind him Stokes was at the carpark entrance. Just as Class opened the door to the station he heard Stokes shout his final three words of warning.

"Trust no one!"

Class entered his office and threw his jacket on his desk then made his way to the window. His office was on the fourth floor overlooking the carpark and from his vantage point he could see Stokes still hanging around the entrance in the vain hope the DI would re-emerge and continue the conversation. Class watched him for a full ten minutes then stared as he eventually wandered off down the road and finally disappear from view. He rubbed his temples, the whiskey dulling his focus but its warmth soothing his anxiety. A double-edged sword, he mused.

The DI slumped himself into his chair and leaned his elbows on his desk, his head resting in his hands. What the hell was he to do now? This case was spiralling out of control and heading into realms of craziness: secret societies, teams of serial killers, corrupt coppers, and smack dab in the middle a nondescript couple from rural Somerset. He was starting to get angry, his frustration finally erupting when he threw his empty coffee mug at the wall; it shattered, sending white jagged shards across the room. His desk phone started to ring. He glared at it as if it were some poisonous snake, his temper still boiling at the feeling of impotence. He wasn't in the mood to speak to anyone; he might just as well give up and go home now. The phone kept ringing. Without thinking Class snatched up the receiver.

"What!" he barked, his frustration vented on the unknown caller. The voice of WPC Lowe was even and un-phased.

"Sorry to disturb you, Sir, but I have a WPC Jones from SOCO on the line for you. She says it's urgent."

Class forced himself to calm down. "Okay, thanks, put her through." There was a faint click on the line followed by silence.

"Hello?" asked the DI.

"Hello Detective Class, this is Jesse Reid," came the reply.

FIFTEEN

Monday, 1500 hrs

Jasper eyed the bound body of Damien Reid with excitement. There was no way this carrion was getting out of this alive. Even if Jesse managed to kill all the members of his team there were already contingency plans in place to finish the couple off and then others would carry on the work. He smiled to himself. The thought of chopping Damien up with a hacksaw really appealed to him.

"I would say 'don't worry' Mr Reid, but in all honesty you really should be worried about now. I'm being straight with you, man to man." He stood and slowly walked over to his quarry who was slumped against the wall of the derelict cellar. "I feel it's my duty to be straight with you and not tell you bullshit to make you feel better." Jasper crouched down, stroking Damien's head. "I am going to kill you in the most horrific way possible and I am going to enjoy it. I can't say it will be fast but I can assure you that your sacrifice will really cheer me up and put a smile on my face."

Damien moaned in defiance.

"I know, I know," replied Jasper. "It sounds really scary but rest assured it's going to be fun," he chuckled. "Obviously not for you, but for the rest of us." He patted Damien on the head as if he were his loving canine companion, stood and walked towards the cellar stairs. He paused then turned to face his captive, whose sobs were audible. "But whatever we do to you is nothing compared to what we have planned for that sexy wife of yours." He erupted into laughter and ascended the stairs.

Damien broke down, his tears streaming at the thought of Jesse in the hands of these bastards; he was breathing heavy, his mouth choking against the industrial tape. He furiously tried to free his hands but the cable ties bit into his wrists, blood flowing from the open wounds. He was helpless. Jasper reached the top of the stairs and hit the light switch plunging the cellar into darkness. As he slammed the door shut he could still hear Damien sobbing. Jasper was having fun.

"How is our guest?" Felix asked as Jasper entered the living room. Jasper looked around the sparsely furnished room. Felix was sat at a table carefully watching his laptop while Denny relaxed on the large couch, sleeping.

"He is as happy as you can be in his predicament," Jasper retorted, his glee evident. Felix shut the lid of his laptop and slowly turned to face Jasper.

"Do we have any idea were Mrs Reid is?" asked Felix.

Jasper sniggered, "Of course. I know exactly where she is. I put a tracker on her car when you were at her house." Felix also started to smirk.

"I'm curious Jasper, where did you learn these skills of yours?"

Jasper stroked his long beard and glared at Felix.

"I thought we weren't to divulge our real names or backgrounds?"

The rhetorical question irked Felix. He shrugged his shoulders. "Usually I pick the team members so I know all about them and from what background they originate, even their skillset, but I did not choose you, did I? You were sent to us by the Council, ergo, I have no information about you and that is annoying to say the least."

Jasper grinned, "I have certain skills that come in useful for our CO."

Felix smiled a wry smile. "CO, eh?" Commanding Officer, not a phrase used by your everyday Jackal. Am I to presume you are ex-military, Mr Jasper?"

Jasper rolled a cigarette and lit it. "You can presume all you want, Mr Felix, but I'm not telling you anything. If the Council wanted you to know they would have informed you. Evidently they deemed you of less importance than you give yourself credit." Felix glared at the bearded man, his anger obvious. Jasper held his gaze.

"Now, now, Mr Jasper. I should warn you that taking that tone with me may lead to unpleasant consequences."

Jasper quickly raised his hand, producing a six-inch blade from the back of his waistband. "Anytime you would like to discuss it further…" he let the sentence trail off, his jaw pulsing with anger.

Felix grinned, "Mr Jasper, I would think very carefully about your next course of action."

Jasper flinched as he felt the blade to his throat and an arm come around his left shoulder seizing his chin in a vice-like grip. He froze.

"Drop the blade," Denny whispered in his ear.

Jasper was secretly impressed; he didn't hear the big man rise and come up behind him. Maybe he underestimated Denny at their first meeting. Jasper started to laugh nervously,

"Come, come friends, let's not be too hasty, just letting off some steam. No harm done." he said. Felix paused then waved his hand, signalling Denny to let Jasper go. He straightened his t-shirt and regained his composure.

Felix returned his attention to his laptop, flicking up the screen, satisfied the encounter was now over. He did however make a mental note to investigate Jasper further when this particular hunt was over.

"I suggest we check where Mrs Reid is right now and plan a little visit. If she stops at a hotel or campsite we can be ninety percent sure she will be there overnight. This should give us enough time to get to her location and finish her. Once we have killed her we will come back here and take care of the husband," Felix snapped without looking at his team members.

Jasper nodded. "I will get a real-time location now. I need to get on the laptop to access my software."

Felix stood up and held out his hand, gesturing Jasper to proceed. Jasper sat at the computer and started to type. Denny eyed Felix, his confusion evident. Felix caught his look and slowly shook his head, the signal that Denny should stand down.

The silent exchange was broken by Jasper, "I have her; she is M6 northbound at the services just past Lancaster. Her engine was switched off ten minutes ago. I can access the hotels system to see if she has checked in," he stated matter-of-factly.

Felix laughed. "Don't bother. She isn't stupid enough to use her real name and she will be using cash to avoid alerting the police to her position." Felix turned to Denny "Get the gear together, we are heading up in five minutes."

Jasper stood and faced Felix. "What about the husband?" he enquired.

Felix shrugged, "We will be back by tomorrow morning. He will keep."

The two subordinates set about their individual tasks, preparing to leave. Felix headed for the back door and exited the house. He stood in the unkempt garden of the grubby terrace house, the property flanked on all sides by similar dwellings. He retrieved his phone from his pocket and dialled a number, then patiently waited for a response.

"Yes," the voice was harsh and to the point.

"Good afternoon, Sir. We have a location on Jesse Reid and are preparing to go after her within the next few minutes." The line was silent for a few seconds.

"Where are you now?" the voice replied. Felix stiffened.

"We are at the safe house in Gloucester, Sir."

Once again the voice made Felix wait for his reply.

"Make sure it's finished tonight. You should have killed her yesterday at the police station, not let her run. You know it's a breach of our rules, Felix. The Council is not happy. You understand there will be repercussions."

Felix gripped the phone, his temper rising. Stupid old fucks, he thought. Who the hell did they think they were talking to? He wasn't some low level Jackal; he was one of The Selected and as such should be shown some respect. He calmed himself before he replied.

"With all due respect, Sir, nothing has changed and in a few hours she will be sent to the Void."

This time the voice was quick to respond. "She has already managed to kill two of your team and we know that an old friend of ours has already visited the policeman in charge of the investigation. He seems to know a lot more than he should."

Felix grinned. "Was that the one I knocked out at her home address?" he asked.

"Yes and he is on your trail, so hurry up and finish it. We will take care of our loose-lipped mutual friend once and for all. This situation is getting out of hand. Don't fail us," stated the voice. The line went dead.

Felix switched off the phone and slipped it in his pocket. He sighed. There was going to be some changes coming, he thought. He wasn't going to put up with this anymore. It was time to elevate himself to the next level, to the position he deserved—but first he had to take care of Jesse. He was beginning to regret letting her go. He came to the conclusion that he had been mistaken and that there was indeed nothing special about Jesse Reid after all, and as such no more games would be played. He looked to the dark clouds circling above. The next time they met he would simply cut her arms and legs off with a machete and that would be an end to it. Felix felt better now. He had realised his error and had come to terms with his momentary lapse of reason. Smiling again, he turned and walked back into the house.

Monday, 1310 hrs

"What the hell are you playing at?" rasped Class down the phone at Jesse Reid. She waited a few seconds before replying.

"I need your help," she stated.

He tried to calm his voice knowing full well the situation she found herself in, although he doubted she understood the full extent of her predicament. He sat down at his desk, holding the phone tightly.

"Listen Jesse, where are you?" he asked as calmly as possible. She hesitated; he continued, "Just tell me where you are and I will come and get you. I can protect you." He heard what he believed to be muffled crying on the line.

"What makes you think you can protect me, Detective Inspector? You saw for yourself what these people are capable of. You were attacked by the same people who have Damien. How exactly are you going to protect me against them?"

In truth he wasn't sure and couldn't give her any definitive answer. He toyed with the idea of telling her about the Order but decided best not to inflame her already fragile state of mind.

"I don't know," he said bluntly. "All I know is we stand a better chance working together than separately." He paused, "Let's meet and we can sort this out once and for all. You're right; I can't make any promises but I'm your only shot to get out of this alive and hopefully get your husband back in one piece."

Jesse remained silent. Class figured she was assessing her options and deciding if he was worth a shot. He knew he wasn't the most approachable man alive and didn't have the best track record with regards to being reliable but he was hoping he had made some sort of an impression to justify her trust.

He continued, his voice as slow and as empathic as possible, "I understand you are scared Jesse. I know these people appear all-powerful but I truly believe we can beat them. We can get out of this."

She snorted in response, then replied. "We? What have you got to do with this? Why would you be worried? They haven't tried to kill you or kidnapped and tortured your husband," she rasped, her voice starting to crack.

Her questions stabbed at him. How could he respond without letting something slip? He let out a sigh. "Look Jesse, these people know who I am and have me marked the same as you. We are on our own. Nobody is going to help us. We have to help ourselves and we haven't got much time." He thought he had reached her and sat silently, waiting for her to respond.

"Okay," she said eventually. "I will meet you at the services Northbound M6 just past Lancaster, tonight at ten. Come alone." The line went dead.

After what seemed like a couple of minutes, Class replaced the receiver and sat back in his chair. He was exhausted, his forehead ached from the alcohol and he was in dire need of a shower. His sweat-soaked shirt clung uncomfortably to his skin. He massaged his temples in an attempt to focus his thoughts. Part of him was relieved that she had made contact but deep down he was feeling apprehensive, his self-doubt crawling ever closer to the surface. You didn't have to be a genius to realise that if he was heading out to meet her there was nothing stopping them from following him directly to her location. That is, of course, presuming they didn't already know where she was, in which case the chances were he would arrive to find a body. He could perhaps phone a station near their rendezvous and get a couple of local lads to babysit until he got there, but could he really trust them? Not only that, the way the killers stormed the police station and killed four trained officers he didn't fancy the local lads' chances considering who they were up against.

"Fuck," he murmured.

He went to pick up the phone but hesitated, his mind tumbling once again, trying to reason who exactly he could trust to help. He replaced the receiver, his paranoia getting the better of him. He jumped up, grabbed his coat and headed out of the office. If he was going into the lion's den he sure as hell wasn't going unarmed, he mused.

Class' shoes squeaked loudly as he paced swiftly down the highly-polished corridor. Struggling to put on his jacket he pushed open the door to the staircase with his free hand and suddenly came face to face with PC Collins.

"Sir," he said, on seeing the DI, straightening himself up before his superior.

Class paused and glanced at Collins. "How long have you been in the service, Collins?" Class enquired.

The young PC beamed. "Out of training three months ago, Sir," he replied.

Class started to grin. "Get your coat, Collins. You have just been selected for a top secret mission," and with that Class walked briskly down the stairs.

Collins hesitated, then duly followed suit, wondering what the secret mission entailed. "Where are we going, Sir?" he called after the DI. Out of view he heard Class reply.

"We are going to visit some friends in the armoury."

SIXTEEN

Monday, 1800 hrs

Archie the Shih Tzu tugged at the stick lodged in the bush, his tail wagging furiously. He bit down hard, turned and took off at top speed, returning to his owner on the far side of the park, happy to show off his retrieval skills. Professor Michael Stokes sat alone on the park bench, intently watching as Archie raced towards him. He smiled to himself. He truly loved that dog, his loyal companion through thick and thin, a little bit of joy in an otherwise bleak and torrid existence. He sighed and rummaged around in his pocket to find a treat for the rapidly approaching dog. Archie skidded to a halt at Stokes' feet and dropped the stick, gazing up heroically at his owner, his breath laboured and awaiting his inevitable reward. Stokes bent down and ruffled Archie's head.

"Good boy, Archie," he said, tossing a chew at the dog, his voice full of praise for his fluffy best friend. Once again Stokes picked up the stick and threw it as hard as he could and once again Archie raced off to claim it. The old man sat back on the bench and looked to the skies. Sodden clouds swirled with a northwest wind; it was getting chilly and it looked like it was getting ready to rain. Even though it was only 6 p.m. he knew it would start to get dark soon and he didn't like to be out once the sun went down. Stokes would give it another ten minutes then make his way home, possibly stopping off at the fish and chip shop to pick up his supper and maybe a little treat for Archie.

He stood up, his bones aching from his seated position or was it something else, he mused. He stretched in an attempt to iron out the creases, aware that his body was deteriorating. You are getting tired, old man, he told himself. These are your twilight years and what have you got to show for it? Stokes subconsciously shook his head in an attempt to wipe the negativity from his thoughts. He was proud of what he had accomplished despite the Order trying to discredit him. Oh, how he despised them, their arrogance and self-righteousness. At first he had been proud to join them and had been overjoyed to be such an integral part of shaping their ethos. He started to cough. He clutched his throbbing chest, then bending slightly he spat out the offending item. A lump of dark thick mucus mixed with blood spewed forth and landed on the concrete pathway. He retrieved a handkerchief from his pocket and diligently wiped his mouth, then after folding it tucked it neatly away out of sight.

"Bloody cancer!" he snarled under his breath, staring at the filthy sludge before him.

He sighed as the first spots of rain started to fall. He pulled his collar tightly and scanned the empty park for Archie. He could not see him. Stokes turned full circle as to get a panoramic view of the park in the hopes Archie was somewhere close by.

"Archie!" he called but no dog was forthcoming. Stokes' heart started to beat faster; he feverishly surveyed the park, willing his companion to appear. He began to walk across the grass towards a set of bushes where Archie had been playing. The rain started to get heavier as he made his way across the increasingly sodden playing field. As Stokes got closer he could see movement at the base of a thick bush directly in front of him. Cautiously he moved closer.

"Archie?" he called in a more sedate and inquisitive tone, his trepidation tangible. With a crash of twigs and leaves Archie bounded out of the foliage complete with stick, jumping up at his owner, oblivious to the anxiety caused. "Bloody hell, Archie!" Stokes exclaimed. "You scared me, you silly little sod!" Stokes started to laugh. "Come on you, let's get some supper." Stokes bent down and slipped Archie's lead on his collar then slowly started to trudge his way back across the field towards the foot path, Archie trotting happily by his side.

Stokes had been thinking about his meeting with the DI all afternoon and had felt slightly miffed that the policeman didn't take what he said too seriously. In truth, Stokes had come to the conclusion that he didn't actually like the DI. He found him arrogant and cocky but had felt somewhat obliged to warn him of the coming dangers, even if he refused to acknowledge them. The Order was not to be underestimated and Stokes thought the policeman was far too incompetent to pose any real threat to them; however, he needed all the help he could get in his quest to bring the Order down, no matter how small. He shrugged at his internal conversation.

It was getting darker now. Stokes tried to speed up, but was aware of his companion's little legs and flagging enthusiasm—that and his own aching bones, he chuckled. Stokes glanced up as he neared the end of the path. Before him, winding to his left, the path continued 'round leading to the small carpark; to his right was a children's play area complete with two swings, a roundabout and a small slide. He seemed to remember a small paddling pool being there at one time but that had long since been removed. He smiled as he reminisced about his younger school days when he would rush here after school to play for a few minutes before running home for dinner. Later he would spend his evenings hunched over science books, studiously working, preparing himself for the bright future he imagined lay ahead of him. All the while his friends would be out playing and chasing girls. He was meant for greater things.

Growing up in the city had its drawbacks but he had always loved Bristol. However, it had changed significantly over the years. It had become plagued with drugs and the inevitable violence that they bring. That's not to say it was majorly worse than any other big city but it was his home and as such he didn't want to see the modern day yob culture ruin the city's welcoming environment. He surmised that all people his age thought the same thing about their own places of dwelling, regardless of location. It would seem the older you get the less tolerant of change you become. He made a mental note to use that in a future thesis. If he was honest, he had always thought this way and this very reasoning was in some part responsible for leading him into the welcoming arms of the Order, that and the incessant need to impress his peers, which he now looked back on with nothing but regret.

He recalled what he had explained to the policeman, that his enthusiasm had waned once he realised their ideals were starting to become separate from his own. After a fractious couple of years it had become evident that sides were being taken within The Order. The inevitable split which occurred still left to this day a vicious wound, unable to properly heal. He truly wished things had been different and that it needn't come to this but time was running out and if he was to succeed he would have to act decisively.

The shout startled the old man. He looked up towards the source, wondering what it was. Stokes saw the figure emerge from the shadows of the playground. The male was about seventeen or eighteen and clutching a beer can, dressed in a dark track suit and baseball cap, his white trainers dirty and caked in mud. He was casually smoking a cigarette leaning against the children's slide and staring directly at the professor. Behind him three other males began to gather like hyenas backing the obvious alpha. With his failing eyesight Stokes couldn't determine age or any other details but sensed they were looking for trouble. Stokes started to feel agitated; the alpha male had a sense of purposeful menace about him.

"Give us a fag, old timer," he snarled.

Stokes quickened his pace, unwilling to engage with the stranger. Archie started to growl and tug against his lead. Stokes pulled him close, not wanting to give any provocation.

"Don't go grandad, I like dogs. How about that fucking fag then?" the yob shouted aggressively.

The thug sprinted to intercept Stokes all the while laughing, whipping up his friends into a frenzy of jeers and abusive taunts. They too came closer, eagerly awaiting the inevitable assault. The old man stopped and snatched Archie up into his arms and grasping his lead tightly. Archie growled, tugging against his collar in an effort to edge towards the threat. The thug brazenly walked up to the professor, his confidence growing with every passing second and pushed him hard against his shoulder, the preamble to an assault, Stokes presumed. Archie snapped at him catching him on the hand, drawing blood and forcing him to recoil.

"Fucking dog!" he rasped and lashed out, punching the dog in the face. Archie yelped and went quiet.

"What do you want, young man?" Stokes shouted, tears welling at the sight of his beloved companion getting savagely attacked.

"Forget about the fucking fag, old man..." the thug sneered through clenched teeth. He turned and looked at his friends, searching for the encouragement to escalate the confrontation. He returned his attention to the professor and squared up to him, his face mere inches away from the terrified dog walker. Archie cowered, too scared after his attack to oppose.

"Just gimme ya fucking money, old man!" he sneered, his mouth spitting, the phlegm spraying Stokes in the face. He winced and pulled away slightly, fearing an attack.

"Okay, just please don't hurt me or Archie," he whimpered.

The lout laughed, his friends gathering close to witness their leader's actions, eager to see violence dished out. Stokes put Archie down but still held tightly to his lead; the dog remained still, cowering to his master's leg. With his left hand Stokes opened his jacket and slipped his hand into his inside pocket to retrieve his wallet.

"Hurry the fuck up, old man, before I die of old age!" the yob sniggered. The rain was heavy now. Stoke raised his head and glared at the yob.

"I can assure you that you won't be dying of old age, son," he growled.

Stokes pulled his hand free from his jacket. The yob stared in terror as he saw the SIG Sauer P226 9mm semi-automatic handgun levelled at his face. Stokes squeezed the trigger. The retort was massive, the slide slamming back as the gun spat out its deadly hollow point load, the muzzle flash-blinding the yob a split second before the round collided with his forehead then erupted out the back of his head, showering his friends with blood and brains. The sound of the empty metal casing hitting the concrete galvanised them into action. Stokes aimed the weapon at them, his stance perfect to take a follow up shot.

"I advise you to leave now," he snarled.

They ran, leaving the body of their leader slumped on the wet floor, the heavy downpour already washing away the blood. Stokes coughed then replaced the pistol back into the covert shoulder holster. He did up his jacket and glanced at Archie.

"Come on then boy, let's get you your supper," he said happily. Stokes walked around the corner and followed the path to the small carpark. As he approached he could see two heavily-built, smartly-suited men standing by a parked black BMW, its windows dark and tinted. Stokes casually walked up to the vehicle.

"Everything alright, Sir?" asked the first man.

Stokes grimaced. "Bloody kids today," he quipped. "Got no respect for anything."

The suited man nodded and opened the rear door of the luxury motor.

"There you go, Sir," he said, gesturing with his free hand.

Stokes got in and the door was closed behind him. The two suited men paused and cautiously surveyed the area with expert eyes one last time, their hands instinctively touching the butts of their own 9mm pistols hanging loosely below their armpits. Satisfied all was well they got into the front seats.

"Where to, Sir?" asked the second man, who had slid himself behind the steering wheel.

"The chip shop, please," Stokes replied whilst attentively drying Archie with a towel.

The suited man started the engine. "Of course, Sir," he said as he slowly steered the vehicle out of the carpark.

SEVENTEEN

Monday, 2135 hrs

Jesse took a hefty gulp of her white wine and closed her eyes, savouring the taste of grape upon her tongue—just something small to remind her of normality. The pub chain restaurant was quiet despite the motorway location and she had glimpsed only a handful of other guests when she booked in to the service's hotel. Of course she had used cash, her paranoia forcing her to ditch her credit cards back in Somerset soon after her escape from the house.

The drive north had been quiet and uneventful and to be honest Jesse was glad of the alone time to be able to clear her thoughts and formulate a viable plan. The whirlwind of horror she had been exposed to over the last couple of days hadn't given her an opportunity to let her circumstances sink in but now the brief reprieve had allowed self-doubt and the feeling of desolation take hold, its hopelessness permeating her very marrow. Even though she had asked for help earlier that day it had taken her most of the journey to accept her decision to contact the DI and ask for his assistance. Deep down she knew she wouldn't last long against the wave of brutality that was coming for her, and in truth she was terrified. Her ego didn't like admitting to the fact that she wasn't the action hero she wished she could be, but rather a scared little girl who had no one to turn to.

Jesse started to cry at the thought of Chloe's mutilated body lying on her kitchen floor, her head ruthlessly smashed open by that killer. She stifled an outburst, tentatively looking around the pub for any sign that someone had heard her and taken an interest. Her guilt was welling up inside her. It was her fault, she mused. She was responsible for her friend's death. Jesse took another swig from her glass, paused then finished it off, her need for the alcohol to wash away her perceived sins paramount. Wiping her eyes she stood up and made her way to the bar. The bartender causally walked over to her, a broad smile on his face.

"Same again?" he asked in heavy Lancashire accent.

Jesse half-heartedly smiled, unable to commit to a full one. "Yes please," she said, not wanting to engage in conversation, her body language defensive.

The barman understood the unspoken request to be left alone and wandered off to refill her glass. Jesse gazed around the restaurant and bar, reading each of the people in turn, assessing if they were a potential threat to her safety. She held her gaze at the young couple in the corner, both smartly dressed and trendy looking, young and fresh in their twenties, with a small baby in a travel buggy. They were enjoying a light evening meal, laughing and smiling with intermittent cooing over the little one. Jesse watched closely as they would subconsciously touch each other's hands, a sign of undying affection. She sighed, her thoughts turning to Damien. She wiped another tear from her eye then turned her attention to the rather obese middle-aged man towards the front entrance. He was sat alone eagerly tucking into a huge burger and chips, his low-cost suit tightly fitted and showing signs of wear. A salesman she assumed, long hours and bad diet taking its toll on his body.

The bartender returned with her drink. She handed over a screwed up five pound note. He smiled again and disappeared to the till to retrieve her change. Jesse sipped the wine, again enjoying the fruity taste. She glanced at the flat screen television perched high up on a shelf out of the reach of the patrons, the images of the news channel flitting from some far away warzone to a politician admitting an affair or fiddling his expenses. The world goes on as normal, she told herself. Again she casually scanned the pub, this time her attention drawn to the middle-aged couple seated close to the bar. They seemed frosty with each other as if in the aftermath of an argument. The husband silently scanned his newspaper whilst the wife checked her social media account on her smartphone. Neither spoke nor looked at each other. Jesse smirked to herself—sign of the times, she thought.

The bartender returned once again and handed Jesse her change; he wasn't smiling this time and didn't hang around for conversation. He scuttled off back to the kitchen, no doubt to engage in some laborious task assigned by his duty manager. Jesse stood up and made her way back to her table, the remnants of her steak and ale pie cold and uninviting. With her fork she toyed with the food, debating whether or not to finish it. She decided not to and pushed the plate to one side, concentrating on her wine instead. Even though the alcohol was welcoming she was conscious of not getting drunk; she didn't want to dull her senses for the impending meeting with Class.

Despite her situation she felt a little more relaxed after checking the building for threats. Of course she couldn't be one hundred percent sure she was safe but she was confidant she had done a good job. The last twenty-four hours or so had taught her a valuable lesson. If any of these people were after her then they were very good at close surveillance and professional enough so they didn't set off any alarm bells. Jesse grimaced at the thought of her imagination running wild. She wasn't some Hollywood superhero after all; this was real life and as such she only had one chance. Her mental illness was her constant unwanted companion and sometimes led her into a false sense of security, thus giving her either more confidence or crushing self-doubt. Some of her doctors had mentioned the term 'bipolar' but Jesse had been too scared to get tested, although she secretly knew she exhibited most of the signs.

She shuddered and took another big swig of her wine, eager to dismiss her growing sense of unease. Jesse rummaged in her pocket and pulled out her pouch of rolling tobacco. She expertly rolled one, stood up and made her way to the front door, already knowing where the smoking area was located. The smell of cooked food and stale alcohol permeated the carpet and furnishings, the décor straining to be inviting and homely but failing miserably. As she passed the scattered wooden tables and chairs she scanned the other occupants for any sign of movement or even the slightest glimpse that they were paying her a little too much attention. She was relieved she didn't see anything untoward and exited the restaurant, heading to the smoking area.

Jesse lit her cigarette and looked around the dark carpark. It was half-full but she expected that more people would arrive during the night. The sound of the motorway gave a low hum in the background, the sky dark and mottled. To her left stood the two-storey prefabricated Travel Lodge hotel, to her right the exit road to and from the services. She took a drag and held the smoke in her lungs, taking her time to enjoy the abrasive nicotine. She exhaled slowly, her body relaxing from the high. Glancing at her watch she studied the time. 2140 hrs. She pondered how far away the DI was and if he would be true to his word and arrive unaccompanied. She shrugged. In fifteen minutes she would know one way or another.

Jesse decided that the best course of action would be for her to go back to her room, take a quick shower and load her gear into the car, then hide somewhere in the shadows around the perimeter of the carpark so she could witness the arrival of the policeman and see if he was alone. If he wasn't she would wait until he entered the hotel, then jump in the car and make good her escape. Jesse smiled at her plan and tossed her cigarette to the ground, then briskly made her way to the hotel entrance.

Across the carpark Denny sat silently and motionless behind the wheel of the white Ford transit van, watching his victim make her way back to the hotel. He grinned, the excitement of the hunt building. Felix sat in the passenger seat slowly sharpening his hunting knife; he too had been watching his prey. When they arrived an hour earlier Felix had gone to the restaurant window to carry out some reconnaissance and to his surprise had seen Jesse sitting in full view. He had chuckled to himself at his victim not having the sense to sit in a location that was out of sight from the windows and doors. Amateurs, he had told himself, and they wonder why they are carrion? He had returned to his team and told them this was going to be easy. Denny went to open his door.

"Wait!" Felix snapped. Denny turned to face Felix.

"Why?" he murmured. Felix started to laugh and reached up, switching off the interior light then covering the plastic with thick black masking tape.

"As soon as you open that door we will be lit up like a Christmas tree." He paused.

"Use your brain, Denny" he said the sarcasm and scorn evident.

Denny glanced over his shoulder at Jasper who was standing up in the back eagerly clutching his vicious-looking fire axe. He was smirking, staring at Denny with utter contempt.

"There, there be a good little doggy," he snipped.

Denny turn away, his temper once again bubbling. He should have killed him back at the safe house, he thought to himself quietly. All three killers got out of the van and slowly made their way to the hotel entrance, all the while using the darkness as cover.

Jesse quickly showered, dressed herself in a black t-shirt, blue jeans and a pair of hiking boots then gathered her rucksack and bag and headed for her hotel room door. She paused to take one last look around to make sure she hadn't forgotten anything. Satisfied, she turned, snatched the handle and opened the door. The sight of Felix stunned her, her body rooted to the floor. Felix didn't hesitate and lashed out with his right hand, the vicious-looking hunting knife making contact and slicing into Jesse's left arm, causing a fountain of blood to gush from the wound. Jesse recoiled but somehow regained her composure. On instinct she ran at him with her rucksack at chest height, using it as both shield and weapon, thrusting all her strength behind the attack. She pushed forward, the momentum slamming Felix in to the wall opposite her room with devastating force. Felix's head smashed into the super structure causing him to lose his balance briefly, then sending him toppling to the ground. Jesse seized the opportunity and followed through with the heavy bag, using it as a battering ram. As Felix landed Jesse raised her right foot and stamped down as hard as she could, her foot colliding with Felix's face. His nose exploded, showering Jesse's boot with blood, the look of surprise disappearing as his head slammed into the carpeted corridor. Jesse screamed with rage and struck again; this time she punted Felix square in the face, his head slamming into the wall.

Jesse grabbed her rucksack and ran down the corridor, not waiting to see if Felix was alive. She rounded the corner and threw herself through the double doors leading to the stairwell. Suddenly and abruptly she was yanked back by the hair. She lost her balance and dropped the rucksack, falling backwards back onto the landing. She crashed to the floor with bone-jarring velocity. She was stunned, her head spinning with the ferocity of the attacks. She couldn't focus. The impact was massive as a large-booted foot crashed into her ribcage, sending her sprawling across the abrasive carpet. She pulled herself to her knees clutching at the wall to steady herself, desperately trying to defend herself from her unknown attacker. As she managed to get to her feet she felt another blow, this time colliding with her jaw, the impact whipping her head back against the wall. She crumpled, blood flowing freely from her wounds. She choked and spat out two teeth, her mouth filling with blood. She blindly struck out but hit nothing but air. Waves of nausea swept through her; she wretched as once again another blow slammed into her face. Jesse lay on the floor dazed by the blows' quick succession. She pulled herself in to protect her stomach, fearing another abdominal attack. Jasper reached down and grabbed her by the throat and dragged her limp body to her feet. He held her against the wall, glaring at her, a vicious-looking axe in his right hand.

Through bloodshot eyes Jesse caught the first glimpse of her attacker. His wild hair pulled back into a ponytail, his long beard to his chest, his breath was a heavy mixture of tobacco and coffee. She stared at him and could see the wanton aggression in his eyes.

"When I'm finished with you I'm going to take care of your husband. I'm going to chop him up with a hacksaw while he is still alive. What do you think about that? " he snarled.

Jesse tried to speak but it came out as a muffled whimper. Jasper laughed at her and released his grip as to hear her plead for her life, the axe firmly gripped should she try to run. As soon as the pressure had diminished Jesse lunged forward and sunk her teeth into Jasper's cheek. He screamed in pain as Jesse bit down with all her force. Jasper tumbled backwards crashing into a small table, knocking off a lamp and scattering the brochures placed upon it. He desperately tried to pull Jesse free by grabbing at her hair but she refused to let go. He swung his right arm in the hopes of hitting her with the axe but due to the close proximity couldn't get the right angle for a cut. Instead the side of the blade hit her on the head but there wasn't enough force to be effective. Jesse merely shrugged it off and held on, oblivious to the blunt, heavy metal, her blood-lust taking hold. She could taste the copper in her mouth as she clenched her jaws together. He screamed obscenities at her as she locked her legs around his waist, her arms tight around his head and neck. He threw the axe to one side and frantically tried to slam her but it was no use. Jesse had locked her legs at the base of his back and refused to let go. She could feel him weaken, his movements less urgent. Jesse could sense he was passing out; she squeezed tighter and kept the pressure on, her survival instinct going into overdrive. Jasper slumped to the floor with Jesse still clinging to him. His body wobbled and went limp; only then did Jesse let go.

She clambered off and stood motionless, her face covered in the Jackal's blood, her shirt torn and ripped. She eyed the body waiting for it to rise; it did not. Jesse tried to catch her breath, her mouth still flowing with blood and vomit. She spat it to the floor and looked around the corridor, her eyes searching for a weapon. She glanced at the axe but decided against it. She wanted to use something else. She spotted a fire extinguisher and calmly walked over to the safety implement. Removing it from its hook she stood above the injured body of her attacker. She looked down on him as he started to regain consciousness. Jasper rolled onto his back, his cheek lacerated to the bone. Large clumps of flesh hung from his battered wound, his beard soaked and sodden. Jesse stared emotionlessly at him.

"How's this for primitive, fucker?" she rasped as she slammed the fire extinguisher down into his face. He managed to let out one scream before she hit him again. His jaw bone cracked and eye socket crumpled as the solid metal object rained down again and again. Jesse screamed as blow after blow connected with the already dead Jackal. She refused to stop, her rage unleashed and unstoppable. Jesse gradually slowed down only after her energy dissipated. She stared unblinkingly at her extinct foe, a mass of crimson sludge were his head once was.

Jesse dropped the fire extinguisher and slowly backed away, scanning around her for possible threats. She snatched up her rucksack and pushed through the doors into the stairwell. Leaning over the railing she checked to see if the coast was clear. It was. Taking the stairs two steps at a time Jesse manoeuvred her way to the ground level. At the bottom Jesse paused to check the foyer. She couldn't see any sign of movement. Silently she opened the doors and made her way into the brightly lit reception area.

"Hello, Jesse," came a voice from behind the counter.

Jesse spun around to see Denny leaping over the counter top, his right hand clutching a heavy meat tenderizer, the wall behind him awash with blood splatter—the remains of the receptionist she presumed. Jesse turned her head, looking at the main door. There was no way she would make it past Denny in time. She twisted her body, preparing to run. The sound of the main doors crashing open caught both Denny and Jesse by surprise. Denny turned to face the source of the disruption, his face a look of surprise. Detective Inspector Lewis Class' large frame charged through the doorway and collided with Denny in the stomach, the force of the brutal rugby tackle sending both men slamming into the receptionist desk. Denny dropped the hammer in the melee, unable to keep hold under the impact of the attack. Both men tumbled to the floor, each trying to stand and gain the upper hand. Jesse ran forward and threw a savage kick at Denny, catching him in the temple. He screamed in pain clutching at his head just as Class managed to throw a brutal right-cross into his face. Denny sprawled backwards from the impact of the simultaneous assault.

"Run!" Class screamed.

Jesse ran for the door. She slid to a halt as the figure of PC Collins appeared in the doorway. For a split-second Jesse panicked, fearing another killer but relaxed as she saw the uniform. Crying, she rushed towards the young PC, her arms outstretched, seeking salvation. Collins stopped and raised his arm, then slammed a vicious punch into Jesse's face, the momentum knocking her to the floor. Class stared wild-eyed at his companion.

"No!" he growled, the shock sending waves of disbelief causing through his body. Denny capitalised on the DI's momentary pause and struck out with a punch directly to the throat. Class collapsed to the floor struggling for air, his face turning red and his body convulsing. Instinctively Class reached up and using his fingers, prised out his Adam's apple, instantly allowing the airflow to resume. He gasped as his lungs filled with fresh oxygen. Collins didn't hesitate; he sprinted at the DI who was now on his knees and rising. Collins grabbed his police issue baton and flicked it out, the heavy duty steel rod ready to damage flesh and bone. He swung at the DI with full force. Class dropped back down onto his back and simultaneously lashed out with his feet, kicking the inwardly charging Collins in the legs. The impact of the kick shattered his kneecap, causing him to tumble forward. Class rolled to one side as the PC's momentum toppled over him and careened head-first into the reception desk. Unable to stop his fall, Collins hit the edge with massive force. His face caved in as the edge of the counter decimated the soft tissue, his mouth torn open as he screamed. Class recovered from his inelegant roll in time to witness Collins's lifeless corpse collapse on the floor. The DI had barely enough time to recover when he was struck from behind, the blow powerful but not enough to knock him down. He spun around to see Denny scrambling to his feet and moving rapidly towards the hammer lying on the other side of the foyer. Class leapt to his feet and once again charged at Denny. Just as he was about to make contact he was blindsided from his right, the force of the blow sending him crashing into the entrance doors, his body weight causing the glass to erupt in a shower of razor-sharp shards. The DI landed hard. He covered his head as his bruised and injured body skidded to a halt, the skin on his exposed face catching glass and concrete fragments.

The DI wearily raised his head, blood flowing freely from his wounds as Denny and Felix walked towards him. Both of them were bloodied and hurt, but they were smiling. Class turned slightly towards the still-unconscious Jesse, whose body was to his right. He tried to stand but couldn't, his legs unable to take his weight. In a final act of defiance he attempted to crawl towards her but couldn't move. The DI started to feel dizzy; his eyes blurry and unable to focus, they started to close. He slumped onto his back, powerless to stop the inevitable attack. Felix and Denny stood above him and gleefully watched as the DI drifted into unconsciousness. Just before he passed out he heard the distant familiar sound of sirens.

EIGHTEEN

Monday, 2253 hrs

Michael Stokes sat behind his antique mahogany desk and listened intently as the voice on the end of the line explained what had transpired only a mere half hour ago. His face remained emotionless but his body taut as it was described how the Jackals had brazenly attacked the Detective Inspector along with a female companion at a Lancashire hotel. The professor thanked the caller and replaced the receiver.

He paused, taking time to stare at the open fire, the orange flames captivating him as they always did, the heavy wooden aroma gently wafting around the room and catching his nostrils. When staring at the flames his mind always wandered and then settled on one single perfect fact: fire just "is", he thought to himself. It is neither good nor evil, just the same as water—he would add to his own internal meanderings—polar opposites yet equally beautiful as they are destructive. The same water that hardens the egg softens the potato he would repeat to himself. He smiled. That saying had always seemed rather poetic to him; how could anyone argue with such simplistic rationale? If this fact stood up against scrutiny then why such logic shouldn't be applied to the human condition, he had asked on more than one occasion. Of course there were always those who would argue against such reasoning, indicating man's evolution into a civilised creature, stating that morals had somewhat dulled and repressed the primitive side and that it was a redundant concept, hence we have no need of it in today's technological society. That being said however, the select few would see the deeper meaning hidden within the question. They would acknowledge that something was "missing" from humanity and that something was obviously the Primitive.

He shook himself from his metaphysical wonderings and picked up the manila folder resting on his desk. He flicked it open, his astute eyes scanning the photo and taking time to read the information collated on his head of security. He smiled slightly, the beginnings of a plan starting to formulate. He swiftly closed the file and jabbed at the intercom button on his telephone handset. A metallic voice answered the hail.

"Yes, Sir."

Stokes quickly cleared his throat. "Mr Stevens, could you come in for a minute, please?" he asked.

"Right away, Sir," came the reply, then the line went dead.

Stokes gently leaned back in his chair, the leather creaking softly, and cast his gaze down at Archie, who was sat happily in his basket radiating in the heat from the fire. The library itself was approximately twenty feet by twenty feet. Oak bookshelves stretched from floor to ceiling around one wall, with either side of the solid wooden door situated directly in front of him and partially on the other wall, only leaving room for the large ornate fireplace. Behind the desk was a well-sized window, its heavy drapes now closed to give privacy at this late hour. Stokes liked to have his back to the window when he worked as he reasoned that staring outside could only harbour distraction, thus stemming his creative flow.

The heavy oak door opened with a well-worn creak and Mr Stevens entered, gently closing the door behind him and made his way to the desk. Archie raised his head then turned away, obviously uninterested with the new arrival. At 6' 4" Stevens was an imposing man. His cropped brown hair and clean-shaven appearance gave onlookers an air of controlled yet underlying aggression. His hardened look was completed by a hefty scar over his left eye. To the professor he was an incredible useful man capable of striking fear into the bravest of opponents by his mere presence alone and as such had been elevated to the privileged position as the head of Stokes' security team some years ago. He truly was an asset, pure and simple. Prior to his employment with Stokes he had been an operative in the SBS, the elite waterborne Special Forces unit within the Royal Navy. Having passed the selection at the top of his class whilst serving in the Royal Marines he had served in the unit specialising in covert operation.

After a rather distinguished career and numerous clandestine missions he had decided to go into the private sector working as an Anti-Piracy Operator, his skillset in high demand across the Far East and off of the African coast. However, his short fuse and heavy hands and the fact he disliked many of his co-workers led him into trouble on more than one occasion. On one such occasion Stevens had found himself in Winchester Prison serving a lengthy sentence for nearly beating a man to death in a Dorset pub for doing nothing more than knocking over his pint. By fate or coincidence it just so happened that Stokes was assigned to the prison conducting research regarding aggression and the study of murderers at the same time at the bequest of the Order; of course the cover story given to the Governor was that he was researching prisoner's welfare and reform for a thesis. After a chance meeting Stokes had had a multitude of lengthy conversations with Stevens regarding many things ranging from philosophy to eugenics. Over time he had come to recognise his impressive and unique skillset, not to mention developing a genuine admiration for his animalistic and somewhat simplistic attitude towards violence—a personality trait much sought after within the Order.

During these formative years the professor had managed to build up an extensive and trusting rapport with the Spec Ops man and after a time had convinced Stevens that The Order was his true calling. The ex-soldier had jumped at the chance to lend his talents to such a worthwhile cause. Utilising their contacts within the Government, The Order managed to obtain his release and he immediately entered the professor's employ, stoically remaining by his side even when the split occurred and Stokes was forced out. There wasn't many whom Stokes liked but Stevens was one of the chosen few. As far as the professor reasoned he was the perfect right-hand man: loyal, without conscious and utterly ruthless.

"How can I help, Sir?" Stevens asked quietly. He stood straight with his arms behind his back, hands clasped.

Stokes stood up and casually gestured the big man to sit. Stevens unbuttoned his suit jacket and sat himself down. Stokes grabbed a decanter and offered Stevens a drink.

"Whiskey?" he asked.

Stevens slowly shook his head. "No thank you, Sir," he replied. The old man smiled and shrugged.

"As you wish," he said, pouring his own glass. The old man replaced the decanter and dropped two ice cubes into the glass, then returned to his seat. "We have a problem, Mr Stevens, and I would be grateful for your input," the professor said cryptically. He paused, watching the big man's reaction. It didn't change. Stokes continued. "It looks like The Order are getting a tad sloppy and I think the time is nearly upon us when we must take the fight to them." He sipped his drink, his analytical gaze never leaving the security man.

"How do you think we should precede, Mr Stevens?" he asked.

Stevens shifted slightly under the questioning. "I'm just a soldier, Sir. You don't pay me to make those kinds of decisions," he replied. "I just follow orders," he added.

Stokes grinned at the big man's honesty, secretly impressed by his blind acceptance regarding his place within the organisation.

"I realise that Mr Stevens, and I appreciate your loyalty but I want you to think outside your remit and just for a minute imagine that you were me. Faced with our current situation do you think it is the prudent course of action to attack and if so, how would you go about finishing them once and for all?"

Stevens shifted once again, a slight smirk touching the corner of his mouth.

"In that case, Sir, I would suggest that we use this policeman and his woman-friend as bait. It stands to reason that the Order will be livid with the Jackals missing their target and as such will make sure that they are the ones who finish the job. I very much doubt they will send any replacements, just expect the remaining two to do all the work. In my tactical experience it stands to reason that these two are viewed as a liability, so if I were the Order I would have no hesitation with taking them out; also, they can't afford any loose ends." The big man stopped and eyed the professor, eager to see if his superior found fault with his reasoning. Stokes was silent but listening attentively. Stevens continued, "Either way our route into The Order is to keep tabs on the policeman and his woman."

Stokes started to laugh. "Then what, Mr Stevens?" he enquired. Stevens also started to smile.

"Once the policeman is dead we get the information we require from the Jackals then go after the Council, finish them off in one hit."

Stokes slowly nodded, took a swig of his drink and stood up. He paced gracefully to the fireplace then paused, once again watching the orange flames dance like amber tendrils.

"How big a team would you need to finish the task, Mr Stevens?" he asked keeping his back to the big man. Stevens shifted his seating position slightly.

"We have a team of four, Sir. We would need to kit them out with TAC gear and high grade MILSPEC assault rifles and we are good to go. Including me, five highly-motivated, professionally trained and well-armed men would give you your desired outcome. In my humble opinion that would be enough, Sir," he stated a matter-of-factly.

Stokes turned to face his right-hand man, his broad beaming smile indicating he was satisfied with his deceptively simple yet highly effective plan of action.

"You don't think five heavily armed men running around the English country side with automatic weapons is a tad overkill and would attract unwanted attention do you, Mr Stevens?"

Stevens remained stoic. "I think these men are professionals, Sir. Zero exposure," he said calmly.

Stokes raised his glass in toast, "Well then Mr Stevens, may I suggest you get your men ready and put them on standby. I anticipate we shall be making our move within the next twenty-four hours. I want to be ready when the opportunity presents itself. Give our contact in Glasgow a call and let him know what equipment you require and he will tend to it; money is no object. I want a swift resolution when the time arrives. Am I clear, Mr Stevens?"

Stevens causally stood up and buttoned up his suit jacket "Absolutely, Sir," he replied.

"Good," stated the professor abruptly. Stevens turned and headed for the door. "Oh, Mr Stevens," Stokes called after him. The big man paused and turned to face his superior.

"Yes, Sir?" he asked.

"No mistakes," Stokes demanded.

Stevens nodded. "Understood," and with that he opened the door and left.

Stokes once again sat back in his chair, his glass nestled comfortably in his grip. The time was nearly at hand he mused; after all these years it was nearly time to take the war to The Order and make them pay for their transgressions. Stokes raised his glass in mock triumph.

"Revenge," he said out loud, then took a hefty swig.

NINETEEN

Monday, 2350 hrs

Class gently eased himself back in the hard wooden chair and winced as the pain in his chest stabbed at him. He paused, closing his eyes, waiting and willing for the pain to subside. It took a couple of minutes before the eventual dissipation brought relief. He wearily looked around the desolate hospital ward, the bright florescent lights making his head hurt and eyes squint.

He didn't remember much after the attack; in fact he had woken up in a hospital bed, naked and hooked up to monitors. His body ached and his senses felt sluggish. Concussion, he had surmised. He had grimaced when they told him he was lucky to be alive and chortled when he recalled being thrown through a glass door. It's not every day you get this much excitement he had quipped, the nurse unfazed nor impressed by the DI's dark sense of humour.

His first instinct was to find the girl, much to the distain of the attending nurse; only after threatening her with obstruction and arrest did she finally cave in and give him the location of Jesse. She had unceremonious mumbled her grievances and opinions and had even threatened to get the resident doctor as he painfully dressed himself and made his way to the private room outside of which he now sat. To the untrained eye one might have thought the hospital to be abandoned; however, he knew full-well that armed officers were stationed at each exit point and that only those with the highest clearance would be allowed to enter the ward. An incident as serious as this would be a hive of activity and speculation and he had no doubt at present it would be splashed across news channels and the internet. There was no one else present on the ward; in fact it was evident that all other patients had been moved prior to his and Jesse's arrival. On top of this he was pretty sure that other armed officers were stationed nearby, should they be needed.

Upon finding her secure location he had gone in to see Jesse and to check up on her. She was awake and apart from some cuts and bruises seemed to be in good spirits considering the night's events. She had politely requested that he wait outside whilst she took a shower and got changed into some fresh clothes, no doubt from her rucksack that some PC had left in her room whilst the doctors attended to her. It was the least he could do, he had muttered to himself. The room door opened and Jesse appeared, her wet hair pulled back into a ponytail, her face bruised and slightly swollen. She smiled as she made eye contact with the DI. He returned the gesture as he ran appraising eyes over her.

"You okay?" he asked his voice slightly gravelly.

Jesse smirked. "What do you think?" she replied, the

sarcasm evident but with also a hint of playfulness. Class smirked then eased himself to his feet, his face grimacing as wounds started to throb.

"Yeah, I suppose that was a bit of a stupid question, eh?" They both laughed, each clutching their sides in pain.

"Best we don't make each other laugh, I reckon," Class added. Jesse smiled once again.

"Want a cup of coffee? I'll get room service," she quipped. Class started to roar with laughter, his head pounding from the concussion.

"Why the hell not?" he replied.

Jesse turned and went back into the room and the DI slowly followed. Before entering he glanced once more both ways down the corridor, the smile gone, replaced now with a look of urgency. Jesse sat on the bed and propped her legs up, the gentle bubbling of the sideboard kettle starting to increase. Class grabbed two cups and dropped two pouches of coffee in each. *Bollocks to it* he thought, after the night they were having they needed a proper dose of caffeine. He glanced up to catch Jesse staring.

"What is it?" he asked. She turned away slightly, obviously embarrassed by her sudden flux of emotion.

"Nothing," she said, her voice low and subdued. Class sat himself on the edge of the bed, gently resting his hand on hers. She pulled away sharply and rubbed her eyes.

"What are we going to do? You can't protect me, can you?" she whimpered.

The DI remained quiet, his own mind struggling with the night's events. He didn't have a plan and was racked with guilt that this woman had placed her trust in him and he had let her down, not just failed her but very nearly got her killed. Could he in all honesty protect her from these people?

"Thought so," she muttered as if reading his mind.

Class lowered his gaze, awash with the feeling of helplessness. He rose and made his way over to the freshly boiled kettle. Remaining silent he filled the mugs, added milk and offered one to Jesse. She turned and took the mug, her eyes red from crying. She gave the briefest of smiles.

"I'm sorry, Detective Inspector. That was unkind of me. I know you saved my life and that if not for you they would have killed me." She started to blush. "I'm sorry," she repeated. Class grinned.

"Don't worry about it Jesse, it is natural to feel this way. Emotions are running high and everything is crazy at the moment," he paused and took a swig of his coffee. "You are an ordinary woman forced into an extraordinary situation. Don't worry about hurting my feelings." She smiled her jaw and face aching from the injuries.

"What happens now?" she asked. Class wasn't sure how to respond. He paused, thinking of a suitable retort but failed to come up with anything convincing.

"Well…" he started, "I think the best thing we can do is to get you into protective custody. Get you to a place that is out of the way of possible threats." Jesse remained silent. Class continued, "In all honesty, Jesse, I don't know who to trust or how far they have influence." Jesse looked stunned, her face changing slightly, a look of bewilderment slowly spreading.

"What do you mean by influence?" She put her cup down and glared at the DI. "Just who the hell are these people and what aren't you telling me? I want the truth, Detective."

Class sighed. He knew there was no way to back track out of this and had come to the realisation that Jesse had to know the truth about the people pursuing her. He sat himself down on the chair opposite the bed and sombrely stared at Jesse.

"They call themselves 'the Order'," he began, his tone low. "Apparently they were started by a group of psychologists and high-powered people back in the sixties. Their main objective is the devolution of mankind into an animalistic state they call the Primitive. They believe that humanity has been softened by technology and morality and that killing is the only pure endeavour." He paused, waiting for Jesse to catch up with the information she was being told. She looked on. Her silence spoke volumes. He continued. "The Order is orchestrated by thirteen men who select others, known as the Selected, who in turn seek out and recruit killers who work in teams known as Jackals." Again he paused, waiting for a reaction. There was none. "These Jackals commit murder on behalf of the Order and take turns choosing their victims, although they refer to them as carrion." He stood and walked to the window, staring out into the rain-swept blackness.

"What the hell has that got to do with me and

Damien?" she finally asked. Class was impressed by her resolve. He had thought that she would break down and descend into hopeless despair but to his surprise she was staying strong. He turned to face her.

"Apparently they have certain rules to work by…" he continued. Jesse recalled the conversation she had with Felix.

"Yeah I know," she said, interrupting Class' flow. "They aren't allowed to use guns and all their murders have to be performed primitively or they suffer the consequences of their masters." It was Class' turn to be shocked.

"They told you this?" he asked her.

Jesse nodded. "Yes, when he called me to tell me they had Damien. They said I had to run and survive. When I pushed him to find out who his masters were he basically told me to fuck off, and hung up on me." Jesse stood up and made her way to the window. Standing next to Class she turned and faced him. "Got a cigarette?" The DI grinned.

"I don't think we are allowed to smoke in here," he said sarcastically. Jesse opened the window.

"I don't really care, do you?" Class let out a slight chortle.

"I suppose not," he replied. He reached into his trouser pocket and retrieved a crumpled packet of cigarettes and a lighter. He popped one in his mouth and offered one to Jesse. She grinned.

"Tailor-mades?" she quipped. "I had you down as a roll-up man," she added as she lit her own.

Class relaxed as he took a lungful of smoke, happy that his chest pain wasn't flaring up with the nicotine rush. Jesse let out her own plume of smoke and returned to the conversation.

"So what the hell have me and Damien got to do with this Order then?" she asked forthrightly.

Class just shook his head. "It would seem you and your husband were at the wrong place at the wrong time, Mrs Reid. As far as we can tell that specific gang of Jackals were at the Wells Police Station to kill one of their own that had been in custody." Jesse coughed and stared at the DI.

"What do you mean, kill one of their own?" she enquired. The DI took another couple of drags on his cigarette and tossed the butt out of the window. Jesse followed suit. He sat himself down again, gesturing Jesse to take the weight off also.

"You know I mentioned that they have to abide by certain rules?" Jesse nodded. "Well it seems that one of the rules is that if one of their team gets captured it is the responsibility of the others to kill them or die in the process," he paused once again to catch his breath. "I believe that they had accomplished their mission then somehow chose you and Mr Reid as their next victims." Jesse looked down and shifted her body weight, eager not to make eye contact. Class could tell she was hiding something from him

"What is it, Jesse? What aren't you telling me? The truth works both ways you know," he said, his voice tinged with a slight pang of annoyance. Jesse looked up at him.

"Damien and I were out celebrating our wedding anniversary…" she began to cry. Class remained quiet. "…when we returned to the car three people, one girl and two men attacked us and we tried to escape but Damien crashed the car so we…" her voice started to break as the memories came flooding back. Class stared at her, his posture still and composed. "Damien told me to run so I did. He followed and we ended up in the police station searching for help, but they were all dead." Class started to chuckle.

"You killed one of those bastards in the station, didn't you?" he exclaimed, a look of excitement on his face. "You were in there," he said. Jesse held his gaze.

"Yes. The female tried to kill me and would have succeeded if it wasn't for Damien…" she let the sentence trail off. Class was chuckling. He didn't need to know the specifics; he knew how the female died. Class reached for another cigarette.

"You my girl are my hero," he said laughing heartedly. Jesse was confused; she stared at the DI, caught unawares by his sudden outburst.

"How so?" she replied.

"No wonder these guys have a major hard-on for you and your husband. You have managed to kill three of these fuckers and made them look like a bunch of muppets in the eyes of their superiors. Twice they have come after you and both times you have beaten them. They are worried Jesse and worried people make mistakes no matter how influential they are." Jesse sat up straight as if excited to absorb some good news.

"You knew we were at the police station?" she asked sheepishly.

Class smirked. "I figured you were both there but didn't have any hard evidence linking you two to the crime scene. We found your car but were going to question you both regarding the abandonment." He paused, his mind turning to PC Collins. "Shit!" he muttered. "That bastard Collins, the one that attacked you at the hotel was assigned to assist me in this case and all along he was one of the Order's little errand boys. He must have been feeding information back to his paymasters about the progress of the case in the hopes that I would lead them straight to you." Jesse stared at him. She wanted to say something to ease his self-guilt but struggled to find the right words.

"Bollocks!" he rasped slamming his fist on to the small table by the bed. He lowered his head. "You were wrong, it's me who should be sorry, Jesse. I led them right to you," Class cursed under his breath, his frustration evident. "Collins knew I was meeting you, he must have tipped them off regarding your location." Jesse stood up and gently held his arms.

"Look at me," she implored. Class met her gaze, his own eyes beginning to well up. "It isn't your fault, they arrived before you. They must have found out another way." Class slowly shook his head.

"I don't see how," he mumbled. Jesse squeezed a little tighter.

"Don't fall apart on me now. I need your help. As

you said, we have to work together if we want to get out of this. It isn't about arresting them anymore, it's about getting Damien back and our survival. They want to kill us Lewis, not scare us or even toy with us; they want to murder us…," she paused to add emphasis on her last few words, "…both of us." Class mentally shook himself. Get a grip, his inner voice screamed.

"Do you have anything that resembles a plan?" he asked flippantly. Jesse gave a half-baked grin.

"And there's me thinking you were the big badass cop with a plan," she joked. Class huffed at her remark.

"Funny," he retorted, a smile returning to his battered face.

The door opening made them both jump, as one they stared at the newcomer. The doctor froze, he obviously had interrupted and felt embarrassed.

"I'm sorry," he stated. Class smiled.

"No problem, Doctor, what can we do for you?" The doctor made his way to Class, his hand open, gesturing a handshake. Class shook it with a firm, positive grip.

"I'm Doctor Baker," he said, a broad smile across his face. "I trust you are both feeling better?" They both nodded. "Now then, Mr Class…" the Doctor began whilst flipping open a folder. "My nurse has informed me that you decided to get out of bed and venture forth on a little adventure without my say-so, is that correct?" He looked quizzically at the DI, who squirmed under his auspicious gaze.

Class grinned. "That is correct, I…" The doctor

didn't let the DI finish his sentence.

"You, Mr Class, are not a physician and as such, not qualified to make such decisions regarding your health. I, on the other hand am, and I am telling you that you have suffered a great deal of trauma and should be in bed resting up." Jesse stifled a giggle at the DI getting a telling-off like some naughty schoolboy. Class turned his head and looked at Jesse.

"And what are you laughing at?" he quipped, his face contorting into a semi-smirk.

Baker looked somewhat flustered at the humorous exchange. "I can assure you Mr Class, that this is no joking matter. Your health is our priority and we can't have you running around the hospital as you see fit." Class returned his attention to the doctor.

"What's the prognosis then, Doc?" he asked. The doctor once again referred to his notes.

"Well Mr Class, you have suffered a broken rib, heavy concussion and numerous cuts and contusions." Class smiled.

"Good stuff then. Thanks for your help, Doc." Jesse coughed loudly to get the doctor's attention.

"What about me?" she asked, a trace of worry in her voice. The doctor composed himself.

"Well then Mrs Reid, you have two broken ribs, lacerations to your arm, head and neck injuries conducive to blunt force trauma and a possible fractured skull." Jesse and Class looked stunned.

"Fractured skull?" Jesse asked, a little more worry in

her question than before. Baker looked directly at her.

"Yes Mrs Reid, in fact we are all surprised you are still mobile and active. To be quite frank, we have seen other people die from these injuries."

"Bloody hell," Class murmured. Jesse remained quiet and sat herself on the bed.

"Doctor…," began Class, in an attempt to divert and steer the conversation away from Jesse's injuries, "who is the senior officer on duty tonight?" Baker closed his file.

"That would be Sergeant Rogan, Mr Class," he offered the policeman. Class rubbed his temple.

"Could you tell him I want to speak to him, please? It is rather urgent." The doctor nodded and headed for the door. "Oh Doctor…," Class called after him.

"Yes, Mr Class?" the doctor responded. "Can you please not tell anyone either of us are awake and only speak to Rogan directly?" Baker nodded once again and left the room, gently closing the door behind him.
"Shit!" Jesse said out loud when the doctor had left.
"Fractured skull, eh?" Class started to laugh. "You're still standing, ain't ya?" he joked. Jesse looked unimpressed. "What's next then?" she enquired. Class sighed.

"Well like I said before, we have to get you into protective custody and hopefully this Sergeant Rogan will be able to help. If not, then we are on our own. I don't want anyone else back in Bristol to know of our whereabouts just in case there are more infiltrators willing to sell us out."

Jesse shuddered, her bravado starting to slip, her mind starting to tumble into her private void. She pinched herself, willing her mind to snap out of it.

"You okay?" asked Class. Jesse forced a smile.

"Yeah I'm okay, just a bit taken back by my state of health." Class smirked.

"Fancy a ciggie?" he asked playfully. This time Jesse really did smile.

Once again the door was abruptly opened, only this time a tall, skinny police officer entered. He was dressed in body armour. Harnessed across his chest was a Heckler and Koch G36 semi-auto rifle and a Glock 17 was holstered at his hip, his pinched features almost rat-like. Class eyed the policeman, his paranoia suddenly rearing its ugly head. Could he be trusted, he wondered.

"I'm Sergeant Rogan. I believe you wanted to see me, Sir," he stated officiously, his accent a deep Lancastrian tone. Class relaxed, satisfied he was no threat.

"That's correct, Sergeant," he replied. "I want to get Mrs Reid to a safe house ASAP. Can you assist?" The armed officer looked at Jesse, then back to the DI.

"I would need to clear it back at HQ, Sir. I don't have the authority to leave or let you leave until my commanding officer gets here and OK's the transfer."

Class exhaled softly. "I understand protocol, Sergeant Rogan, but we really need to get Mrs Reid out of here and into someplace safe. You do understand what has happened this evening, don't you?"

The sergeant shrugged, "Sorry Sir, not my concern. I have strict orders to keep you both here." Class could feel his temper rising.

"Now listen here, Sergeant, I am a senior officer and I am ordering you to assist in the safe relocation of a vulnerable witness. There are very serious people coming after her and this hospital is a target. Do I make myself clear?" he rasped. Once again the sergeant remained emotionless, his body language unchanging.

"I will contact my SO, Sir, but can't make any promises." He turned and exited the room, leaving Jesse somewhat confused and Class irritated.

"Bloody jobsworth," he snarled when the sergeant was out of earshot. Jesse let out a deep sigh.

"Guess it's going to be a long night," she offered and settled herself on the bed, preparing for a night in the hospital. Class admitted defeat and succumbed to the fact that they were not going anywhere this evening. He slumped into the chair and gazed out of the window. He secretly hoped the armed officer's CO was more reasonable than his subordinate was.

TWENTY

Tuesday, 0745 hrs

Jesse awoke with a jump. Her mind raced as the remnants of the dream resonated in her subconscious. She frantically scanned the hospital room fearing her dream was in fact real and that Felix was there with a blade dangerously poised over Class' throat. Jesse let out a gasp of relief as she realised all was well and the DI was sound asleep in the chair, undisturbed from where she last saw him the previous night. She rubbed her eyes and looked at the clock on the wall. She had slept well despite the dreams and still ached from her injuries. She felt stiff from the bed rest yet somewhat refreshed. She stared at the DI happily sleeping, a slight sound of snoring breaking the otherwise quiet room. She relaxed as her senses returned from her slumber and felt comforted by his stalwart presence.

"What time is it?" Jesse snapped back from her daydream and smiled at the now awake DI.

"Seven forty-five" she replied softly. Class stood up and stretched. His entire body ached, not only from his injuries but also from the night spent in an awkward sleeping position.

"Bloody chair," he mumbled under his breath as he tried to shake off his slumber. Jesse pulled herself out of the bed and picked up the kettle, eager to kick start her body with some much-needed caffeine.

"Wanna cup?" she asked. Class grinned.

"Of course I do," he jested.

Jesse padded over to the sink and filled the little kettle with water, then returned to the bedside table and switched it on. They both remained silent, each of them lost in their own thoughts, their musings only broken by the click of the freshly-boiled kettle. Class sorted out the coffee whilst Jesse popped to the toilet. When she was alone she gazed at her reflection, the bruises on her face now purple and vicious looking. She turned her head to the side revealing a freshly stitched cut on her head. She winced, remembering Jasper's attempt to hit her with the blunt side of the axe. At the time she didn't feel anything, her rage dulling any pain inflicted, but now after the event she could feel every blow. Jesse started to cry, the tears flowing freely down her cheeks. She turned on the tap and splashed her face with cold water, an attempt to wash away her tears and try and bring her back to some sort of normality.

"You okay, Jesse?" she heard Class call from the other side of the bathroom door. Jesse wiped her eyes and stared defiantly at her battered reflection.

"Yeah, I'm fine," she retorted as confidently as she could muster. Jesse heard the ward door open, then muffled voices in her room. She strained to make out what was being said. She heard Class' distinctive voice then others.

She wiped her face dry with a towel, took in a deep breath and opened the bathroom door to face the newcomers.

The room was now occupied by Class and three other policemen, all in uniform. She didn't recognise any of them. Class turned to her and gently gestured for her to join in the conversation.

"So this is Mrs Reid, I presume," stated the closest policeman. Jesse eyed the speaker. His overweight frame and fat face made him look somewhat comical, his uniform tight around his chest and stomach. He smiled broadly at Jesse.

"Good morning, Mrs Reid. I am Chief Superintendent Blake of Lancashire Constabulary. I trust you are feeling better after your ordeal?"

Jesse didn't reply but held his gaze. The CS felt uncomfortable and let out a nervous laugh, then returned his attention to Class.

"As I mentioned to you just a minute ago, Detective Inspector, we are prepared to offer Mrs Reid and yourself temporary protective custody at a safe house located in our district. Until, that is, we have conducted a thorough investigation regarding the incident at the hotel. Of course neither you nor Mrs Reid will be able to leave, pending the results of said investigation," he paused and glanced quickly at Jesse. "I hope you understand," he added.

Jesse looked imploringly at Class, her unspoken question being understood by the DI.

"What are your contingency plans if the safe house becomes compromised?" Class asked directly. The CS huffed abruptly.

"I can assure you, Detective Inspector, that neither our safe house location nor any details of the operation will be leaked. My officers are one hundred percent trustworthy."

Class smirked. "Forgive me Sir, but my cynicism is based on factual evidence and thus far has been proved right. The people after Mrs Reid and me have infiltrated the police service and god-only-knows what civil service offices." He looked at Jesse and nodded. "I'm sure Mrs Reid would rather have a backup plan should anything go wrong."

Blake sighed, his face contorting a little. "What rank am I, Detective Inspector?" he asked roughly. Class rolled his eyes, he knew what was coming.

"You are a Chief Superintendent, Sir," he said curtly.

"That is correct, Mr Class. My rank is beyond reproach and to have a Detective Inspector of all things call it into question is boarding on insubordination. I tell *you* what is going to happen and you do what you are told regardless of your personal feelings or what your bloody gut instinct tells you. This is my constabulary and you are a mere guest. I am doing you a favour by housing you here and don't you forget it." He glared at the DI, his face starting to turn scarlet. "Do I make myself clear?"

Why are all senior officers such a bunch of tossers, Class mused to himself whilst refraining from biting back at the fat, pompous CS. He smiled politely.

"Understood, Sir," he replied softly, struggling to

keep his temper in check. Jesse remained silent, not wanting to inflame the situation further. Blake broke the uneasy silence.

"Good, I'm glad we cleared that up. Right then, my men here will wait for you both to gather up your belongings and then are tasked with taking you to our safe house in Preston." Jesse and Class glanced at each other. Blake continued, "Upon your arrival we will send out for food and provisions to see you through the next couple of days, then we will see how the land lies before proceeding further. Whilst staying there I will have two officers standing guard twenty-four hours a day. Any questions?" Class shifted slightly.

"Are these officers to be armed, Sir?" he asked as politely as possible.

Blake sighed under his breath. "No, Detective Inspector, they will not be armed. I see no point in wasting taxpayers' money on the assumption that these criminals know where you are. My officers are highly trained in control and restraint and carry standard issue pepper spray and batons." He puffed out his chest as if proud that his officers carried such pointless weapons.

Class couldn't help but snap back this time. "With all due respect, Sir, I'm not quite sure you understand the level of violence these people are capable of. Didn't you see the mess they made of the hotel? Pepper spray and ASPs are going to do fuck-all when these guys come mob-handed. The chances of your officers getting butchered are pretty bloody high…" he paused, wanting his words to hit home.

"I strongly urge you to use armed officers, not just for our sakes but for your own men's safety."

Blake glared at Class, his temples throbbing with anger.

"I decide what threat level is appropriate Detective Inspector, not you!" he growled. "Now get ready, you will be transported in five minutes," he added. Blake turned and marched out of the room, taking his two officers with him. Class slumped down on the chair, his head cradled in his hands.

"Jesus fucking Christ!" he snarled. "What the fuck is wrong with these people?" Jesse sat on the bed and held his hand.

"Come on, let's just get the hell out of here and worry about the rest later, eh?"

The DI tried to smile. "Okay, let's do that, shall we?" he joked.

Jesse stood up and made her way over to her rucksack and began gathering her clothes and other personal bits up, stuffing them in, not bothering to fold or place neatly. She was eager to get going. Class jumped up and headed for the door, he turned to face Jesse.

"Okay, I'll be right back, just going to get my jacket from my room. Don't leave without me," he said, winking at her and with that he opened the door and left.

Jesse looked around the room, pleased that she was escaping the claustrophobic confines of the sterile, makeshift prison cell. No matter where they were going she knew it had to be better than this place. Jesse checked the room once more and made her way into the corridor, relived to see the two police officers waiting patiently. They nodded but remained silent. She turned to see Class walking briskly towards her.

"Okay, let's get going, got everything?" he asked, sounding a little out of breath. She nodded. Class turned to the policemen.

"Over to you then boys. Let's go."

Without saying a word the two officers started to walk away. Both Jesse and Class followed, their eyes scanning to and fro. They walked down the long corridor, took the stairs down three flights and then exited from a side emergency door. One of the officers started to talk into his two-way radio. Neither Class nor Jesse could hear the reply due to the covert earpiece worn but they presumed he was talking to the driver of their waiting vehicle. Upon exiting the hospital they gathered on the pavement. Class surveyed the small delivery courtyard, searching for any threats. The yard was secluded with seven-storey buildings on three sides, which left only one way into the space. Jesse looked to what little sky was visible. It was blue with no rain clouds. She smiled to herself, pleased that it wasn't raining again. She inhaled deeply and could smell fresh laundry and disinfectant. As strange as it sounds, Jesse found the mixed aroma somewhat intoxicating, a little slice of normality once again.

Class gave Jesse a cursory glance then turned to his left as a black Mercedes swung into the yard and proceeded to turn in the little space as to be facing out towards the exit. The two officers immediately opened both rear doors for Jesse and Class to get in. They both did so, eager to seek shelter. The policemen jumped in and no sooner as the doors were closed the driver accelerated out of the yard and onto the hospital's main road. Within minutes the Mercedes had left the hospital grounds and pulled out onto the main ring road, heading out of town.

Nobody in the car had noticed the dark blue Vectra pull out of a side street and staying three cars back, start to follow them.

TWENTY-ONE

The night before Felix and Denny were just about to finish Class and Jesse off when the sirens started. They were left with little choice but to flee the scene without finishing the job. They had sat concealed in the back of their transit watching the emergency services arrive, unaware that the perpetrators were still nearby. It appeared that the police were more concerned about dealing with the aftermath within the hotel than to conduct a proper search of the area. They must have presumed that the attackers had fled. If so, it stood to reason that they would concentrate their efforts in having roaming patrols up and down the motorway. The Jackals had watched intently as Jesse and Class had been spirited away by ambulances, still unconscious as far as they could see. Felix had been vexed that they had come so close to finishing the job and the carrion had managed to escape, yet again.

Maybe he shouldn't have let Jesse run back in Somerset, he told himself. This truly was a different sort of hunt. Normally the carrion would be dead within minutes of the hunt beginning but this was turning into a complete disaster. Felix had sighed deeply at the realisation that he alone would be held accountable for the whole fiasco. He also reasoned that it was only a matter of time before Denny would challenge his authority and try to usurp him as leader.

After waiting a couple of hours they decided to leave the scene. They drove a couple of junctions up the motorway then found a nice secluded spot where they set fire to the transit, after which both had walked over a mile before Denny managed to flag down a young couple in a blue Vectra. Unfortunately for the good Samaritans, only a mere ten minutes into the journey Denny had hacked them both to death and dumped their bodies in a culvert at the side of a quiet B-road. Only then had they decided to head back into civilisation on the assumption that Jesse and Class would have been taken to a main hospital to have their wounds treated. In theory all they needed to do was to check out some of the hospitals and see if there was any heighted police activity. If there was then it was in high probability the right location.

The final part of the plan would be to reach out to their police contacts and find out when they were going to move them to the inevitable safe house, then follow them and finish them. It was simple and effective. They had both decided to park the car a little way from the suspected hospital so as not to arouse suspicion. Despite portrayals to the contrary in films, security is quite effective at hospitals in the modern age and two men sitting in a car does tend to raise eyebrows—unwanted attention they could do without. Felix grabbed his mobile phone and punched in a number; he waited as the line rang.

"Yes?" came the answer.

"It's me. Any confirmation where they have being taken yet?" Felix enquired. A brief silence, then the voice answered.

"We should have some information for you soon. Your instructions are to stay off the radar and keep a low profile. Do not engage with anyone—repeat—do not engage with anyone. There are not to be any civilians killed and all other hunts are hereby suspended. Your only concern is to follow then terminate Detective Class and Jesse Reid."

Felix nodded as if the voice was in front of him. Denny sat in the passenger seat staring blankly out of the window, uninterested in the conversation.

"Are there any other instructions from the Order?" Felix asked tentatively, trying to gauge his own mortality or lack thereof.

"The Order is disappointed with you, Felix. They expected more from their protégé," the voice replied.

Felix suddenly realised how precarious his future looked and was desperately trying to figure out a way to win back favour.

"Could you please pass on my sincere apologies to the Order and assure them that this matter will be dealt with as soon as we have the correct information with regards to their extraction plan?" The voice remained silent for a few seconds. Felix started to feel awkward, waiting for a reply.

"I will pass your comments on to the Council," the

voice finally said. Felix felt a little better.

"Thank you," he replied, but the voice had already hung up. Felix closed the phone and tossed it on the dashboard. He slumped back, his head throbbing with the growing strain of the situation. Denny faced him.

"What's going on then?" he grumbled. Felix closed his eyes and rubbed his head.

"We have to stand down and await instructions. As soon as they know, we will know," he replied. Denny shrugged.

"Can we kill anyone else while we wait?" he asked, flippantly. Felix opened his eyes and stared at his companion.

"No Denny, we can't. No civilian casualties, okay? We just finish off those two, then we take a little break. The Council's orders."

Denny hadn't replied, just returned to staring blankly out of the window. Felix started the engine and glanced at his watch. It was 0540 hrs.

"Fuck it," he said. "There's a café around the corner, let's go and get some breakfast." Deny didn't reply. Felix pulled away and headed for the café.

Felix slurped the remnants of his cold mug of tea and glared at Denny across the table, his annoyance steadily increasing. Denny refused to make eye contact; in fact he held his head low, still brooding over last night's events

"Tell me again how you managed to get fucked up by an overweight copper, Denny" Felix snarled. Denny slowly raised his head to face his questioner.

"He was pretty fast, got the drop on me, Felix," he said quietly. Felix grunted, unimpressed by his team member's explanation.

"I can't believe those two are still alive. We both look like a right pair of wankers. I will be surprised if we don't get green lit ourselves," Felix snapped, recalling the telephone conversation.

Denny started to get angry. Why was he getting blamed for them getting away? Denny had been stewing for hours ever since they had escaped the hotel. He had been close to expressing his feelings to Felix but was unsure just in case Felix got mouthy, causing him finally to lose his temper. There would be no going back once that happened. Denny stared at Felix.

"I'm not the one who got done in by a woman," he growled.

Felix was speechless. How dare he talk back to him, a mere Jackal speaking out of turn to one of the Selected was unheard of, especially to Felix.

"What the hell did you just say, Denny?" Felix asked quietly, his voice even and emotionless but his rage barely contained. Denny swallowed hard. He wasn't going to put up with this any longer; it was time to tell Felix how it was.

"I said, I'm not the one who got fucked up by a woman," Denny replied, his voice full of aggression.

Felix tried to stare him down but the big man held his glare. For the first time Felix felt uncomfortable around his subordinate.

"Now now," Felix quipped, trying to impose his intellectual will upon his soldier. "You wouldn't want to do anything stupid, would you Denny?" Denny remained silent, his gaze never leaving Felix. Felix swallowed. "Look around Denny, do you think this is the best place to be having this conversation? Do you really want to start something in here?" Denny glanced around the room, scanning everybody in there. The 24-hour café was busy. Lorry drivers, workmen and a few of the general public were busy snatching some greasy food before getting on with their lives. There was at least seven other people sitting in the Café, some of them rough-looking, who could pose a threat. Denny shrugged and returned his attention to Felix.

"I don't care Felix. I'm happy to kill every single person in here and I will tell you something—you will be the first one to bleed out," he rasped.

Felix started to panic; he could feel the vehemence in Denny's voice and see the intent in his eyes. He wasn't joking. Felix subtly tightened his grip on the knife beside his empty plate. Denny noticed the manoeuvre and discreetly pulled his own knife from his waist band, resting it just by the lip of the table, its blade ready to strike. Felix glanced down at the weapon and grinned.

"So this is how it's going to be eh Denny? You want to be in charge do you? You want to be the big cheese?" Denny didn't reply; he just simply stood his ground, eyeing the other man, poised for an attack. Felix continued. "You think you have what it takes to lead, Denny? You think you have got what it takes to carry out the Order's wishes?" he scoffed.

"I know I would do a better job than you, Felix. After all I'm not the one who has been out-smarted by a woman on more than one occasion. You have had plenty of chances to finish her off yet you toy with her and let her escape. You should have killed her at the police station and saved us all a lot of aggravation," he snapped.

Felix simply smiled and released the grip on his knife, knowing full well he wouldn't stand a chance if it kicked off now. He would choose his battle ground, not Denny, he mused. Felix cautiously surveyed the room one last time. Too many witnesses in the café, he silently said to himself. He returned his attention to his subordinate.

"I'm not going to fight you Denny, not here anyway. We have instructions to clean this mess up with zero civilian casualties. That means no one else dies unless they are preventing us from finishing off Jesse and that copper." He paused and leaned back in his chair. "I'm sure even you can grasp the reason in that decision, can't you?"

Denny slowly replaced his knife and glared at Felix.

"One day your fancy words aren't going to save you, Felix. On that day me and you are going to have things to sort out once and for all," he whispered, as not to arouse suspicion from anyone in the café. Felix merely shrugged as if unconcerned but made a mental note to kill Denny sooner rather than later.

"As you wish Denny, but first shall we attend to the task at hand?" Denny nodded in agreement. They both stood up and headed for the exit, each man still brooding over the confrontation, each of them making plans to kill the other.

Felix decided to park the car in a different side road located around the corner from the hospital and await the phone call. His instinct told him they were at the correct location. He was starting to flag and needed some sleep but doubted if he would get any. Without saying a word both men got in the car and travelled the short distance to their layup point to await instructions.

0815 hrs

The sound of the phone ringing woke Felix from a deep sleep. He shook himself in an attempt to regain his faculties. He glanced over at Denny who was still snoozing, unaware of the incoming instructions. Felix grabbed the mobile and answered the call. He recognised the abrupt voice instantly.

"You are at the correct location; they will be leaving in five minutes. Their destination is a safe house in Preston. They will be travelling in a black Mercedes E Class. We don't have an index number but it should be easy to spot. It will be moving quickly. No other support vehicles are with them. We suggest you wait until they reach the safe house as we have been informed that the security detail at that location will be unarmed."

Felix smiled. Unarmed? This will be easier than he first envisaged. Sometimes he wished the Jackals could use firearms.

The voice continued. "I have been instructed to inform you that should you not complete this mission you and your companion will be targeted and hunted down by Internal Security." The line was terminated.

Felix felt a pang of fear and his palms started to sweat. Unlike Jackals and the Selected, Internal Security was totally clandestine, allowed to use firearms and pretty much had permission to do what they wanted without fear of repercussions. Rumours of their savagery were legendary within the Order and apparently took barbaric atrocities to a whole different level. These were the people even the Jackals were scared of, although Felix had never had anything to do with them or met one, to his knowledge. The only solid information Felix had regarding Internal Security was that they had been started in response to a rebellion of German Jackals in the mid-80s who had decided that they were owed more power and wealth since they were the ones doing the Council's dirty work. The insurrection had cost the lives of three Council members and sixteen Jackals. So by way of a deterrent, the surviving members had ordered the formation of an Internal Security section, apparently made up of former Special Forces soldiers and private contractors from around the globe. Their main remit was to keep the Jackals in line and respond to any threat from within its ranks.

It was obvious to Felix that the voice was passing on the message that the Order now considered Felix and Denny at best threats or at worst, liabilities. This didn't bode well for either man. Felix started the engine and slowly edged the car forward towards the junction about twenty yards in front of their current position in an attempt to get a clear line of sight to the hospital exit. Denny was awake now and sensed something was about to happen, the anticipation growing. He subconsciously touched the hilt of his blade; he glanced at Felix who was busy concentrating on the main road ahead of them.

With the engine running both men silently waited for their quarry to reveal themselves. Felix smiled as the black Mercedes E class finally exited the hospital and drove at speed past their vantage point heading east out of town. Felix slowly pulled out and dropped in behind the target vehicle, three cars behind as not to draw attention. Both men could smell blood. It was now just a question of waiting.

TWENTY-TWO

Tuesday, 0830 hrs

Felix gripped the wheel tightly as he gracefully manoeuvred his way through the traffic to keep up with the Mercedes. He watched as his target slowed down due to increasing congestion and the belief that they were not being followed. The traffic was heavy but luck seemed to be on the Jackals' side as nothing barred their view of the target vehicle and at each junction or set of lights they managed to get through unhindered. Felix glanced over at Denny in the passenger seat. He was hunched forward in his seat as if to will the car faster, no doubt eager to inflict pain on their carrion and anyone else that got in his way.

"Let's just run them off the road and finish them now," he suddenly said, breaking the silence.

Felix huffed. "That's not the plan Denny. We have to follow them to the safe house and then we deal with them," Felix replied. Denny chuckled at Felix's perceived lame response.

"I thought you were supposed to be some sort of alpha male, a great killer, scared of nothing and dancing to nobody's tune but your own? Not some lackey who obeys the orders of a bunch of old men!" he hissed defiantly.

Felix smiled. "What would you have me do? Just run them off the road in rush-hour traffic, then both of us jump out and butcher them in the middle of the street in front of a ton of witnesses?" he retorted, more than slightly annoyed by Denny's put-down. Denny started to laugh.

"That's exactly what I am proposing, Felix," he rebuffed. "You used to say that we are the predators, those at the top of the food chain and that every time we kill we get closer to attaining the Primitive. Well don't you think that this would create such a wave of publicity that everyone on the planet will know our names? We would be considered legends, not just within the Order but everywhere. People would be lining up to join our cause, hailing us as the newfound messiahs. It could very well be the catalyst of bringing the Primitive to the masses." He paused, letting the words permeate Felix's easily-caressed ego, then grinned, Felix's silence speaking volumes. "They would see your sigil, Felix. It would be the flag used to usher in the evolution, the new age would come about because of us. The Order are thinking long-term whilst lining their pockets in the present but what if this is an opportunity to kick-start it early, for us to bask in the limelight instead of those old fools tucked up safe in their ivory towers?"

Felix hated to admit it but the more Denny explained his reasoning the more he agreed with the plan. Sure, the Order was planning to kill them anyway so why not go out on a high? Why shouldn't Felix attain the fame he deserved? He paused, thinking about the possible outcome should they proceed with Denny's plan. They would get to kill Jesse and that copper, kick off the next stage of human evolution and send a message to the Order. He always knew he was destined for greatness and maybe this was it. A sudden bout of paranoia swept through him. He wanted to make sure Denny wasn't playing games, considering their fragile relationship.

"What about the Order?" he asked sheepishly, testing the water. Denny smiled.

"Fuck the Order, fuck those old men in their ivory tower; they have no idea what it's like to get bloody, to take a life and send the meat to the Void. They sit back and watch us further their agenda and never give us a second thought..." He paused, watching Felix's reaction. He continued. "Why settle for being a member of the Selected when you can be a God?" he sneered, inwardly knowing he had won Felix over.

Felix looked at his companion and started to laugh uncontrollably.

"Denny, I think you may have a point. We are Gods, you and I, and now is our time to shine. Fuck the Order; we now work for a higher power..." Denny started laughing.

"What's that?" he asked rhetorically, knowing full well what the answer would be.

"Us!" Felix screamed and slammed his foot on the accelerator, catapulting the car forward. Denny howled as Felix swung the car out into oncoming traffic forcing a Mini to stamp on its brakes and skid helplessly into a crowded bus shelter, the massive impact shattering the framework and sending exploding glass across the pavement and road. Pedestrians dived for cover as the Mini flipped onto its side, its driver crushed under the impact. Felix kept going, oblivious to the shouts and jeers from other car drivers and the screams from those on foot. Denny was hanging out of the window now, hollering at passers-by. He was clearly enjoying himself, aimlessly waving his knife and shouting obscenities.

Up ahead the Mercedes was two cars in front and keeping at a steady speed, apparently oblivious to the carnage happening behind them. Felix clenched his teeth and gunned the Vectra once more, smashing the front end into the rear of a Ford Escort in front, the driver tossed by the jarring impact and barely able to keep control of the under-powered vehicle. Felix roared and hit it again determined to clear the way, this time the Escort jack-knifed, causing it to spin and end upside on to the Vectra. Felix eased off, dropped it down a gear and slammed into it again, this time crashing into the side of the car, its front offside wheel arch imploding from the manoeuvre; the tyre exploded causing the spring to collapse. In a shower of sparks and rubber Felix kept going, forcing the Escort along the road, the sound of metal on metal deafening, the driver frantically holding on.

Up ahead at a set of lights the crossing glowed red. The Mercedes slowed to a stop and was first in the queue. Felix took his chance and powered past the Escort, sending it sprawling into an off licence window. The window erupted as the Ford hammered through the frontage. Bottles of wine and beer exploded, sending a tidal wave of alcohol in all directions. With its engine screaming it finally came to a standstill, its front half in the shop and rear on the pavement. He kept going closing in on his target. He swung the Vectra out into the oncoming traffic as far to the right as he could, his off side tyres raking the pavement, the stench of burnt rubber filling the air. He floored the car, forcing the rev counter up, hitting red, the engine screaming under the strain. Felix's timing was impeccable; when the front of his car was roughly five feet away, he viciously tugged the steering wheel to the left forcing the car to skid towards the rear passenger door of the Mercedes. The lights turned green and now alerted to the killer's presence the policeman dumped the clutch, causing the luxury car to leap forward. It was too late. Felix's Vectra careened into the rear end, the driver's passenger door buckling from the impact. The back end of the Mercedes spun around clockwise, causing the car to skid across the junction right into the path of an oncoming artic. The terrified HGV driver hit the pedal with both feet, causing the heavy rig's air brakes to kick in, the fully loaded trailer shuddering to a stop and smoke bellowing from the overheated tyres, but it was too late to stop the collision.

Inside the Mercedes Class was recovering from the Vectra's hit. He glanced up, his head swirling to see the HGV bearing down. He turned and grabbed Jesse, pulling her tightly to his body, bracing for the impact. The lorry smashed into the side of the Mercedes. Class and Jesse were thrown to the other side of the vehicle. The driver screamed as the door frame gave way and slammed into his chest, ripped through his back and embedded in the seat, his face splattered with blood as the force of the blow shredded his internal organs. Jesse closed her eyes as she felt the car roll over onto its roof, her torso hanging by her seat belt, Class tightly gripping on to her upper body.

The HGV kept going, pushing the twisted wreck of the Mercedes further across the junction, the air awash with the fragrance of petrol and scorched metal. Felix jumped from the wreckage of the Vectra and watched as the Mercedes came to a halt halfway across the junction. He glanced to his left to see Denny emerge from the car. Both men smiled as they cast their eyes over the scene before them. Denny sprinted to the Mercedes, his gaze focused on a policeman slowly clambering through the smashed passenger front window.

A Lycra clad passer-by dumped his pushbike and leapt at Denny in an attempt to subdue him, realising what was happening. The big man side-stepped then threw a punch which collided with the pedestrian's throat, sending the would-be hero tumbling to the floor, grasping his windpipe. Denny stomped on his face for good measure, making sure he was down. He glanced up, willing anyone else to tackle him. They didn't. Pedestrians ran screaming from the scene. Shop owners furiously scrambled to lock doors, ushering in the terrified to seek shelter.

Felix looked around as other drivers cowered in their cars, not daring to intervene with the horror playing out.

He smiled to himself. *Bow before your God*, he mused. Denny kept going. Reaching the car as the policeman was on his knees, he launched a vicious kick that collided with the policeman's jaw, sending him sprawling into the twisted car door. With his left hand he gripped his throat and hefted him up, the law man's head flopping from the concussion.

"Witness the Primitive!" Denny bellowed, his body flooded with adrenaline. With one fluid movement Denny grabbed his knife in his right hand and slammed it into his victim's temple, the sound of bone splitting as the blade punctured his skull and slid effortlessly into his brain. Denny whooped as he felt the body go limp, blood showering the glass-scattered tarmac. He let go, letting the body fall to the floor.

From the back seat Jesse could only see Denny's lower half and the crumpled body laying discarded in a heap. She was stuck, her seat belt holding her battered body in place. She desperately tugged at the belt but it wouldn't release. Starting to panic she turned to Class who was slowly coming to.

"Class!" she screamed, desperately trying to arouse the DI from his crash-induced slumber, shaking him roughly. She frantically turned her head searching for any approaching threat, still pulling at the belt. There was a popping sound as the belt released and Jesse's body collapsed onto the roof of the car. She winced as her hands scuffed the broken glass littering the confines of the vehicle.

Class groaned as he, too, fumbled with his seat belt.

It came loose with ease and he dropped to the floor, his back taking the brunt of the fall. He rubbed his head, the realisation starting to kick in. He glanced up just as Jesse screamed, her body being dragged backwards out of the car by the hair. Felix's face stared back, beaming as he yanked with all his strength. Class reached out to grab Jesse but was too late, missing her ankles and swiping mid-air. Jesse's feet kicked out as she tried to escape, her hands clutching the pavement to stop her backwards momentum. Felix grabbed her by the throat and spun her around, slamming her into the wrecked Mercedes. He lashed out with a devastating knee to the abdomen, causing Jesse to sink forward, the air forced from her lungs. She gasped for breath as another blow struck her in the face. Denny stood motionless, then he too joined the barrage of violence aimed towards her.

Inside the car Class crawled out of the opposite passenger window and dragged himself to his feet. He stared at the front of the HGV mere inches away, steam and smoke gently rising from the broken engine, the smell of mechanical carnage clinging to the air. He turned to see Felix and Denny mercilessly taking turns throwing blows at Jesse and leaping onto the top of the car, he raced forward and threw himself at Felix.

Denny glanced up just as the policeman caught Felix by surprise. Class screamed in rage as he collided with the killer, sending them both tumbling to the floor. Felix landed on his back, the impact winding him and giving the DI enough time to take advantage. Class managed to stay on top and started to rain down heavy blows to the Jackal's face. Denny ran at the policeman, throwing himself into a rugby tackle. Class saw the attack and threw an elbow. The appendage crashed into Denny's nose causing him to crumple, blood cascading from his devastated face. Class kept up the attack on Felix who was now lying unconscious in a pool of his own blood. Denny started to rise and yanked his knife from his belt. He reached forward and plunged the blade into the DI's shoulder. Class screamed in pain and fell to one side, clutching at the embedded metal. Denny whooped as he struck out a heavy stomp to the policeman's head, the sound of the collision massive. Class fell onto his back, the blade forced further into muscle. His head was spinning; he desperately tried to get to his feet but was unable to move. He stared upwards to see Denny standing over him, gleefully embracing the moment. The Jackal suddenly screamed, his head pulled backwards. Class looked on in disbelief as Jesse yanked his head back hard and from behind thrust a shard of broken glass into the left-hand side of his neck, then slowly and savagely raked it across his throat. The cartilage started to snag but Jesse kept going, her rage unstoppable. He gargled as Jesse added more pressure to her attack; his pupils dilated as the glass eviscerated the flesh and unleashed fountains of blood from the cavernous wound. Class screwed his eyes shut as the downpour saturated him. Jesse let the body fall to the floor and stood motionless as Denny gave out his death rattle, the breath causing bubbles from his exposed oesophagus.

Class opened his eyes and looked around him, the road awash of blood and glass. People had ventured from their places of safety and stood transfixed, unable to believe the events before them. The DI suddenly remembered Felix. A surge of panic coursed through him. He turned, expecting him to have vanished but was relieved to see his still-unconscious body lying on the floor. Class got to his feet and moved slowly towards Jesse. Her hair was soaked with blood, her face battle scarred. He put his arms around her and gently pulled her close.

"It's okay. It's over," he whispered. Jesse remained silent. Class hadn't noticed the sound of sirens or the fact that there were now six marked and unmarked police cars surrounding them. He held on tightly, feeling her body shaking. Even as the shouts of, "Armed police, get on the floor!" resonated, he refused to let her go.

TWENTY-THREE

Tuesday, 1515 hrs

"How many times do you want me to tell you the same fucking story?" rasped Class.

The officer across the table remained silent. His body posture relaxed. Class looked around the small interview room, the artificial neon light hurting his eyes, forcing him to squint. Class looked down and gently rubbed his heavily bandaged arm then stretched his back, the fresh knife wound in his shoulder sending agonising waves of pain through his body. He winced as he took a swig from the warm bottle of water in front of him.

"Let's go through it again shall we, Detective Inspector?" his interviewer asked stoically. Class sighed deeply and rubbed his head, then raised his eyes to the policeman.

"Where's Jesse?" he asked, trying to remain calm and keep his frustration in check.

"Mrs Reid is fine; she is in the medic centre resting," came the reply. Class chuffed.

"Medic centre? Why the hell isn't she in the hospital? I hope you have armed guards at her door!" he growled.

"Don't worry Mr Class, I have spoken to Mrs Reid

at length and she is in good spirits, considering. And to answer your question, no, there aren't any armed officers guarding her from the bogeyman."

Class stared blankly at the smart arse before him. Across the table Detective Inspector Calum Horsley remained calm all the while studying the battered policeman's body language. On Class' arrival at Lancashire Constabulary HQ he had looked into his service record and to be honest wasn't impressed with what he found. Not only was he aggressive, but judging by his personnel records he was a bit of a let-down, some would even say, useless. And judging by his own experiences Horsley would have to agree. In an effort to dig deeper he had even contacted some of Class' work colleagues to gather their impressions of him and it had come as no surprise that they had little or no time for the anti-social detective who sat before him.

Horsley gently sighed, not wanting to hear his bullshit story again, but knew he had little choice if he was to find any glaring holes that could shed some light on his case. He rolled his eyes at the highlights so far—secret societies, clandestine killers, animal worshipping sects—this was just a complete work of fiction and fantasy, he thought to himself.

"You do realise we are charging Mrs Reid with three counts of murder with intent, don't you Mr Class?" He paused. "And you with accessory," Horsley said smugly.

Class glared at the young DI. His modern, dark blue three-piece suit, his neatly fashioned beard that was all the craze these days and his slicked back hair. What a total wanker, thought Class. He grinned at his inner joke and took another swig of water.

"I want my commanding officer here right now; he knows what's going on and will vouch for my story," he replied to the hipster policeman.

Horsley smirked. "For your information, Mr Class Chief Superintendent Wallcott is already here and is currently having a nice cosy chat and some biscuits no doubt with my boss, and from what I've heard he isn't too impressed with you or Mrs Reid..."

He glared at Class, baiting a response. Class remained silent, unwilling to rise to his goading. Horsley continued, the smirk fading slightly, "Something about a load of coppers getting done-in down some back-water yokel station. Apparently it's all a bit hush-hush, and rumour has it your Mr and Mrs Reid are the instigators." Class could feel his jaw muscles tighten, his temper starting to simmer.

"You think you know what's going on here, don't you?" Class asked gravelly. "You think what I have told you is a load of bollocks and to be honest so did I when I was told, but after the last few days I have witnessed some of the most fucked-up shit I have ever seen!" He slammed his fist on the table, making Horsley jump. "These people are everywhere. They have the backing, logistics and funds and have access to real-time intelligence. They are without doubt some of the most dangerous people out there and the worrying thing is that ninety-nine percent of the population doesn't even know they exist!" Horsley shifted under the DI's outburst. Class continued. "What happened to the one I dropped? Is he dead?" he enquired.

Horsley cleared his throat. "No," he replied quietly.

Class frowned. "Please don't tell me he is here in this building as we speak?" he asked, his voice full of concern.

Horsley smiled. "As a matter of fact he is and I have offered him a deal. He says he will stand witness to Mrs Reid's actions. He has sworn under oath that he attacked Mrs Reid at the road incident through fear for his own safety and that he was, in fact, only trying to help Mrs Reid from the car crash."

Class was visibly stunned. "You are fucking joking, right? What about CCTV? Witnesses to the incident? Surely there was some sort of surveillance at that junction?" Class' mind was racing—this couldn't be happening. Horsley shrugged.

"No witnesses would come forward due to the brutality of Mrs Reid's actions. The only CCTV was privately owned but when canvassed all the shop owners stated that their systems weren't working that day. It would appear that Mrs Reid has put the fear of God in them. Witnessing someone have their throat slit with broken glass isn't conducive to volunteering information, it would seem."

Class rubbed his eyes "What else is he saying?" he said, once again trying to hold his temper. Horsley stood and started to walk to the door. He paused and looked at Class.

"For a reduced sentence Mr Smith is willing to testify that he was under the direction of Mr and Mrs Reid at the Wells Station massacre and that after a crisis of conscience he went after her, knowing full well she would continue with her murderous rampage."

Class threw the plastic bottle at him in temper. It bounced harmlessly off the door frame, inches away from the policeman. Horsley remained still, unfazed by the attack.

"Mr Smith? That's not his real name, is it? You really think that Jesse and her husband could do such a thing? An accountant and dental receptionist from bloody Somerset? I'm telling you that Mr Smith is full of shit and you are being played. What are going to do with him, anyway?"

Horsley straightened his back and adjusted his suit jacket. "Mr Smith will be placed in protective custody awaiting the trial."

Class slumped back in his chair in disbelief. "You are out of your mind. Jesse is in grave danger and her husband is being held hostage somewhere, that's if he isn't already dead." He took a breath. "I want to see Walcott now!" he rasped.

Horsley opened the door, then glanced at Class.

"Chief Superintendent Walcott is the one who signed off on the deal," he said and walked out, slamming the door behind him.

Jesse tugged at her cuffed arm attached to the bed's side rail. It didn't mysteriously unlock. She sighed and flopped back into the pillow. The small room was stark-white with just the bed and a wardrobe for furniture, the window covered with wire mesh. Obviously it was a secure medical room within the HQ. She had not been able to take much in on her arrival, still traumatised from the accident. The building had been a hive of activity with officers and staff whispering, "cop killer" and "bitch", among other things, as she was wheeled past. She closed her eyes. The face of Denny appeared, his mouth open in a silent scream and then his throat opened up, slashed by an invisible knife.

Jesse opened her eyes again; it had been the fourth time that had happened. It would appear that sleep would be a fickle companion for the foreseeable future. The door opened and Horsley causally walked in. He stood for a moment, gauging if Jesse was asleep.

"What do you want now?" she asked her tone bitter. Horsley closed the door and walked to her bedside. He glanced at the cuffs.

"I would apologise for the excessive bling but seeing as you have killed half of the UK's population in the last couple of days I thought it prudent to secure you..." She glared at him. "...For our own safety, of course," he said with a slight smirk on his face.

"You know damn well I'm not responsible for those murders," she retorted, facing the other way, not wanting to make eye contact.

Horsley laughed quietly. "I think you will find that it's not me you have to convince little lady, it's the twelve jurors in the Crown Court that will decide your fate, and as it stands the evidence is mounting up."

She turned to face him, her face contorted. "What evidence?" she asked forcefully.

Horsley chuckled. "Well, for starters we have a star witness, one of your subordinates as a matter of fact. I think you know him well. He's going to share all the juicy gossip." Jesse looked confused.

"What the hell are you talking about?" she replied, her patience being tested.

"Mr Smith," he retorted, a broad smile on his face. Jesse slowly shook her head.

"Who the hell is that?" she enquired.

Horsley's face dropped. He started to grimace, annoyed with Jesse's games. He leaned forward.

"You know whom I'm talking of Mrs Reid, the man who you ordered to kill all those innocent people, the man who valiantly rescued you from the wrecked car. The man who has been trying to stop you and your husband's brutal killing spree."

Jesse spat at him; a thick globule of phlegm hit him in the eye. He pulled back, disgusted by the attack.

"Fuck you!" she screamed as he retrieved a handkerchief from his waistcoat pocket and gently dabbed his cheek. Jesse slumped back, too weary to continue her defence.

Horsley grinned and leaned forward once again but this time aware of her method of attack. She turned her head, the refusal to engage the only act of defiance left at her disposal. Horsley came close to her ear, his breath hot with a slight smell of mint tea.

"You are finished Jesse—you and your husband, when we find him of course, are going down for life."

Jesse started to cry. Horsley moved closer. "By the way Jesse…" he said, a slight whiff of smugness emanating from his lips, "…the Order says 'hello'."

He pulled back, anticipating her attack. She turned and lashed out with her free arm but he was out of reach. Horsley leaned back, clutching at his chest and roaring with laughter. He slowly moved towards the door, all the while playfully pointing at Jesse.

"The Order loves you, Jessie baby."

She looked around for something to throw at him. There was nothing. Horsley stood by the door. He tried to speak but couldn't contain his laughter.

"Hang on, I'm sorry, Jesse. This is just so damn funny." He managed to gain control, coughed then continued, "There is no need for games anymore, Mrs Reid. This is what's going to happen." She glared at him, her whole body shaking with rage. "Firstly," he started, "we are going to stitch you up and send you to prison for a very long time. We already own the jury and the judge. Then whilst you are inside we are going to arrange some nice people to visit you in your cell. You will be systematically beaten and raped every single day of your sentence." Jesse kept quiet, unable to find the words. "Whilst you are inside we are going to torture your husband and then feed him to the dogs bit by bit." He started to laugh again. "Hell, we might even take a few pictures and send them to you, keeping you updated on our progress."

Jesse was shaking, her mind starting to tumble into her dark place but this time she welcomed it. She sought sanctuary from this never-ending nightmare. Horsley stepped forward.

"Oh and let's not forget your good friend Detective Inspector Class. We have something a little special in store for him." Jesse closed her eyes willing him to disappear, unable to listen to anymore of his vile rhetoric. "We are going to drum him out of the service for drugs and possibly a good old-fashioned rape charge and then we are going to have him sent down for a nice case of brutal kiddie porn, some proper sick shit, maybe a pinch of bestiality thrown in for good measure. Then we are all going to kick back with a couple of beers and watch him get torn to pieces in a Category A security prison. He will end up being big bubba's C-wing bitch." He stroked his beard in mock epiphany. "Do you know what happens to kiddie fiddlers in jail Jesse, let alone an ex-copper to boot?" He was laughing heavily now, tears rolling down his cheeks. He opened the door and completely changed his persona, an act for anyone walking by or within earshot.

"I'm sorry Mrs Reid, but if you change your mind we are here to help." He winked at her as he went to leave.

"Horsley!" she called after him.

He turned to face her once again. "Yes, Mrs Reid?" he replied politely.

"I'm going to force feed you your own heart," she growled.

Horsley smiled. "We will see," he replied and left the room.

TWENTY-FOUR

Tuesday, 1830 hrs

Chief Superintendent Sir Harris Walcott stared blankly out of the third-storey conference room window. He watched as the dark clouds started to roll in, the light fading and the staff carpark lights activating with the anticipation of night. He sighed and ran his hand through his thinning grey hair. He looked exhausted, his dark grey suit straining against his slightly overweight stomach.

"What do you think, Harris?" a voice asked from the dark mahogany table behind him. Walcott turned to face the voice.

"I'm sorry, what?" he asked, aware that he had drifted off half-way through the conversation. Chief Superintendent Jeremy Blake repeated his question.

"Do you think the case is solid enough on Jesse Reid to achieve a conviction? Or do you think we should contemplate a different solution, maybe one that is a bit more permanent?" Walcott tugged his suit jacket and strolled to his empty leather chair. He carefully sat himself down, his arms resting on the highly polished table.

"I think to take a more permeant course of action would only bring more attention to the whole sordid affair." He glanced around the table; the other six people sat, nodding silently. Blake huffed noisily in protest.

"Sorry Harris, but I think that would be a mistake," he paused, gauging the others reactions. Nobody agreed. Blake continued, undeterred by the lack of support. "I personally think we should just finish off her and her husband, save ourselves anymore hindrance. It is only prudent considering the amount of attention she is receiving."

Walcott eased back in his chair, looking directly at Blake. "Jeremy, I understand your reservation regarding the Reid's but consider this..." he stood up and began to pace slowly around the table. "If we have her convicted we can control the environment in which she stays. It stands to reason that no one will take anything she says seriously. By monitoring her we can keep tabs on any further threat rearing its ugly head due to the fact that if anyone else starts investigating us they would surely reach out to Mrs Reid as a likely ally. Thus giving us a distinct tactical advantage."

Blake stood up in anger. "Harris, that is folly and you know it. Keeping her alive is nothing but stupidity. We need to eliminate the threat immediately and as for your lap dog Detective Inspector Class…" he let the sentence trail off. Walcott glared at his companion.

"I seem to recall, Jeremy, it was your idea to have Class investigate the Wells Station attacks. I distinctly remember you stating that he was so inept that he couldn't possibly reach the truth, yet it appears he was a lot more astute than you gave him credit. No other person has single-handedly gotten this close to us." There was a slight chuckle among the attendees.

Blake started to turn scarlet. "Be that as it may Harris, wasn't it you who suggested Class in the first place? Maybe you let your own personal feelings cloud your judgement? I only agreed with your idea to make Class the scapegoat. Even you thought he would balls-up the investigation, giving you ample excuse to drum him out of the service," he rebuked.

Walcott chuckled and faced the now-seated Blake.

"Come, come Jeremy, let's not play the blame game; we are all on the same side after all," he paused as a gentle knocking on the table resonated from the silent six members. Walcott smiled in acceptance. "Class has indeed caught us off guard. His tenacity surprised every one of us. But let's not forget who gave him the head start and pointed him in our direction." A slight ripple of groans echoed in the plush meeting room. Walcott continued, "If it wasn't for our old friend Professor Michael Stokes, he wouldn't have had any idea we existed."

Blake relaxed in his chair. "Finally we agree on something, Harris. What is your plan of action regarding that traitor, may I ask?" Blake enquired. Walcott smirked. He addressed all in attendance.

"I think it is about time we retired Mr Stokes once and for all. What say you?"

All eight men stood as one and gently rapped on the

table, acknowledging the decision. Walcott smiled, basking in the adulation. He held his hand up, indicating he wasn't finished. The others settled down once again.

"I will task two teams of Jackals to hunt him and his friends down and kill them. They will stand as a testament to what happens when you rise against the Order." Walcott paused, awaiting any disagreements. Only Blake appeared to have something to say. Walcott turned to him, willing him to voice his grievance.

Blake coughed slightly. "What about that mad dog of his, Stevens? Shouldn't we be worried about him and his cronies? Walcott suddenly felt a little apprehensive at the mention of Stevens' name.

"I can assure you that two teams of Jackals is more than enough to take care of Mr Stevens and his band of merry men," he said, trying to hide the doubt in his voice. Blake smiled, knowing full well his colleague was nervous.

"So Harris, you aren't at all worried that Stevens commands a team of four ex-members of Internal Security and that their very existence was designed to take out Jackals, should the need arise?" he beamed. Walcott shifted slightly, his relaxed visage slipping.

"Mr Blake, I am aware of Mr Stevens' credentials and I am most certainly aware of the qualifications his team possess but do I have to remind you that we still have fifty members of Internal Security at our disposal, should the need arise?" He paused to catch his breath, then continued. "I, for one, think such deployment should be the absolute last resort as their methods are somewhat excessive, for which could attract even more attention to our Order. I am confident that the Jackals are up to the task." He was sweating slightly, his tone giving a glimpse of his apprehension. Blake gently nodded, agreeing with Walcott's explanation.

"Okay Harris, we will do it your way. At least we have a backup plan should anything go wrong. What about Felix? What do you want to do about him?" retorted Blake. Walcott curled his lip. The mere mention of his name angered him.

"As far as I am concerned that man is no longer affiliated to our Order and in my opinion should be taken care of forthwith." Once again the silent members nodded their approval. Blake smiled.

"I shall deal with our friend. Perhaps a case of custody suicide is in order," he quipped. This time everyone at the table laughed. Walcott grabbed a gavel from the table and knocked it gently on the hard surface.

"Thank you, gentlemen. I hereby bring this meeting to a close. Thank you for attending and I trust you have a safe trip back to your respective areas."

The six silent men rose from their seats and after shaking hands with both policemen quietly left the room. Walcott and Blake sat alone, eyeing each other suspiciously.

"Why do you constantly try to undermine my authority, Jeremy? Are your ambitions to rule so all-consuming that you are willing to risk the entire Order?" Walcott asked bluntly.

Blake got to his feet and glared at the other man.

"Harris, for too long you have wielded power without the slightest notion of what it means to lead or further our objectives. In my opinion you are the one who wishes to bring about our demise not me." He moved towards the door. "...and furthermore it pains me to see the others appear blind to your actions. You speak of external threats but as far as I can see you are the greatest threat to our continued existence and I make no apologies in my attempts to bring you to heel." With that he opened the door and left briskly without waiting for a reply.

Walcott let out a sigh of relief and slumped down in his chair. He gazed at the telephone on the table, contemplating his next move. Blake had been correct in his analysis. Walcott had been secretly planning to disrupt the Order and thus far had been working in the shadows; it now appeared that he would have to take more assertive action. He snatched up the receiver and dialled the custody suite. The line beeped then a voice came on the line,

"Custody suite, Sergeant Billings speaking."

Walcott composed himself. "This is Chief Superintendent Sir Harris Walcott. Could you please bring Mrs Reid and Detective Inspector Class to board room three please?" he asked, officiously.

"Certainly Sir," came the reply.

Tuesday, 1910 hrs

"Come in!" called Walcott, replying to the heavy knock on the door.

He glanced up to see Jesse walk in, hands cuffed and her head hung low. Behind her Class sombrely followed, his eyes surveying the room. He grimaced when he caught sight of Walcott. Finally Detective Inspector Horsley strolled in at the rear, their escort from the cells. He was grinning, obviously enjoying his power trip. Walcott rose to his feet and gestured for them to sit. Jesse and Class glanced at each other then attentively sat themselves down, facing the window and the senior policeman. Horsley went to sit down but Walcott coughed. The DI looked at Walcott with suspicion.

"You can go Horsley; I will call you if needed." The junior officer scowled, his annoyance evident. Jesse glared at him, a slight smile touching her lips. Horsley turned and walked out, slamming the door behind him.

Class eyed his superior. "What the fuck do you want?" he snarled, his respect all but gone. Walcott stood and gazed out the window.

"I'm sorry you both find yourselves in this situation. I had no idea it would get this far." He turned and addressed Class. "I honestly didn't expect you to get anywhere with this case, Class," he stated.

Class shrugged indifferently. "Wouldn't expect anything less from you Harris, so it comes as no surprise. You have been waiting to get back at me for years." Jesse looked at Class, her expression more than a little confused. Class smiled at her. "It's a long story," he jested, then returned his attention to Walcott.

The Superintendent let out a hefty sigh. "A few

years ago I was approached to join the Order as a senior member."

Class chuffed. "Now there's a surprise," he muttered.

Walcott remained silent at his remark, then continued. "At first I thought their ideals were correct; however, I later discovered that their true motivations were nefarious. I instructed you to investigate the Wells Station murders because I wrongly assumed that you would get nowhere in the case, thus shielding the Order from the actions of the Jackals. I never expected you to get this deep."

Walcott paused and turned his attention to Jesse. "And you, Mrs Reid, were just at the wrong place at the wrong time. You were never to have lasted as long as you have. In fact, no one has ever survived as long as you and to be honest, it has caught the Order off-guard."

Jesse started to laugh. "Whoop whoop!" she replied sarcastically, gently fist-pumping the air. Class laughed at Jesse's defiance. Walcott looked annoyed.

"I'm glad you find your current circumstances amusing, Mrs Reid," he said sharply.

Jesse started to giggle. "Oh fuck off, will you? You are going to bump us off anyway so why not have a bit of a laugh on the way?" she retorted, flippantly.

Class joined in. "Yeah Walcott, she's got a point. You have to admit a sense of humour helps you through the difficult times," Class offered.

Walcott appeared flustered. He snatched up the phone and stabbed at a button.

"Mr Horsley, can you come in, please?" He slammed

the receiver down, glaring at the two in front of him. "Let's see how funny you find the things Mr Horsley is going to do to you, shall we?" he snarled.

Jesse and Class looked at each other. Class started to laugh uncontrollably.

"Hey Walcott, you sound like some dodgy James Bond villain," he quipped. Jesse giggled at his off the cuff remark. She stared at Walcott.

"No, Mr Bond, I want you to die," she said in a comical German accent.

Walcott's jaw ached, his temper starting to boil. The door opened and Horsley strolled in, his cocky swagger winding Class and Jesse up, his mere presence an affront to their nerves. He casually walked around the table and stood next to Walcott, gleefully watching them victimised. Jesse glared at the hipster DI; she wanted to kill him there and then, her very essence yearned for the chance. Class gently touched her leg, urging her to stand down.

"Why the hell are we here, Walcott? You are framing her and probably going to stitch me up or more than likely kill us, so why drag us in here to gloat? To tell us how clever you lot are for beating us? Just get the fuck on with whatever you're going to do; I'm bored of this game," he barked.

Walcott undid his jacket button. "Thank you, Mr Class. I shall take your advice."

For a big man his speed was impressive. Class hardly saw the Superintendent move. Walcott reached into his suit jacket and pulled out a cutthroat razor, spun his body and with one quick motion slashed Horsley's throat. The

DI staggered backwards, clutching at the gushing wound. Jesse and Class looked on speechless as the smarmy DI fell against the window then slid to the floor, the blood soaking into his trendy blue suit. He was dead before his body hit the floor. Walcott chuffed and turned to his prisoners.

"I hope that goes a little way to prove my resolve, Mr Class," he said wiping the blade on Horsley's jacket.

"Okay, now I'm really confused," replied Class.

Jesse remained silent, secretly annoyed that justice had been taken from her.

"Why would you do that?" she croaked.

Walcott reached into his jacket and retrieved a handcuff key, then tossed it across the table.

"I have been working with Professor Stokes with the intention of bringing the Order down," he stated frankly.

Class started to smile. "Holy shit!" he exclaimed, his voice full of genuine surprise. "You have been working with that crazy old bastard all along?"

Walcott grinned. "Yes, Mr Class. Ever since he was drummed out I have remained good friends and allies with him and stand beside him in the hopes of bringing the Order down. I have lived a double life for many years now but have had to keep my loyalties hidden for fear of reprisals. But alas, I fear some have realised my true intentions and time is now short."

Jesse un-cuffed herself and threw them on the wooden table. She gently rubbed her wrists, glad she was free from the constraints.

"What now?" she asked. Walcott reached into his

jacket pocket, this time retrieving a plain white envelope. He tossed it at Class.

"In that envelope is an all-access security pass and the keys to my Range Rover parked in row A, level one of the staff carpark. I suggest you put as much distance between here and yourselves as quickly as possible. Stay off the main roads and motorways if you can. I have taken the liberty of releasing your rucksack and belongings. You will find them in the boot. I have also left five hundred pounds cash in the glove box. I'm sorry but that's all I could get at such short notice." Walcott paused awaiting questions; there wasn't any thus far. He continued. "The plan is for you two to disappear, giving Stokes and his team a clear window in which to take out the Order. Once he is successful we will find you and give you the all-clear."

Class looked confused. "What about Jesse's husband and the charges against us?" he asked. Walcott scratched his chin.

"We think we know where Mr Reid is being held and as soon as the Order is taken care of we will send in a rescue team. As for the charges we will plant evidence that point to Felix and his little gang. This will get you two off the hook. After all that, you are free to get on with your lives as you see fit."

Jesse started to cry. "Damien is still alive?" she asked quietly.

Walcott nodded. "As far as we know, yes."

Jesse stood up, wiped the tears from her cheeks and snatched the envelope out of Class' hands. She ripped it open and examined the keys and security pass.

"Let's go," she said, walking towards the door. Class stood up and held out his hand to his superior.

"Thank you," he said.

Walcott shook his hand firmly. "Just get out of here Class, before I change my mind." Class smiled and walked to the door. Jesse opened it and after making sure the coast was clear made her way out into the empty corridor. Class followed suit.

Class and Jesse made their way down the heavily lit corridor then down three flights of stairs to the bottom floor. In with the security pass was a piece of paper with a map scribbled on it. It showed an emergency door that led directly out into the staff carpark. Obviously Walcott had strategically chosen board room three for its accessibility. Class confirmed that the door they now stood by was the correct escape route and with one swift movement pushed the heavy bar down, releasing the doors. They slowly walked out fearing an ambush but there was no one in sight. Jesse scanned the rows of vehicles looking for the Range Rover. She spotted it on the far side of the dully lit carpark. Nudging Class she pointed to the location. He nodded and together they moved between the cars, keeping as low as possible.

They reached the dark blue Range Rover and Class was relieved that the keys actually worked. They slid in, closing the doors behind them. Jesse checked the back for her rucksack whilst Class checked for the cash. Both were happy when they found their respective goods. The

DI started the engine and slowly pulled out of the parking space all the while scanning the structure for possible threats. Jesse sunk down in her seat, anxious to limit her exposure.

The DI steered the heavy vehicle onto the inner complex road and headed for the exit. The long sweeping road seemed to go on for miles. Class and Jesse remained silent, their hearts feeling like they were going to burst through their chests. Finally Class saw the exit gates; he kept his speed normal, not wanting to attract attention. He slowed down as he approached the junction then manoeuvred the 4x4 gracefully out onto the carriage way. Jesse exhaled loudly as he accelerated. She glanced back to see if anyone was following. Satisfied they were clear she settled back in the seat. She glanced over at Class. He was smiling.

"What's the plan?" she asked eagerly.

Class thought for a second. "We are going off-grid. No safe house, no city. We are going somewhere that I haven't been for about twenty years. Somewhere they would never think of looking," he replied. Jesse looked bemused.

"Where?" she asked. Class indicated the rucksack which contained her camping gear.

"Somewhere we need that little set up," he said cryptically. Jesse glanced back at the rucksack then back at Class.

"Go on then, the suspense is killing me," she pleaded.

The DI started to laugh. "Ever been to the outer Hebrides?" he asked excitedly. Jesse frowned.

"Where the hell are they?" she asked.

Class smirked, "The Isle of Lewis, my dear girl. An island off the West Coast of Scotland."

TWENTY-FIVE

Tuesday, 1955 hrs

Walcott closed his laptop, stared at the blooded body of Horsley slumped on the floor then turned his attention to his mobile phone. He scrolled down his contacts then after choosing the correct one pressed 'call'. The line rang and after a few seconds a voice answered.

"Yes?" came the reply.

Walcott hesitated. "It's me. Things have gone according to plan; they are in my vehicle. I have sent you the log-in details of the on-board tracking device so you can keep tabs on them. I'm pretty sure the Order will send the Jackals after them once they find out where they are going but at this time I have no idea where they are heading."

The voice was silent for a few seconds.

"You have done well, Harris. I am proud of you. We will keep you updated."

The phone went dead. Walcott felt nervous but was sure he had done the right thing. It was only a matter of time before the Order found out he had helped Jesse and Class escape and he was pretty sure they would kill him.

He was living on borrowed time and he knew it. He didn't, however, care that Jesse and Class were bait to entice the Order to commit more of their forces, thus leaving the Council vulnerable. It was a bold plan but wholly necessary to bring about their demise. He psychologically shrugged at the thought of his bait dying. They were expendable. The end justifies the means, he mused.

He sat back, wondering how long it would be before the Order realised what had happened. He suspected it would take a maximum of a couple of hours. He wearily stood up and made his way over to the mini bar and pulled out a bottle of cognac. He popped the lid and hastily filled a thick glass tumbler. He eyed the brandy for a second then downed the fiery liquid. Walcott smacked his lips and refilled the glass, eager to taste more of the beverage. It could well be his last drink, he thought to himself. The door swung open and the familiar face of Blake strolled in, flanked by four armed officers. Walcott spun around, unsurprised by the unannounced visit. He smiled graciously at his companion and raised the bottle.

"Drink, Jeremy?" he asked jovially. Blake ignored the offer. He turned and ordered two of his men to remain outside and two to stand guard inside should the Superintendent try anything.

"What the hell are you playing at, Harris? I always suspected you were up to something but this..." Blake growled. He threw a set of CCTV stills onto the table.

Walcott casually walked over and gave them a cursory glance. He smiled at the black and white photos of Jesse

Reid and Class driving out of the main gate in his own Range Rover. He shrugged.

"What does it look like, Jeremy? I helped them escape. I gave them my keys and some cash and let them walk out of here." He replied, seemingly unconcerned with the situation in which he found himself.

Blake slowly shook his head. "You are working with that traitor Stokes, aren't you Harris?" he roared. Walcott simply shrugged and took another huge gulp of brandy.

"Yes I am, Jeremy," he stated proudly. "I am working with Stokes with the intention of bringing the Order down, to finish it once and for all. That includes you, old chum," he said smiling. Blake sat himself down.

"Have a seat, Harris," Blake retorted calmly. Walcott made his way around the table and flopped down in the chair opposite his former companion.

"You know we are going to kill you, don't you Harris?" Blake asked sedately. Walcott grinned.

"Of course I do. I'm not an imbecile," he replied, his brain starting to ache from the alcohol. Blake shook his head in disbelief.

"The manner of death and the amount of pain inflicted will be dictated by how much useful information you give us. I implore you to tell us everything and I give you my word it will be quick," he stated emotionlessly.

Walcott sniggered at the offer. He knew full well they couldn't be trusted and the chances were they would inflict as much pain as possible as a warning to others not to rebel. Of course, because of his high-ranking position those above him may want to question and torture him in secret before finishing him off. He smirked at the irony of the Head of Avon and Somerset Constabulary being completely helpless. Blake slammed his hand on the table.

"I am going to ask you some questions, Harris. And I want you to take your time and consider your options before you answer." He clicked his fingers, demanding Harris' attention.

Walcott stared at him unblinkingly. Blake continued, his voice low and deliberate.

"Where are they going, Harris? Where can we find them? And what do they know about us?" he asked.

Walcott shrugged. "I'm not going to tell you anything Jeremy, so just get on with what you have to do but just remember one thing…"

Blake leaned back in his chair, curious to what Harris had to say. "Pray tell, Harris," he replied.

Walcott sighed, "When the time comes, and it's coming soon, when you find yourself staring down the business end of that maniac Mr Stevens' gun, I want you to remember this moment, Jeremy. I want you to remember my words. The Order is finished. Stokes is going to dismantle everything you hold dear. He and his men are going to destroy your entire world. He…"

The retort of the gun was colossal within the small board room. The heavy grain .45 calibre bullet smashed through Walcott's right temple and tumbled out of the back of his head, taking half of his brain with it. His body fell backwards with the impact, sending him and his leather chair crashing to the floor. Blake remained still calmly holding on to the Glock 21, its barrel still smoking from the discharge.

"So much for not using firearms," Blake muttered. He turned to his two body guards. "Get rid of these two bodies. Make sure you dump them somewhere where the news channels will get wind," he paused, his face contorting into a sly smile. "Maybe dump them in a school playground. That should prove amusing," he added, a broad smile on his face.

The two uniformed men hastily proceeded to carry out their instructions. Blake stood up and walked towards the door.

"Shall we put out an arrest warrant for Reid and Class, Sir?" asked one of his subordinates.

Blake turned. "No. We want to get to them first. Activate the Jackals; I want at least three teams ready to go as soon as we get a static location," he barked. The officer nodded.

"What about his laptop, Sir?" he enquired.

Blake paused then returned to the table, grabbed the computer and opened the lid. The screen fired up, still logged into Walcott's email account. Blake smirked.

"Stupid man," he thought to himself. Blake scrolled the sent files and opened the latest mail. "It would appear these are the log-in details for his on-board tracker!" he exclaimed. Blake copied the details and brought up the tracker application. He pasted the password and silently waited for the site to load. "Bingo," he said under his breath.

"Get the teams ready. I want them on the road in an hour. It would appear they are heading for Scotland." Blake flipped the lid shut and tossed the laptop to his guard. "Make sure they keep this activated. They have no idea we can track them," he stated confidently.

The security man snatched the laptop and continued with wrapping up the two dead bodies.

"Carry on with your assignments then contact me when you are on the road heading north," he snapped and headed for the door. There was one more person to speak to, someone who may still prove useful.

Felix lay on his cell bed with his hands behind his head, staring at the ceiling. The past few days had been taxing to say the least. He had enjoyed his little car chase but was now wondering if he had made the right decision. Maybe he had been foolish to think Denny's plan would work. He should have known better than to go against the Order's instructions.

He was, however, secretly impressed with Jesse's termination of Denny though. In fact, if things had been different Felix might have moulded her and welcomed her into the fold. He would have enjoyed shaping her into a fearless Jackal. She might also have even been a good choice for a mate, he mused. Felix smiled as his mind filled with thoughts of blood-soaked sex with the alluring Mrs Reid. Felix wasn't sure he had made the right decision to agree to be a witness and despite the reassurances of that hipster copper he was pretty sure the Order would eventually have him killed. The stark reality was that he was expendable and on his own without any back up, his entire team dead.

Felix reminisced about all the team members he had lost at the hands of Jesse and Class. He silently growled as the realisation hit him that he would never get a chance to send them to the Void. The nearest he would get to hurting them now was to see them sent to prison for crimes they hadn't committed. The hipster policeman had explained in graphic detail what would happen to them once they arrived in their new home and this pleased Felix to a certain degree. It wasn't the same as killing them but at least they would suffer.

He stood up, stretching his aching body. His face was heavily bruised from Class' attack. Class, the only man that had very nearly stopped him, the one who had come closest to killing him. Class was the real one he wanted now, the one he wanted to brutalise more than anyone before. Felix nodded at his own internal voice. He intended to devote the rest of his short life to making him suffer. Felix started laugh.

The sound of the heavy keys rattling the cell door snapped Felix out of his daydream. He watched as the door swung open to reveal a high-ranking officer flanked by two heavily armed subordinates. Felix swallowed, convinced his time had come.

"Hello Felix, how's the accommodation?" the stranger asked.

Felix smirked. "The room is presentable but the menu is frightful," he retorted smugly.

Blake laughed and entered the cell. He casually looked around at the barren room.

"Something tells me you might want a chance to escape such diabolical dwellings. Am I correct?" he asked cryptically. Felix had to admit that his curiosity was panged.

"And who might you be, friend?" he asked quietly, his predatory eyes studying the newcomer.

Blake turned and ushered his men out of the cell. They hesitated.

"Fear not, gentlemen. I'm sure Felix here harbours me no ill will..." he turned to once again face Felix "...Isn't that right, Felix?" he added, his confidence high.

Felix considered jumping on the stranger and thrusting his thumbs into his eye sockets but decided to hear him out first. He smiled gently.

"Why of course. As it stands I am to be considered a pussy cat. However, that may change if I don't find your next few words favourable."

Blake swallowed hard. Insolent pup, he thought to himself but kept the smile on his face.

"Do you know who I am, Felix?" Blake enquired. Felix shook his head slowly.

"I am Chief Superintendent Jeremy Blake. I run Lancashire Constabulary and I am here to make you an offer." Felix's surprise was evident and Blake was enjoying it. "May I sit?" he asked politely. Felix grinned and gestured him to take a seat on his bed.

"What can I do for you, Mr Blake?" Felix replied, eager to learn more. Blake settled himself and began his sales pitch.

"I am near the top of the food chain regarding the Order; I believe you are aware of them?"

Felix remained quiet, unsure if it was a trap. He didn't know this man and he had met a third of the thirteen Council members. It was possible he was telling the truth but Felix decided it was prudent to keep his mouth shut for the time being. Felix shrugged non-comital. Blake chuffed, unimpressed with Felix's refusal to comply.

"I will put it bluntly, Felix. Earlier today I was coming down here to hang you in this very cell. Your suicide would have been a very sad end to a rather horrific day," he paused for dramatic effect. "Now, I'm sure you are aware that you are currently still breathing, thus it should convince you that our plans for you have changed somewhat." Felix remained silent.

Blake started to laugh softly. "I take it from your silence that you understand the gravity of your situation and that you have come to realise I am the only person who can keep you alive. Do you understand?"

Felix suddenly felt afraid; it was now painfully obvious this man was who he claimed to be. Felix nodded in response.

"Jolly good, Felix," Blake said, his voice tinged with sarcasm.

"What exactly do you want Mr Blake, no more games?" Felix enquired, slightly apprehensive about the coming answer. Blake tapped him on the knee playfully.

"How would you like to gain favour with the Order

once again? Better yet, how would you like the opportunity to get out of here and kill Jesse Reid and Lewis Class?" probed Blake, the policeman knowing full well he would take the bait.

Felix smiled broadly. "Things would return to how they were before? I get to have my own team?" he asked cautiously.

Blake stood up, reaching out his hand to the still-seated Felix. "Come back to us, Felix. Show us what you are made of," he stated boldly.

Felix jumped to his feet, his head giddy with excitement. "Without a doubt," he replied.

Blake lowered his gaze. "There is just one other thing, Felix," Blake responded sheepishly. Felix cocked his head, wondering what it was. "There will be others going after them, not just teams of Jackals but an old adversary and his associates; they are all former Internal Security. Does this make you reconsider? These gentlemen are highly skilled and you are a single man, do you think you can handle such odds?"

Felix slowly nodded. "It would be an honour to die trying, Mr Blake," he exclaimed proudly, inside feeling sick that he had to play the masterful servant to this man.

Blake started to laugh. "Splendid. Follow me then," he turned briskly and banged on the cell door. It opened and he ushered Felix into the corridor. He handed the Jackal an envelope. "In there is money, a mobile phone and a set of car keys for a BMW outside. In the boot you will find a variety of weapons for your pleasure. I want you to head north into Scotland. We will phone you with further instructions."

Felix accepted the envelope gleefully. He tugged it open, inspecting the contents. Blake signalled his men.

"These gentlemen will see you to the car." Felix nodded and started to walk off, his enthusiasm starting to build. "Oh, Felix?" Blake called after him. Felix stopped and cocked his head towards the Superintendent.

"Yes, Jeremy?" he asked flippantly.

Blake smirked. "Please bear in mind that should you try and run the Order will hunt you down and flay you whilst you are conscious, then most probably keep you alive just long enough for us to feed you your own entrails. Do you understand?" he stated happily.

Felix grinned.

"I wouldn't expect anything less." He turned and carried on walking towards the exit.

much with the appearance or character of its supplier.

"Nice bit of kit, Mr Fraser. What's the damage?" he enquired, trying to hide his deep-seeded repulsion. Fraser scratched his short cropped hair, his scruffy track suit stained and grubby, a heavy gold chain hanging from his neck.

"Five grand for each of the Scorpions, another thousand for five hundred rounds of ammunition, including two spare magazines for each gun," he replied sheepishly, only too aware of his customer's distain, his tone tinged with a slight twang of trepidation.

Stevens reached inside his jacket and pulled out a thick, padded envelope. He tossed it at Fraser who fumbled to catch it.

"There's twenty-eight grand in there—Mr Stokes' way of saying 'thank you' considering the short notice."

The Glaswegian sniggered as he opened the envelope, thumbing the thick wad of notes.

"A pleasure doing business with you..." he paused, debating whether to say anything else, unsure if his customer was in the market for things of a more exotic nature. He decided to take the chance. "I have some nice rocket propelled grenade launchers if you are interested?" he added chirpily.

Stevens glared menacingly at the Scotsman. "With all the terrorist shit hitting the headlines you want to offer me grenade launchers? This is England, not fucking Afghanistan," he seethed.

The Glaswegian lowered his gaze, more than a little

TWENTY-SIX

Tuesday, 2220 hrs

The large semi-derelict warehouse was dimly lit; the vast open space was devoid of goods and furnishings, its heavy steel girders flaking and rusting, the smell of dampness and mould clinging in the air. The four figures gathered in the middle flanked by two vehicles, their headlights illuminating the clandestine meeting. Stevens leaned forward and eagerly flicked the metal latches on the heavy duty polymer flight case and eased the lid open. He diligently reached in and pulled out one of the five CZ Scorpion EVO 3 A1 sub machine guns secured within. Hefting the weapon with his right hand he pulled back the charging handle and released it, smiling as he heard the reassuring click as the gun's action was worked. Stevens brought the weapon up to his eye and slowly squeezed the trigger, the hammer slamming down on an empty chamber. He grinned and replaced the weapon in the case.

"I trust you are happy, Mr Stevens?" asked the fat Glaswegian standing to his left.

Stevens turned to face his contact; he was suitably impressed with the level of hardware on offer but not so surprised by Stevens's reaction.

"Sorry, Mr Stevens. I thought you may have been in need of a little extra fire power. Generally my customers don't take this kind of hardware unless they are going to war. An RPG always gives you a distinct advantage should you find yourself in a sticky situation," the Scotsman replied cautiously.

Stevens ignored him and turned to his two subordinates who stood quietly by a black Land Rover. He pointed to the two flight cases.

"Strip and check these over then load them up. I want to be on the road in fifteen minutes." They both nodded and set to work.

Stevens returned his attention to the Scotsman who was remaining silent, not wanting to aggravate the situation. "What else have you got on offer?" he asked. Fraser grinned.

"What are you in the mood for, Mr Stevens?"

The big man stepped closer, his posture aggressive. "Information, Mr Fraser. Information."

Fraser started to feel uneasy. Stevens unnerved him.

"I...I don't know what you mean, Mr Stevens," he muttered, his brow starting to shine with sweat. "That's not my line of work," he added.

Stevens held his gaze and moved closer, again forcing the fat man to take a step backwards.

"Oh I think you do, Mr Fraser. I have it on good authority that you have been singing like a little bird to the authorities regarding your customers. I have even heard of some of these said customers being detained. But you wouldn't know about any of this, would you Mr Fraser?" he paused taking a moment, enjoying making the Scotsman squirm.

Fraser swallowed hard, his mouth dry. "I can assure you, Mr Stevens, that I have done no such thing and I would ask you to convey that to Mr Stokes when you see him next. You are some of my very best customers. I am a businessman, not some sort of gutter trash grass. I value the trust between seller and buyer. What kind of businessman would I be if I squealed on my customers?" he retorted, puffing his chest out, trying to sound confidant.

Stevens smirked, clearly unimpressed by the Scotsman's explanation but not letting on.

"Fair enough, Mr Fraser," he stated smiling. Fraser relaxed, secretly glad things had been defused. The last thing he wanted was to be on the wrong side of this man and his companions.

"Do you have any grenades with you, Mr Fraser?" the big man asked.

Fraser beamed at the prospect of another sale. "I only have two with me but can have more within six hours. How many do you require?" he enquired, the unpleasantness seemingly forgotten.

Stevens sighed. "Only two for now. What type are they?" he enquired.

Fraser reached down into a smaller flight case at his feet and retrieved a small black object. He handed it to Stevens.

"This is a Russian made F1 anti-personnel hand grenade. A big bang in a little package." he stated proudly. Stevens took the grenade and inspected the explosive.

"Not bad. How much?" he asked. Fraser hesitated before answering. "Five hundred each," he replied, testing the waters. Stevens laughed.

"You are joking aren't you, five hundred quid each? I can get them for two-fifty elsewhere. After all of Mr Stokes' generosity, you are still trying to fleece him," he snipped. Fraser appeared flustered.

"Okay, okay. Two-fifty each but that's a onetime offer. How many do you want?"

Stevens was just about to answer when one of his men approached.

"All good, Sir. Loaded up and ready to move," he stated officiously. Stevens slowly nodded, then stared at the Scotsman.

"You know what, Mr Fraser? I have come to the realisation that I don't think I really like you," he said, his voice low. "In fact, I think you are a lying piece of shit that would sell his own mother for a pound. You have neither honour nor morals and that angers me, Mr Fraser."

The Glaswegian started to panic sensing the growing menace in the big man's voice. He slowly started to back up then quickly spun around ready to break into a sprint, hoping to reach the safety of his Nissan Skyline parked ten feet behind him. He didn't see the blow coming. Stevens' second man hit him in the face with a heavy torch, sending the fat man crashing to the floor. There was no need for a secondary attack. He was already unconscious.

Fraser came to, his forehead bleeding heavily. It took a couple of seconds for him to realise where he was. He looked around the confines of his car, wincing when he saw his hands zip tied to the steering wheel, his wrists lacerated and bleeding. He tugged viciously, screaming more in panic than in rage.

"Now, now," came a soft voice from outside the vehicle. He looked up to see Michael Stokes flanked by Stevens and his two men. Stokes was smiling.

"What the fuck is going on!" bellowed Fraser demandingly, still frantically trying to release himself. Stokes slowly paced forward towards the car's passenger window and casually popped his head in, all the while feigning interest in the Scotsman's lurid mode of transport.

"Well, this really is a stereotypical vehicle for a low-level creature such as yourself, isn't it Ryan?" he asked sarcastically.

Fraser turned his head and spat at the old man, the projectile catching him on his suit front. Behind the old man Stevens lunged forward for an attack but Stokes held his hand up, stopping the big man from intervening. Stevens stopped and returned to his position.

"Good little lap dog, ain't he Mr Stokes?" Fraser stated, his growing desperation masquerading as bravado. One of Stevens' men handed Stokes a handkerchief which he diligently used to wipe the grog from his breast. He smiled at the bound Scotsman, unfazed by the dirty protest.

"You know full well why you find yourself in this

predicament don't you, Fraser?" he asked. Fraser turned away and fell silent, not wanting to incriminate himself or make eye contact. Stokes carried on despite the fat man's refusal to admit his misdemeanour or engage in civilised conversation. "I'm sure I am correct in recalling that we had an understanding regarding the sale of your merchandise—the understanding being that you wouldn't supply the Order with any weapons, or is my memory a little hazy? It has recently come to our attention that you have gone back on said arrangement and have surreptitiously supplied various handguns to them. This of course is a serious breach of etiquette regarding our business relationship, wouldn't you agree Fraser?"

Fraser lowered his gaze and started to cry softly, all trace of his bravado gone.

"I'm sorry Mr Stokes. It was only a few handguns. I didn't see the harm—you know I save all the good stuff for you," he whimpered, the realisation of his short future beginning to sink in.

Stokes smiled, reached in through the window and gently patted his arm.

"I was in the Land Rover the entire time, dear chap. I was watching you, watching your body language. I really hoped it wasn't true, but alas, I fear our business relationship must be severed."

Fraser remained silent, knowing full well the futility of convincing these people otherwise or the hopelessness of lying his way out of it. Stokes started to chuckle softly.

"The funny thing is I don't even mind you ratting on

your other customers. We turned a blind eye to that sordid little affair, but betraying us of all people is just damn right rude."

Fraser looked up, his eyes pleading for mercy but knowing full well the finality of the situation. Stokes sighed and playfully pinched his cheek.

"It's okay, Fraser. I forgive you," he said grinning. He stood up, put his hat on and briskly walked towards the Land Rover, nodding at Stevens as he passed by.

Stevens casually walked over to the incarcerated Scotsman and with one hand pulled the pin from the F1 grenade and tossed the metal pineapple through the open window. Fraser looked on in horror as he watched the grenade bounce off of the seat and tumble into the foot well, the safety spoon releasing with a loud metallic ping, arming the explosive. Stevens cheerfully waved at him through the window then causally walked away, his experience knowing full well the amount of time he had to make good his escape before detonation.

Fraser was still screaming when the explosion detonated within the car. Glass was viciously strewn in all directions. The car's bodywork was reduced to a mass of twisted scorched metal, the blast spewing forth a mushroom cloud of thick, black toxic smoke to the warehouse ceiling. Stevens re-joined Stokes and his two men and got into the Land Rover, slamming the door behind him, the heat from the blast still hot on his skin.

"Well?" he asked, looking in the rear-view mirror, directing his question to Stokes who was sitting in the back seat.

Stokes rubbed his chin with one hand as he flipped the lid open of his laptop. He waited a couple of seconds for the machine to fire up then scanned the tracking information on the site.

"Looks like they are in Scotland," he stated smiling. Stevens chuckled.

"What the hell are they going to do up there?" he asked. Stokes shook his head.

"I'm not entirely sure, Mr Stevens, but I suggest we start to make our way across the border. Mr Blake was good enough to help acquire this information and I think it is pretty safe to assume that the Order have by now put a bullet in his head and by virtue have access to the same intelligence as us. I am in little doubt that they have already deployed Jackal teams to intercept," he replied.

Stevens grimaced. "I was under the impression that the plan was to bring down the Council whilst their forces were tied up dealing with the copper and that girl and for us to attack whilst they were vulnerable?" he enquired respectfully. Stokes shook his head gently.

"It was at the time, Mr Stevens, but now I think it would be better if we pop up and pay the DI and Mrs Reid a visit first. We can take out some of the Order's soldiers whilst we are there," he replied stoically. The big man seemed confused. "Don't worry, Mr Stevens. There are a few high-ranking members of the Order located in Scotland ripe for the picking, so rest assured we shall be paying them a visit also." He paused. "Please don't forget to get two of your men to attend to that other bit of business back in the Southwest, my good fellow," he added.

Stevens nodded. "I have already sent word, Sir," the military man replied.

Stokes laughed softly. "Then let us get underway," he ordered. "I haven't been to Scotland for ages," he added, his laugh getting gradually louder.

The driver started the engine and slowly pulled out of the warehouse. Stevens glanced in the wing mirror and watched the flames still licking the walls, imagining the final thoughts of Ryan Fraser. He grinned. He never liked him anyway.

TWENTY-SEVEN

Wednesday, 0043 hrs

Class lit a cigarette and tossed the match out of the window, annoyed by the fact that his lighter had run out of fuel, the aromatic smell of sulphur fresh in his nostrils. He squinted, struggling to see out of the windscreen, the rain gentle but consistent. He sighed gruffly, exhaling a large plume of smoke. The weather and the fact that it was nearly one in the morning meant he was denied the view of the breath-taking countryside around them, he thought to himself unhappily. He slumped back in the seat and cocked his head towards Jesse who was snoring quietly in the passenger seat, her head resting on a rolled-up jacket wedged against the window. The DI took another hefty drag and once again attempted to take in his surroundings, secretly annoyed that he had been left to his own personal demons and erratic thoughts. He mentally shook himself, annoyed by his own selfishness.

They had reached Fort William half an hour ago and had decided to park up in the carpark on the banks of Loch Linnhe, just off of the town centre. At this time of night it was relatively empty, a few camper vans were sporadically scattered but none close to their current laying-up point. Just the way he liked it. Jesse had fallen asleep quickly; Class, however, had been denied the sweet embrace, hence his quickly-deteriorating mood. The DI huffed to himself in frustration and opened the car door. He swung himself out and quietly shut it as not to wake the exhausted Jesse. He tossed his butt and immediately pulled out another cigarette and once again toiled to light it with a match, the icy Highland wind making the job even harder than before.

He breathed in deeply, filling his lungs with not only smoke but also the crisp Highland air. He smiled, reminiscing about his childhood visits to Fort William and the surrounding mountains, his father taking him deer stalking and supposed crocodile hunting in the murky lochs and wild glens. He smiled thinking about his triumphant return to school after the holidays, enthralling his friends with tales of his reptilian adventures, unknowing that most had thought him crazy or worse still, lying. He had been mortified to find out some years later that his father had been misleading him all along. A child's imagination was a marvellous yet fragile thing, he thought to himself. Having said that, despite the embarrassment and juvenile ridicule he wouldn't have had it any other way. Like a floodgate, once he had recalled fragments of these memories others began to flow freely, each one like a wave crashing upon his subconscious, some good but others he would sooner forget.

"A penny for your thoughts," the voice stirred Class

out of his recollections. He turned to see Jesse standing by the car pulling her jacket around herself to beat off the rain.

"What are you doing up?" he asked, his concern evident. Jesse strolled towards him. She too breathed in the night air, filling her lungs with the pollution-free oxygen. She smiled sleepily.

"It's amazing, isn't it? Even though I live surrounded by the countryside the air up here smells and tastes different, almost better. It's as if the very ground is alive and breathing. It feels good to be surrounded by such untamed wilderness; it focuses the mind." Class smiled softly, understanding full well what Jesse was trying to say.

"I know what you mean," he replied quietly, his mind still reminiscing. He turned to face the Loch, the gentle lap of the water almost hypnotic. "People say that the Highlands are the last true wilderness left in this country and I would have to agree. I haven't set foot up here for years but as soon as I return all the memories come flooding back. I can remember the smells, the very feel of the place and the air; it's all logged in my mind, like some sort of psychological muscle memory. Even though I am a city boy at heart and I love living in Bristol I truly feel alive up here, away from the hordes of people and mindless consumerism. It really does put your life into perspective when you are surrounded by nothing but nature," he paused and turned to face Jesse who stood motionless allowing the DI to talk, not wanting to disrupt his flow. He continued, "I think everybody thinks like that when they visit up here. The wide open spaces of the moors and the rugged mountains seem to captivate even the most hardened city dweller. It makes all of us question our choices."

He stopped talking, feeling embarrassed that he had opened up a little too much. Jesse smiled warmly at him.

"I think we all crave for the wild to some degree. Modern life has us brainwashed into thinking we must work, pay bills, then die, that we must be happy for what we have and should never question the bigger picture. Either that or that we must worship money as if it was the one true religion, obtain it at any cost. Everyone is so concerned with the trivial stuff being force-fed to us via the television or media that they are blinded to the real problems surrounding them…" Jesse paused, her mood suddenly somewhat sombre. "Maybe the Jackals aren't that crazy after all," she said, lowering her gaze.

Class looked stunned; he shook his head vigorously. "No Jesse…," he snapped, "…they are nothing more than killers, pure and simple. They can dress up their actions in as much psychological rhetoric or spiritual bullshit as they like but when it comes down to it they are just bat-shit mental. They belong in prison. No normal morally-adjusted person would willingly go out and kill for the sake of it or to get some sort of perverse kick." He stopped, aware that his tone had started to become somewhat aggressive.

Jesse walked up to him and reached out her hand. "Got a spare ciggie?" she asked, hoping to diffuse his rant. He smiled.

"Yeah," he replied, reaching into his pocket.

JACKALS

Jesse took the cigarette and Class fumbled with a match, once again cursing his lack of lighting implements. Jesse took a drag and walked over to the railing, struggling to make out the environment through the gloom. She felt his hand on her shoulder.

"I'm sorry Jesse, I shouldn't have snapped at you like that. I was out of order," he said mournfully.

Jesse sighed. "Don't worry about it, it's been a mental few days," she replied, hoping to appease his self-inflicted guilt. "Do you think they are coming after us?" she enquired sombrely. The DI shrugged his shoulders in an attempt to be non-committal; Jesse scowled knowing full well what he was doing. He lowered his gaze, all too aware that his rouse wasn't working.

"Yes Jesse, they are coming after us, and I fear that after our miraculous escape they are going to be sending everything they've got. Hunt or no hunt they can't leave us alive—we are on borrowed time," he replied.

Jesse huffed out loud. "Do you think we stand a chance?" she asked pleadingly. Class grinned.

"There is always a chance Jesse, we are still breathing and we ain't going down without a fight," he retorted, almost sounding convincing.

The rain started to get heavier; Jesse flicked her cigarette and made a run for the warmth of the car. Class followed suit. They managed to slam their doors before the heavens opened, the deluge cutting down the visibility even further.

"Are you married?"

The question caught Class off guard. He turned to face Jesse.

"I'm flattered but you already have a husband. Mind you, I am a good looking man and I don't blame you," he quipped, winking at her. Jesse laughed and gently punched him on the arm.

"You know what I mean," she said playfully, inwardly soothed by the normality of the banter. He shook his head.

"Nope, no woman was stupid enough to have me," he replied, his demeanour taking a darker tone.

"But you came close, didn't you?" she said.

The DI looked thoughtful. "Yes, I was close once but I turned my back on her and walked away."

Jesse shifted her position and stared at Class, willing the policeman to explain further. He felt agitated under her gaze, knowing full well what she expected.

"I was engaged to Samantha Walcott, the Avon and Somerset Chief Constable's daughter, but after a turbulent four years I dumped her at the altar," he stated matter-of-factly. Jesse remained silent; Class was surprised by the lack of female vitriol in response to his ungentlemanly admission.

"Why?" she finally asked. Class huffed softly.

"I want to tell you that I didn't love her and that I did it because I fancy myself as some sort of male gigolo, irresistible to the opposite sex, but I would be lying. The truth is I did and still do love her," he rubbed his forehead in an attempt to wipe away his memories. "… I left because she deserved better," he added.

They remained silent for a few seconds, each one reflecting on their own marital troubles. It was Jesse who broke the pause in the conversation.

"Then why leave? Surely you have some redeeming qualities?" she asked with a slight smirk.

Class started to laugh softly. "Do you moonlight as some sort of marriage councillor? If so I'm not impressed with your people skills," he joked back. They both began to laugh. The DI composed himself. "I'm a fuck-up, Jesse," he said blankly. "Everything I touch turns to shit. I'm a crap copper, I drink heavily and I am a trustee of modern chemistry. I wasn't good enough for her then and I'm certainly not good enough for her now…" he paused, not making eye contact. "She is perfect, compassionate and kind. I didn't want my shit to bring her down to the gutter where I belong."

Jesse sighed. "Why didn't you just talk to her, tell her how you felt? If she loved you I'm sure she would have understood whatever demons you had or at least tried to help."

Class huffed and turned to face his companion.

"The shit I see day-in, day-out is the type of stuff no one should ever witness let alone share with the ones you love over dinner. In my mind I was protecting her from all the crazy fucking things that happen every day to good, honest people. I wanted to lock her away to keep her safe, but in the end I turned to alcohol and drugs, my way of dealing with the constant barrage of filth I found myself wading through." He wiped his eyes. "I was secretive and moody and took it out on her. I ended up backing away when I should have done what you said and talked to her but my male pride wouldn't allow me. In the end I felt the best thing to do was to walk away and let her be happy."

The car fell silent, neither one adding to the conversation. The only sound was the heavy rain against the vehicle metal work. After a few minutes Jesse spoke out.

"Sorry, but that's bullshit," she said scathingly. "You fancy yourself as the victim, and that excuse sounds like the plot to some dodgy Hollywood movie, the down-beaten cop whose marriage is on the rocks. This is real life, not some sort of action flick. Every couple have issues, not just you!"

Class glared at Jesse, his temper suddenly rising. "What the hell do you know about pain? You got a perfect little life going on, a perfect house and husband. Before all this nightmare you had never experienced the full weight of the shit that life can throw at you," he rasped angrily.

Jesse scoffed, "You have no fucking idea what you are talking about!"

Class paused, taken back by the venom in her voice.

"Well?" he asked. Jess turned to face out of the window, tears starting to run gently down her cheeks.

"When I was at school I was bullied continually. I went to a private all-girls school, the kind of school that costs thousands per term and that rich parents ship their kids off to and to forget about them so they don't become a burden to their social life."

Class sighed. "Poor little rich girl, eh?" he said sarcastically. Jesse glared at him. "I never asked to go to this school and unlike all the other girls my family lived just down the road. They didn't ship me off and forget about me."

Class started to chortle. "Wow, mega trauma in the Jesse Reid household. I take it all back. Was daddy some sort of banker or politician? You didn't get the pony you wanted for your tenth birthday?" he quipped, secretly annoyed by her privileged upbringing.

Jesse once again glared at the DI. "My father is Sir Rupert Devine, a big shot in the business world and an all-round self-centred wanker," she hissed. Class shrugged his shoulders.

"Am I supposed to know who the fuck that is? If so you are barking up the wrong tree, lady. I've never heard of him."

Jesse started to giggle. "I didn't expect you to know who he is but I bet your Chief Superintendent Walcott does," she replied stoically.

Class stared at her, his expression slightly confused. "How so?" he asked, his curiosity getting the better of him. Jesse held his gaze.

"He is the founder and managing director of Devine Tactical Industries, the UK's largest defence contractor for textiles and tactical equipment. He not only supplies the Ministry of Defence but also every police force in the country with everything from stab vests to armoured vehicles…" She paused, allowing it to sink in. "He is the go-to guy; he runs in the very highest circles of power."

Class rubbed his chin, it would appear he was a heavyweight after all.

"If your father is such a bigwig and has the ear of the government why the hell haven't you asked him for help? I'm sure some of his Secret Service chums could have helped you out of this shit storm. Instead you got lumbered with a washed up, sorry excuse for a copper, who has done a pretty crappy job of protecting you thus far," he scoffed.

Jesse once again turned away from the DI, her eyes welling up.

"I haven't spoken to my father in nearly twenty years," she replied softly.

Class felt he had hit a raw nerve and immediately regretted acting so flippantly. "I'm sorry," he mumbled, embarrassed by his stupidity and lack of diplomacy "Can I ask why?" he enquired gently.

Jesse turned once again to face him; she wiped her eyes on the sleeve of her jacket.

"I was raised on the Mendip hills, just outside of Wells. My father was rich and somewhat feared within the business world so inevitably a lot of the girls at my school were jealous. Every day I was tormented and bullied. They used to shout at me that I thought I was beautiful because my maiden name was Devine. Every day I was tormented, it was never ending. I didn't fit in with any groups or clicks and was a bit of a loner. The only friend I had was a girl called Miranda. She was my one and only best friend. We used to go riding on the hills and imagine life outside of Somerset. In truth she was the reason I didn't commit suicide. I had come close many times, you see. Anyway, for five years Miranda and I were inseparable and she used to stay over at my house on the weekends. One afternoon my mother and I came home early from a ballet class and found my father having sex with my best friend in my parents' bed. Miranda was even wearing some of my mother's lingerie and perfume. We were both eighteen at the time. They didn't even try to explain or lie. It was obvious that my father didn't care about my mother, and my so-called best friend Miranda was smirking at me, enjoying the drama. My mother didn't say a word. She quietly made her way to the gun safe and proceeded to load a shotgun. I screamed at her to stop but she wouldn't listen. She put the barrel up to her chin but before she pulled the trigger she looked at me and said softly, "Tell your father I will see him in hell." Then she killed herself in front of me." She started to cry again.

Class remained silent, unsure of how to respond; a subdued, "Fucking hell..." was all he could manage to muster.

Jesse composed herself and continued.

"My father even had the cheek to bring Miranda on his arm to my mother's funeral; she was all glammed up like some gold-digging whore. We had an argument after the wake and I stormed out. I gave him an ultimatum. I told him it was either his slut or me and he chose her. He disowned me there and then and to this day I haven't forgiven him for what he did to my mother."

Class reached out and held her hand. "I'm sorry, Jesse," he said, his tone conveying his sincerity. Jesse shrugged.

"For a split second I thought about contacting him when all this shit started but I just couldn't bring myself to do it. The thought of him makes me feel physically sick." she added.

Class pulled out two cigarettes and handed one to his companion. "Here," he muttered. "I'm no good at counselling but these have never let me down," he jibed. Jesse smiled and accepted the token.

"You're right," she said, smiling, "…you are a shit counsellor." Class grinned.

"I really am sorry if I've spoken out of turn Jesse, I had no idea about the shit you have been through."

Jesse sighed. "It affected me badly. The rejection, the fact he chose his tart over his own flesh and blood. For years I have suffered with depression and a myriad of psychological issues. It took me years to admit to myself that it did affect me. I despise him for what he did but on the same token crave for his admiration. Does that sound crazy?"

Class gently shook his head. "Nope, not at all Jesse. I'm no Brainiac but even I know the human mind is a deep complex thing, so much so that we have only just scraped the surface regarding how it works and why. We all have our issues Jesse, mine— if I'm honest with myself—is that I drink way too much and take far too many drugs. I know I'm a fuck-up yet can't seem to stop myself. I have an addictive personality, hell; maybe I'm just addicted to the drama created by my own addiction."

Jesse stared at him. "Bloody hell, Class, that's deep," she said, grinning. Class huffed.

"Not just a pretty face, you know," he quipped. Class glanced at his watch. It was two a.m. He stretched his back and yawned. "I think we should try and get some shut-eye, young lady. We have a few mores hours' travelling tomorrow to get up to Uig on Skye. The ferry leaves at eleven."

He leaned back and closed his eyes, eager to drift into oblivion. Jesse did likewise but not before straining out of the window into the gloom, silently praying that their pursuers wouldn't find them. She too closed her eyes, the anger towards her father still boiling inside of her.

TWENTY-EIGHT

Wednesday, 0713 hrs

Class woke with a jump. It took him a few seconds to realise where he was, his senses frantically clambering to take in and rationalise his surroundings, his brain still reeling from his nightmare. With one hand he wearily rubbed his face and through tired eyes looked about him, his body still shaking. Class gently sighed and relaxed slightly when he saw Jesse sleeping soundly next to him, blissfully unaware of the horrendous end they had both come to in his dream.

It was daylight outside and he was relieved to see the rain had stopped. In truth he hadn't realised he had fallen asleep; it had taken a long time for him finally to switch off. He was tired but the glow of the sun was a welcome sight. He causally looked at his watch and quietly chuffed at the hour. It would soon be time to make a move if they were to get to the ferry port in plenty of time, but for now Class decided that the best course of action was to let his companion sleep for a little while longer. She would need it he reckoned; it was only a matter of time before their pursuers caught up with them and all hell broke loose.

JACKALS

The DI gingerly opened the car door and swung himself out into the chilly morning air, his body aching from the cramped confines of the vehicle. He stretched himself feeling his muscles expand from their slumber, dull waves of pain finding their way to the nerve endings. He gazed across the loch and stood silently taking in the beauty of the mountains, a brief respite from the horror they found themselves in, he mused. Class suddenly felt a wave of crippling self-doubt. Would he ever see this view again, he found himself wondering. Almost immediately he shook his head in response, eager to drown out his trepidation. He had to remain strong for her; she was relying on him, no time to show any cracks in his resolve or weakness.

Class rummaged in his pocket searching for his cigarettes. He swore under his breath when he found the packet to be empty. He looked behind him towards the town centre; if his memory served him right there was a newsagent or convenience shop just up the hill. He glanced back to the vehicle were Jesse was still sleeping. He decided not to leave—his paranoia getting the better of him—they could be close. He started to feel a surge of panic; he frantically scanned the carpark for anything that posed a threat. Once again the nausea came, his inner voice warning him of the futility of the coming battle. The odds were no way in his favour; they were going to die, he reasoned. They could be anywhere, anyone. They could be watching them right now, waiting to make their move.

Once again Class scanned the car park, his mind

turning to the journey ahead. There was a lot of open road between their current position and the ferry terminal, plenty of places they could be ambushed, their car pushed into a loch, never to be found. He scratched his chin straining his eyesight for any tell-tale signs they were being watched. Don't be ridiculous, his rational side exclaimed. The Jackals modus operandi was that they were to kill primitively. Ramming them off the road and ditching them into the dark, murky depths wasn't really in keeping with their ethos, but then again all bets were off after earlier events. The DI was tired of trying to second-guess these bastards; they had limited options. Their only play was to make it to the island, turn the tide in their favour, try and dictate the battle ground and work it to their advantage.

"Fuck!" he said out loud. The reality hit him like a hammer. Just who the hell did he think he was? He wasn't some Special Forces hero, some kick-ass action man—he was just some over the hill Somerset copper who had a drinking habit and a fondness for good quality cocaine.

"Morning." The voice startled him. He turned to see Jesse standing a few feet behind him.

"Bloody hell woman, that's the second time you've managed to sneak up behind me. I must be getting old," he exclaimed jovially, desperately trying to disguise his ever-diminishing optimism.

Jesse smiled and stretched her arms out to her side; no doubt she also felt the aching sensation from their night in the vehicle.

"What's the plan then, hero?" she enquired. Class

grinned, amused by her choice of words.

"Now you are up I think we are going to head off soon. I don't like being stationary for too long. The ferry isn't until eleven but I don't want to be caught napping…" he paused and for the third time scanned the carpark. "…I'd rather be on the move; a mobile target is harder to track and catch." he added. Jesse frowned.

"How far behind us do you think they are?"

The DI shrugged. "Not far, but I don't want to take any chances. The more distance we can put between us and them the better," he replied, his voice edged with a slight hint of fear. Jesse nodded in agreement.

"Well let's get going then, shall we?" she stated, turning on her heels and heading for the car.

Class smiled. "We will stop off at the next garage for fuel, some food and supplies then get on the road," he said, reaching for the door handle. They both got in and Class started the engine. Slowly he pulled the car out of the space and made his way to the exit. He paused at the junction waiting to see if any vehicle followed; there wasn't any sign of surveillance. Class breathed a sigh of relief and pulled out on to the main road.

There wasn't much traffic so in theory any tails would most likely stick out, thus alerting them to any danger. Class drove down the main road and at the next roundabout noticed the petrol station situated next to a McDonald's restaurant, behind it a little industrial estate ambled its way down to the banks of the loch. He made his way onto the forecourt and turned to Jesse.

"Let's make it quick. I will put fifty pounds in the tank whilst you go and get supplies and pay. No messing about, in and out quickly. We have to minimise our exposure...," he paused, looking around the station, "...those fuckers have access to a lot of databases and I wouldn't be surprised if the garage's ANPR system will ping us and alert them to our location. There isn't much we can do about that so let's make it quick."

Jesse grinned and jumped out of the Range Rover. She turned and stared directly at the surveillance camera located just above the store entrance. In one slow motion she stuck her middle finger up and mouthed the words, "*Fuck you*". Laughing she turned to Class who was still sat in the driver's seat staring at her, his face grimacing.

"Well if they know we are here we might as well send them a little message, wouldn't you agree?" she said giggling, then quickly turned and headed for the entrance.

Class couldn't help but admire her fighting spirit, her refusal to shrivel up and die without a fight. Maybe he should take a leaf out of her book he thought to himself, embarrassed by his momentary lapse of courage only a little while earlier. He got out and started to fill the tank. Once finished he gave the thumbs up and jumped back into the vehicle. He was still smiling when she returned with a plastic bag full of bottled water, chocolate bars, a couple packs of sandwiches and two packs of cigarettes. She slumped into the passenger seat and tossed a pack of Camel onto his lap. Class grinned.

"You are a fucking life saviour," he said as he started

the engine. They both laughed as he pulled out and headed north towards Spean Bridge and ever closer to their destination.

Felix grinned and drained the remnants of his coffee cup all the while watching intently from the McDonald's restaurant situated alongside the petrol station. It went without saying of course that he had known they were held up at the carpark. When he had arrived during the night he had driven slowly past them and had even debated whether to attack straight away as to catch them off guard whilst they slept but after a few minutes had finally decided to lay up further down the road, just off of the main drag. The little industrial estate located behind the fast food chain acted as a concealed static OP whilst maintaining good vantage points and lines of sight should they make a move.

Having looked into the policeman's past it wasn't a stretch to reason he was heading for the Highlands, possibly the Outer Hebrides. Of course the target vehicles built-in tracker had gotten him to their current location but his intuition played a big part regarding their future plans. Felix always took great pride in his ability to foresee and pre-empt his prey's next move, usually before they had even thought of it themselves.

He watched closely as Jesse clambered into the Range Rover then followed with his eyes as they left the forecourt and disappeared out of sight. There was no rush, he thought to himself; he could track them on his smart phone. He figured that the signal might drop out now again due to the geographical location but he was confident he could stay a safe distance behind them as not to alert them to his presence. The only time he may become exposed or compromised was at the ferry terminal, if that was where they were heading, of course. He would have to give that particular problem some thought on route.

Felix stood up, gathered his phone and causally made his way to the car park. Just as he put the key in the ignition his phone started to chime, indicating an incoming call. Felix glanced at the screen, an unknown number. Felix sighed; there was only one person who had the number. He jabbed at the accept button.

"Hello, Mr Blake," he stated as cheerily as he could muster.

"Good morning Felix, how are you this glorious day? I trust you are enjoying your little holiday north of the wall?" the voice replied. Felix could feel his heckles rise; he really didn't like this pompous prick.

"Indeed I am, Mr Blake. In fact, I am so close to the wild life I can smell them," he bragged.

"Jolly good show, Felix, I had a feeling you were the right man for the job. Now then. Just to make you aware that three teams of Jackals are not far from your current position and will more than likely be chomping at the bit to get in on the action, so to speak."

Felix rolled his eyes, he was getting fed up not only with playing nice but pandering to those he deemed sub-human.

"Of course," he said flatly. "Is that all?" he added. There was a slight pause.

"We have it on good authority that others are also on their way."

Felix grinned. "Let them come," he threatened.

"That's my boy," Blake retorted. "Happy hunting." The phone line went dead.

Felix tossed the phone onto the passenger seat and twisted the key. The BMW's engine roared to life. Felix manoeuvred the luxury car out of the car park and onto the main road. As he gunned the accelerator he smiled at the traffic sign announcing he was on the route to the Isle of Skye. Felix was happy. The sun was shining, he was feeling excited about the hunt once again and to top it all off he had a boot full of implements to assist in sending that copper and his bitch into the Void with their entrails hanging out. Today was a good day, he mused.

TWENTY-NINE

Wednesday, 0850 hrs

Stokes stared out of the Landover window and stifled a yawn, silently mesmerised by the high mountains flanking the road, the early morning sunlight radiating from the heather and peat, thin wisps of mist gently floating sporadically amongst the dotted sheep. The journey had been uneventful, yet tiring. He had tried to sleep but was denied its sweet embrace; instead his mind raced at the thought of what lay ahead, and in truth he was both excited and terrified, not terrified in the traditional sense but of the opportunities that would present themselves should the mission be successful.

Throughout the journey he had been secretly impressed with Stevens and his driver's resolve. Both had kept going regardless of the lack of rest, their zeal and loyalty keeping them focused, the perfect blend of gentlemanly refinement with a subtle underlining brutality. If the Jackals were akin to blunt force trauma, his men were a surgical scalpel. The professor was pleased they were on his side.

Stokes had a soft spot for Scotland, especially the Highlands. In his humble opinion only well-educated and learned men could truly appreciate the magnificent splendour of the wilds. The mere plebs should be content with their place in the crime-ridden cities where they belonged. This was no place for such weak people he mused; only hunters thrived in such a hostile environment. Life was a gift that many did not deserve. He sighed and brought his attention back to Stevens who was busy in the front passenger seat studying a map.

"How far are we, Mr Stevens?" he asked mournfully. Stevens turned in his seat to face his employer.

"We are just coming up to Fort William, Sir. It would appear they are heading for Inverness or possibly the Isle of Skye. When we get past Fort William we will have a better idea of their destination and make plans to suit."

Stokes grinned. "Excellent," he said, a little happier than before. "Are your men still with us?" he continued. Stevens nodded.

"Yes Sir, they are about a mile behind us. They are carrying the spare weapons and will be providing logistical and tactical support."

Stokes chuckled. "You say that like this is a military operation, Mr Stevens." The mercenary smirked.

"If not an operation of military prowess what then should I term it? We are a smaller force about to engage a larger one. I think it is only prudent that we look upon it as warfare, no mercy or rules of combat are to be expected nor given. They have the numbers but we have the capability and the fire power," he retorted smugly.

Stokes let out a hearty laugh in response to his subordinate's dry wit and forthright delivery.

"Bravo, Mr Stevens. I shall allow you to have that one and bow to your vast experience and military skillset."

Stevens returned his attention to his map. He reached for his Motorola SRX 2200 encrypted two-way and pressed the call button.

"Delta One receiving?" The radio crackled with static.

"Delta One receiving. Go for transmission."
Stevens grinned. "Comms check. You boys lonely back there? Still with us?" he said.

"Eager to get stuck in, boss" came the reply.

The big man grinned. "Stay on point. We have inbound hostiles in unknown numbers. Your orders are to terminate on sight if engaged. Zero civilian casualties, if possible. Receive." A slight pause.

"Copy that, Boss. Delta One over and out." Stevens placed the radio in the door well and turned once again to face Stokes.

"All good to go, Sir. Don't worry, they are professionals," he stated with absolute confidence. The old man smiled.

"That's why I have you around Mr Stevens, a true professional if ever there was one. I think the Order won't know what hit them…" he paused and once again gazed out of the window. More and more dwellings appeared, no doubt due to the fact they were getting closer to a settlement "This has been a long time coming, Mr Stevens. It's time they paid for their transgressions," he whispered more to himself than to his companions.

Stevens listened intently but remained silent, not wanting to distract his superior, all the while his hand subconsciously touching the butt of the Springfield XD-9 Semi Auto pistol resting on his lap.

Jesse ripped open a packet of pickled onion crisps and thrust the packet under the nose of Class, who recoiled in mock disgust. She giggled at his playful stupidity.

"How can you not enjoy pickled onion crisps?" she quipped.

The DI chuckled. "I hate them, in fact I hate onions altogether," he jested.

Jesse slumped back in her seat and propped her feet up on the dashboard.

"You've got some serious issues, Class" she jibed.

The DI smirked. "Says the one," he retorted.

Jesse remained silent, her thoughts turning to Damien.

"Do you think they've killed my husband?" she asked quietly. Class sighed; his silence spoke volumes.

"Thought so," she said sedately.

Class ignored her, not because he was heartless but because he didn't know what to say. He wanted to tell her that her husband was alive and well and that everything was going to be okay but in his stomach he knew it was bullshit. The chances of Damien surviving were near to zero and the likelihood of both of them getting out of it was only a little better. He figured she wouldn't believe him even if he tried to lie, so why bother? Neither of them spoke again for about half an hour, Jesse content with watching the passing scenery and Class focusing his attention on the winding and twisting road which snaked its way through the Western Highlands. Jesse's mind swirled and danced in her self-induced solitude, her fears ringing in her subconscious, her mind's eye recalling the brutality of the situation. She cursed under her breath.

"Those bastards!" she thought to herself. She hated them for what they had done to her and her husband. This wasn't their fight; they had nothing to do with any of it. They had been innocent. The image of Chloe dying on her kitchen floor flashed before her then the image of Felix standing there, grinning. She started to cry but turned her head away from Class, not wanting the policeman to see her tears.

"You okay?" he asked, aware that Jesse was having a moment. Jesse wiped her cheek and forced a smile.

"Yeah, I'm good," she muttered.

Once again both sat in silence, both knowing that the cracks were starting to appear but neither one wanting to admit it nor show the other. They were falling apart and it was only a matter of time before something gave. Class struggled to find any words that could encourage or motivate her, in truth not just for her but for himself also. The act of speaking out loud may have a calming effect, he reasoned. Alas, the words were not forthcoming so he decided to keep quiet. He just wanted to get to the island and hide.

JACKALS

Jesse broke the uneasy silence. "So when we get to the Isle of Lewis what exactly are we going to do? Where exactly are we going?" she asked inquisitively.

At last Class smiled. "We are going to hide out in a shieling way out on the moors just north of a village called Tolsta. It's in the Northeast of the island. Lord Leverhulme owned the island from 1918 to 1923 and decided to build a road from Tolsta to Ness on the most northern tip of the island, but abandoned it after the Great War. All that's left is a bridge that goes nowhere; in fact it's called the Bridge to Nowhere by the locals. The only thing after it is some remanence of a peat trail that runs along the cliffs up to Ness. It's barren, desolate and we will be able to see anyone coming for miles."

Jesse grinned. "What the hell is a shieling?" she enquired. Class started to laugh.

"It's a stone and corrugated hut used by the locals for staying in when they were out cutting peat!" he exclaimed happily. Jesse's smile faded.

"You mean to tell me you have dragged us all the way up here to hide in some mouldy shack in the middle of nowhere, freezing cold with only the sheep to keep us company…" she paused "…that is your great masterplan, is it?" The DI started to chuckle.

"I said it was the best plan I could come up with, I didn't say it was perfect. But believe me when I say the islanders will know strangers are about before anyone else, the jungle drums will start beating when those bastards turn up. We will know and have the advantage. Luckily I still have a few contacts and friends on the island should we need assistance but I would rather keep them out of it. We have the right gear; we just need to pick up some supplies, bunker down and see if we can wait it out."

Jesse smirked. "Wait it out? This isn't some fairytale where the good guys always win. This is real life, with real killers coming after us whose only mission in life is to cause pain…" she rasped. She paused, waiting for a response. There was none.

"Hiding isn't going to do any good, Class--how long shall we wait? One week, two months? They are relentless, they are just going to keep coming until we are dead and no one can help us."

The DI remained silent and concentrated on the road. Once again the silence was tangible. For over an hour neither spoke, each occupant lost in their own thoughts, each facing their own personal demons.

"Look." stated Class.

Jesse looked up to see the road fall away into a long downhill sweeping bend. To her left she could see far below the sea loch and a small ferry terminal, the surrounding mountainside loosely scattered with cottages. From their vantage point the water looked inviting and on any other day Jesse might have thought this place appeared magical.

"Uig!" exclaimed Class. "This is our jumping off point to Lewis. We get the ferry from here over to the Isle of Harris then drive north up onto Lewis. A few more hours and we will be there," he added.

Jesse chose not to respond, content with taking in

the scenery. Class slowly pulled into the terminal carpark and switched off the engine. There were already a handful of cars parked in the loading lanes, some empty, the occupants obviously stretching their legs in the nearby surrounding area. Class scanned the vehicles looking for threats then slowly took in their surroundings. To his right sat the low tatty building acting as the ticket office and reception; to its right a small scruffy looking garage complete with what looked like a makeshift café. Directly in front of them, situated at the beginning of the embarkation ramp sat what looked like a single storey pub, its outside desperately in need of a lick of paint. Behind the pub were a small collection of dwellings, no doubt cottages belonging to local fishermen, their gardens strewn with lobster pots and nets.

A sudden shriek made him look back towards the ticket building to his right. A small group of young adults burst out of the door giggling and whooping as one of their group dropped his ice cream much to the amusement of his friends. Class watched the group slowly walk towards a mini bus parked just to his left a few lanes over, its roof rack stacked with mountain bikes and pulling a trailer full of canoes. He stared intently as they opened the side door, the words BLACK COUNTRY ADVENTURE LTD emblazoned on the side.

"Nice to see kids getting outdoors instead of stuck on their bloody computers all day," Jesse suddenly said. Class grinned.

"They're hardly kids, late teens early twenties I'd say,

but I know what you mean."

Jesse couldn't help but laugh. "You really are a smart arse, aren't you Class?" she joked.

Another cheer went up from the group as one of their female members lost her boarding card, a sudden gust of wind whipping the paperwork away. She frantically started to chase it across the carpark. It came to a halt next to Jesse's window; she was just about to jump out and help when the young girl managed to get it before it disappeared once again. The blonde-haired girl stamped on it then reached down and snapped it up. Jesse smiled warmly at her; she returned the gesture then turned and held up her absconding ticket in triumph. Once again her friends cheered as she rushed back to join them.

"Oh, to be that age again, eh?" Jesse said. The policeman nodded.

"Yep. No worries, no hassle, life hasn't even begun to fuck them over yet," he said matter-of-factly. Jesse looked at him in disbelief.

"I can't even believe you said that. How can one so young be so cynical?" she said in mock rebuke. Class smiled and opened his door.

"I'm going to get our tickets. Stay here and keep your eyes open," and with that he slammed the door and made his way across the carpark, finally disappearing into the ticket office.

Jesse lit a cigarette and slowly blew out a stream of smoke. She felt like she was in a dream world. All around her life went on as normal whilst hers and Class' was a whirlwind of violence and brutality, everyone else oblivious to what was going on and what true horrors stalked the streets. She huffed to herself. It's not like in the movies when you see the hero in such a predicament and you shout at the telly that he is doing things wrong, convinced that you know what you would do or how you would react in similar circumstances. Mocking the protagonist for poor choices from the confines of your armchair was safe, but this was real life. If they made a wrong move here they would die. It was that simple. The door opening made Jesse jump. Class clambered in and slammed the door behind him.

"Any problems?" he asked. Jesse shook her head.

"All good here," she replied.

Class nodded. "Okay, then. It's 10:00 a.m. now, so the ferry is on its way. We should be boarding soon. We just have to keep our heads down." Jesse agreed.

A long toot of a horn made them both look up and to their left. Appearing from the bend out to sea was the ferry approaching the dock. They both smiled. They were nearly there.

THIRTY

Wednesday, 1050 hrs

Class eased the Range Rover along the boarding ramp and down into the metallic hull of the ferry loading bay. He gently pulled up behind the mini bus. He cast his gaze around the ferry. The boat wasn't packed but there seemed to be a steady flow of passengers making their way to the Outer Hebrides. It shouldn't be too hard to find somewhere quiet to lay low on board. He sighed gently and tugged on the handbrake, then glanced at Jesse.

"Right then, let's find a nice quiet spot and have a coffee. Hopefully we can get some rest before the last leg of the journey."

They both nodded in agreement and jumped out of the vehicle. Jesse and Class joined the other car passengers moving towards the exit points and in single file they slowly made their way up the narrow stairwell into the lounge area of the ferry. Just a few people in front of them Class could see the mini bus group of young adventurers squawking and laughing amongst themselves, their noisy joviality resonating off the super structure, their good nature somehow infectious. He smiled and glanced behind towards his companion. Jesse held onto the railing tightly and could feel the vibrations of the engines, her stomach churned slightly at the gentle waft of diesel. She wasn't really keen on sea travel and had decided not to alert Class to this fact; she was a country girl not a mermaid, she reasoned. It appeared that the DI had no issue with it at all and even appeared to be excited about going to sea. Jesse thought the best course of action was to just sit down and try to get through it, hopefully without throwing up and making herself look stupid.

At the top of the stairs the youngsters darted off in different directions, eager to explore the ship. Other passengers looked on in disgust as they cheered and screamed their way around. The deck was spacious and surprisingly clean, the dark mahogany trim polished but the carpet appeared threadbare and well worn. The obligatory fruit machine pinged and beeped as the captain came over the loud speaker welcoming everybody aboard followed by the mandatory safety briefing. Jesse wondered if anyone actually ever took any notice.

Class made a beeline for the rear of the ship, no doubt to a quiet, sparsely-inhabited seating area. The policeman looked around. Satisfied this would suit their needs he invited Jesse to sit down.

"I will get us a brew; try to get some rest," he said.

Jesse slumped down and reclined her chair. It was a damn sight more comfortable than the night spent in the Range Rover, she thought. The ship started to fire up its engines and slowly made its way out into the Minch. The

DI returned with a tray, on which where two large cups of coffee and a plate with two sticky buns. He placed the tray on the table and followed Jesse's lead by flopping down into his chair. He closed his eyes and smiled.

"Mmmmmm super comfy," he said playfully.

"How long is the crossing?" she asked.

"About two hours," he responded without opening his eyes.

Jesse relaxed a little. That isn't so bad, she thought.

"…of course that depends if we hit bad weather. They get some serious sea storms out there," he added.

Jesse suddenly felt her stomach lurch and stared out of the window in a bid to distract her mind and ever-increasingly gargling stomach. She watched as the land slowly disappeared and gave way to the swell of the Atlantic. Class opened one eye slightly watching her reaction and started to chuckle.

"Don't worry Jesse, we will be fine. You know what to do; you listened to the safety announcement, didn't you?" he added, this time keeping his eyes shut knowing full well how she would be reacting.

Jesse felt sick, the motion of the boat increasing as they hit open water. Class couldn't help but grin.

"Oh my God, I think I'm gonna puke," she stated and jumped to her feet. "Where are the toilets?" she asked desperately.

The policeman chuckled. "Down the hallway, on the left," he replied, not opening his eyes.

Jesse darted off, her hand clutched to her mouth.

JACKALS

Jesse burst her way into the toilet and threw herself into a cubicle just in time. She vomited into the bowl, her head spinning from the velocity. Gently she steadied herself and flushed, dabbing her mouth with tissue paper. With the motion of the boat rocking her side to side she carefully made her way to the sink and splashed her face with cold water. The momentary relief was greatly received. Jesse gazed at her reflection; her pasty-coloured face stared back at her.

The door suddenly swung open and bounced off of the sink with a crash. Jesse looked up to see the young blonde girl from the mini bus rush in and make a dash for the cubicle. Jesse winced at the sound of her throwing up, followed by the toilet flushing. She grinned.

"At least I'm not the only one," she thought to herself, suddenly feeling less embarrassed by her lack of sea legs. Jesse turned to see the young girl slowly exit the cubicle, her face pasty and pale.

"Are you okay?" Jesse asked her. The young girl nodded slowly.

"I hate boats," she said sheepishly.

"Me too, I prefer dry land," Jesse retorted.

The young blonde tried to force a smile. "I'm from Birmingham, not much call for sea travel in the Midlands," she said, obviously starting to feel a little better.

Jesse laughed. "Couldn't agree more," she replied, then turned to splash a little more cold water. Jesse doused her face, then glanced up to see if her complexion had returned.

The force of the blow sent Jesse's head slamming into the mirror, the force smashing the glass, and needle-point shards tumbled into the sink. Jesse tried to turn but her hair was yanked back, then once again her head was rammed into the broken glass. Jesse felt a slice open up across her cheek, the blood cascading down her chin and onto her shirt. Jesse was reeling from the consecutive blows and her brain tried to compensate for the momentary disruption. She spun around to face her attacker. The young blonde grinned menacingly at her.

"The Jackals send their regards, bitch!" she yelled as she threw a punch at Jesse's face. Jesse tried to block the attack but the blonde was too quick. The blow connected with her nose which erupted under the impact; her head jolted to the left as a jet of blood sprayed across the wall behind her. Her legs gave way and she crumpled to the floor just as the blonde threw a vicious kick. Jesse instinctively covered up to protect her head but the kick landed in her ribs, winding her and knocking her back into the sink surround. Jesse could feel herself falling in and out of unconsciousness; she reached up, desperately trying to grab hold of anything that would help her to her feet. She had to get up and fight, she yelled at herself internally. The girl whooped as she levelled another kick, this time towards Jesse's head. Jesse managed to duck and was relived as the attacker's foot sailed harmlessly above her and slammed into the fixtures, a bone snapping loudly on impact. The blonde screamed in pain and tumbled backwards as she tried to put weight on her shattered ankle. Jesse saw her opening and yanked herself to her feet. She screamed at her attacker with rage and with all her force lunged forward, her shoulder barging the girl into the cubicle door, sending them both sprawling into the confines of the tiny toilet. The young blonde lost her balance and fell sideways, her head smashing off of the toilet seat. There was a deafening crack as the impact caved in her cheek bone, the snap echoing in the metallic basin. Jesse braced herself and raised her right leg and whilst steadying herself viciously stomped downwards onto the blonde's temple. Her skull ruptured and her neck snapped; her eyes rolled back as blood gushed from her nose and ears. Jesse didn't take any chances; she kept going, raining down blow after blow onto the girl's face and head, her upper body reduced to crimson mush. Jesse screamed as her battle-lust subsided.

The sound of the door opening made her spin around, ready for another attack, but she wasn't fast enough. She only just saw the metallic flash of metal before she felt the searing pain as the blade sliced into her upper shoulder. She screamed and threw her arms up in an effort to defend. She stumbled backwards trying to escape the onslaught, her feet slipping on the blood-soaked lino flooring. Jesse felt the blade being retracted, the serrated edge causing more trauma on the way out, then immediately forced into her body once again, this time into her upper arm, the wound sending shock waves of pain through her body.

Jesse glared at her assailant. The second attacker was also a young female but this time with brown hair. Jesse vaguely remembered her as one of the young adventures. The realisation hit Jesse that in all probability all of the members on that mini bus were indeed Jackals; she had counted at least eight, possibly more. Her mind raced—she had to warn Class.

The second attacker didn't speak. It would appear she wouldn't be making the same mistake as her friend; she slashed wildly at her target. Jesse lunged at her and grabbed her in a headlock, then tugged with all her might, pulling the girl off her feet and into the cubicle. The girl frantically struck out with her blade, trying to stab at Jesse but couldn't get any meaningful blows due to the confined space. Jesse could feel non-lethal superficial cuts opening up all about her body but held on regardless, her adrenaline now in full fight or flight mode. Jesse rammed the Jackal's head into the wall trying to force her to drop her weapon but she clung on to it, once again lashing out, trying to hit vital organs. Jesse grimaced as more cuts opened up. She could feel the hot, sticky liquid soak into her clothing, her back sodden with sweat. Jesse grimaced as she felt the tip of the blade puncture her thigh. In one last-ditch attempt and in a fit of rage she threw everything she had at the girl—elbows, rabbit punches—anything to distract and give her an opening. Jesse finally saw her chance and with her left hand grabbed her attacker's hair and pulled downwards, exposing her face. Jesse pulled back her head and then thrust forward, head-butting her full force in the face. Jesse grinned as the Jackal winced in pain, her nose and top lip savagely ripped open, her head starting to flop uselessly to the side. Jesse took full advantage of her misery. With one fluid movement Jesse slid her hands up the Jackal's face and plunged both her thumbs into the girl's eye sockets, her fingers clutching at the face, locking her hands into position. The Jackal screamed and jolted, her limbs uselessly flailing in an attempt to shake Jesse off but it was of no use. Jesse kept pushing with all her strength; she rose to her feet, allowing more of her body weight to thrust downwards. Jesse laughed as the Jackal's eyeballs finally gave way and popped under the enormous pressure. Jesse could feel the sockets rupture and the cavities fill will fluid but Jesse kept going, forcing her blood-stained digits into the killer's brain. With one last gasp of breath the Jackal finally stopped moving, the blade tumbling from her grasp. With a sickening squelch Jesse pulled her thumbs free, allowing the body to fall limply to the floor.

Jesse tried to move but had sustained many wounds. She looked around her, there was so much blood she couldn't tell how much she had lost. She grabbed the door handle and dragged herself to her feet. Each time she moved another part of her body would hurt, making her wince in pain. She made it to the sink and started to wash her face. Gently Jesse pulled up her shirt to inspect her wounds. Luckily most were just shallow cuts and should stop bleeding soon. To her surprise her arm seemed to have stopped bleeding already but her shoulder and cheek would need attention. Jesse made her way to the exit door and slowly opened it. She peered through the crack to see if anyone else was in close proximity, guarding the room.

There was nobody there.

Across the hallway Jesse could see another door, the white cross on a green background signifying a first aid room was a welcoming sight. At last something went her way, she inwardly joked. Her body started to shake from the shock, the adrenaline dump subsiding. Jesse wiped her brow. She had to warn Class but couldn't exactly roam around the decks in her current state, so her first priority was to get into that first aid room and get herself patched up. She was confident that she could do a good enough job as to not arouse too much suspicion. For one final time Jesse intently listened to the sounds outside then casually stepped into the corridor. She looked back at the toilet door to see a bolt latch; she locked it, then snapped the bolt handle off. It wouldn't keep the maintenance crew out but should deter other passengers and hopefully buy them some time to get off the ferry without the alert going up. The last thing they needed was the police to be waiting for them when they made landfall.

Jesse glanced down the corridor and swiftly moved towards the target door. She twisted the handle, praying it was unlocked—it was. Jesse stepped through the doorway not knowing if anyone was in there but she had no choice. She closed the door, took a sharp intake of breath and turned around, ready to do some quick explaining. It was empty. Jesse paused for a second to catch her nerve. She exhaled slowly. The room was small, approximately twelve feet square; on the far side was a bed with crisp white sheets and to the left a large cabinet, with a sign proclaiming MEDICAL SUPPLIES; to her right a small sink and mirror. Jesse made her way to the cupboard and tugged at the door; it was unlocked. She was glad someone had not done their job properly and had forgotten to keep it secure. Jesse quickly rummaged around in the supplies and found what she was looking for. She took off her shirt and applied gauze, then pressed down a thick dressing to her main wounds; finally she strapped it up with surgical tape. It wasn't pretty but it would suffice until she had more time to sort it properly.

She heard voices outside. She turned towards the door but to her relief the sounds dispersed. As she turned back Jesse caught her full reflection in the mirror. She was stunned by her wounds. Her body appeared battle-scarred and broken. The last few days had been agonising. Her body may be battered but it was her mind that had sustained the most damage. In truth she didn't know if she would ever recover from her ordeal but for now her will to survive and get Damien back was the most important thing. Second, of course, was her desire for revenge or at least attain some sort of reciprocity upon those who had ruined her life. If she was going to die then she will damn sure take as many of those bastards as she could with her.

She shook off her apathy and tugged on her shirt. She snatched up a small first aid kit and made her way to the door. This time she didn't even check to see if the way was clear. Jesse exited the room and made her way back to the rear seating area. Class was asleep, snoring loudly. She slumped down and shook him on the arm; he jumped.

"What?" he asked, still half drowsy. He stared at Jesse, his face changing when he focused on her wounds. "What the fuck happened?" he asked desperately, the concern in his voice overwhelming. Jesse told him.

Class listened, his guilt ever-mounting that he wasn't there to protect her. "Fucking bastards!" he rasped under his breath.

Jesse grabbed his arm in an attempt to calm him down. Class looked up, his face snarling at something behind her. She turned to see the remaining ten Jackals walk slowly past them, five male and five female, each of them smirking in turn. Class stood up, preparing himself for the attack but none of them made a move. The DI glared as the killers sat on seats opposite their table, five of them covering each exit from the seating area. A tall, skinny male that Class put at early twenties casually walked over and sat at their table. He smiled at Jesse.

"Well, you have been a busy little carrion, haven't you?" he sneered.

Jesse held his gaze. "And I'm not finished yet!" she fired back.

The Jackal chuckled. "Do you really believe you are going to make it off this island alive? What chance do you think you have against us? There are ten of us and two of you…?"

Class glared at the Jackal. Without saying a word he threw a right jab. The speed was impressive. It collided with the leader's face, drawing blood from his lip. Both Class and Jesse were smiling.

"Maybe so, but I'm going to take some of you fuckers with me, you skinny little cunt!" Class growled.

The Jackal wasn't impressed by the policeman's show of aggression and remained smiling.

"Tut-tut, Mr Class, such anger, it must be all those drugs you take. No wonder your work colleagues hate you and your ex-fiancé thinks you are a waste of space," he retorted. He turned to Jesse. "And you, Mrs Reid. Such a lovely young lady who has missed out most of her life due to daddy issues..." he paused, and then continued. "...Oh and by the way, how is your husband?" he asked, grinning.

This time it was Class' turn to hold Jesse back. Jesse started to smirk, not rising to the bait.

"Did you see what I did to your little bitches? I hope one of those sluts was your girlfriend or maybe you prefer boys?" she quipped. Class started to roar with laughter. He looked at Jesse.

"Now that was a good come back," he said.

Jesse smiled. "Glad you liked it," she replied with a smirk.

The skinny man remained silent, then abruptly stood up and straightened his jacket. Class and Jesse flinched, ready for violence but the leader remained stationary.

"Just to let you know that my name is Rupert and I will be the one who sends you both to the Void. The others are all extremely proficient of course, but I really am something unique." He smiled at Jesse and Class in turn, then nodded. "Until we next meet," he said cheerfully, then made his way back to the nearest table.

Class was shaking, his temper at boiling point. "We have to attack them now, kill as many as we can while we still have a chance. They won't expect it," he said quietly.

Jesse shook her head. "No, look," she replied.

The DI looked behind his seat as two families, complete with five small children entered the area. They walked past Jesse and sat themselves down one table away from the nearest five Jackals.

"Fuck!" Class snarled quietly. He looked up to see one of the small children smiling and waving at Rupert who in turn was pulling funny faces, making the child giggle uncontrollably. All ten Jackals were laughing and smiling. Jesse stared at Rupert who nodded towards his companions. Jesse and Class looked down to see the other nine Jackals produce blades and axes from under their jackets out of sight from the children and parents, but made sure they were seen by the prey.

Class eyed Rupert and mouthed the words, "*You're a dead man.*"

Rupert grinned and winked at him. He suddenly stood up and jumped on the seat, then addressed his group.

"Okay gang, let's sing our team song, shall we?" he asked gleefully. The others responded with fake joviality and sickening happiness; clapping and cheering they began to sing.

"We are the Jackals, and we snarl and bite; we are the Jackals and we're coming for you tonight!" At the end of the sentence they all held their hands up and made growling noises. Jesse looked around in horror as the kids were joining in and the parents looked on smiling, unaware of the situation. Over and over again they repeated the words until Rupert held his hands up.

"Okay, okay teammates that's enough singing and making merry. Let's leave these nice people to enjoy their final moments on this vessel in peace and quiet, shall we?" Immediately the parents and their kids started clapping and cheering. Rupert took a bow and sat down.

Jesse looked at Class, her face contorting in fear. "What the hell are we going to do?" she enquired nervously.

Class sat back. There was no way they could fight in here; the toll on innocent lives would be unimaginable. By the same token they couldn't get off the ferry so the way Class looked at it was they had to make a run for it when they landed. He glanced at his watch—12:17 p.m. Just over forty minutes left aboard. His gut instinct told him they wouldn't attack again, they had no reason to. All they had to do was to wait then follow, then finish them off at their leisure. Jesse stared at the policeman.

"It was your idea to come to an island and now we are trapped and outnumbered. What's our plan?" she implored. Class stood up and stretched.

"Well, I'm going for a fag. Wanna join me?"

The confines of the Jaguar Estate were stifling and the two corpses in the boot had begun to smell. No one had noticed that the late arrivals hadn't left their vehicle to join the other passengers in the upper saloons. The ferry workers had been eager to set sail and had locked down the car deck in the belief that everything was clear. The car itself had tinted windows so nobody could see in anyway and that was just perfect. The car would just merge into the traffic when disembarking and disappear onto the island. The owners hadn't suspected anything when the well-dressed stranger approached them at the terminal; in fact they had been eager to help. And help they did. The last car on the vessel was high-end and the new driver didn't seem out of place behind the wheel. Felix smiled and stroked the blade of his knife. It was nearly time.

THIRTY-ONE

~~~

Wednesday, 1410 hrs

The AS355 Twin Squirrel helicopter gently touched down at Stornoway Airport. The rotor continued to spin as the pilot disengaged the engine. The co-pilot exited and immediately held open the rear door for his passengers to disembark. It had been a last minute rush job and the client had paid top money for an express service –a quick hop across the Minch from the Isle of Skye to the Isle of Lewis. During his time working for Falcon Express Helicopters Dan Woollens had come across a lot of rich folk willing to spend obscene amounts of money for their service, but this had to be the easiest money he had made. The flight only took ten minutes but the price tag had been in the thousands. During the short flight he had wondered who these guys were. They were most likely London businessmen up here for a stag hunt or a round of golf, but at the end of the day he was getting paid good money for not only his flying skills but for his discretion. He held open the door and the first of his clients stepped down from the chopper.

"Please mind your heads, gentlemen; the rotor is still

turning!" he shouted, trying to be heard above the declining engine whine.

Michael Stokes stepped onto the concrete and walked purposefully towards the waiting taxi; behind him Stevens kept pace, clutching a black canvas holdall. Finally, four other men disembarked, each carrying similar holdalls. Dan smiled at each in turn but none returned the gesture. When they were clear Dan slammed the door and jumped back into the front seat.

"Any tips?" Rich Baker asked through the helmet intercom. Dan shook his head.

"Nope. Didn't even get a fucking 'thank you'."

Baker shrugged his shoulders. "Rich bastards," he replied. Dan gave the thumbs-up and Rich powered up the engines.

"Let's get back," he said. Dan watched the six men get into the minibus taxi and as they banked he wondered again whom they were and why they had been instructed to fly back to Inverness, pick up three more passengers then return them back to Stornoway. Baker grinned.

"I know what you're thinking and it isn't any of our business. We get paid to fly so let's just do that, shall we?"

Dan laughed. "Okay Number One—let's go get our other clients."

"Where to, gentlemen?" the driver asked as the last man got into the taxi.

"Do you have any four wheel drive hire companies in Stornoway?" Stevens asked abruptly.

The taxi driver nodded. "Aye, just the one," he replied, just as curtly.

"Then take us there please, driver," Stevens retorted.

The driver nodded and started the engine. As he pulled away he looked in his rear-view mirror. The stern face of Stevens glared unflinchingly back at him. He decided to keep his mouth shut; after all it was a short fare and was only going to be for a few minutes. He had a sense that these men didn't want to engage in idle chitchat.

Class jumped in the Range Rover and fired up the engine. He had made a point of coming down five minutes earlier than Jesse to check his vehicle and to put his plan into motion. His fingers drummed quietly on the steering wheel, his foot tapping nervously. Jesse remained quiet, her attention focused on the ten Jackals silently boarding their mini bus directly in front of them. Rupert was the last to climb aboard. He paused and waved at them, the sickly grin once again present. Jesse stuck her middle finger up at him.

"*Fuck you*," she mouthed. Rupert laughed and blew her a kiss. Class clenched the wheel in temper.

"I'm gonna kill that fucker," he growled.

Jesse huffed. "Not before me you won't," she stated. "What's the plan?" she asked nervously.

Class smiled. "Get off the boat, get on dry land and put the pedal to the floor. Get out of Dodge as fast as we can," he stated. Jesse giggled.

"That's your master plan, eh? Drive like a loony...,"

she started to laugh louder, "…on an island, with no escape." Class also started to laugh.

"Yep, it's a doozy ain't it?" he quipped.

Jesse shrugged her shoulders. "Oh well, could be worse I suppose," she retorted. They looked at each other and laughed even harder.

Ahead of them orange strobe lights began to flash, signalling the lowering of the ramp. One by one other vehicles started their engines, their drivers eager to get moving. The driver of the mini bus turned the engine over but nothing happened. They tried for a second time but once again nothing happened. Ahead cars were starting to disembark. Class slammed the 4x4 in reverse then when clear pulled out around the stationary mini bus. Rupert jumped out and glared at Jesse as they passed. The DI stuck his finger up as they sailed by. Behind them vehicles blasted their horns in anger at the broken down bus blocking their exit. In the rear-view mirror Class could see Rupert and one of his companions under the bonnet hitting and lashing out in frustration. Jesse started to laugh.

"What the hell did you do?" she asked excitedly.

The policeman grinned. "I'm no mechanic but I reckon if you pull out lots of random leads and cut other wires your car won't start," he said happily, a sense of pride flowing through him.

Jesse couldn't stop laughing. "Bravo, Mr Class! I applaud you and your sneaky ways. You had me doubting but it turns out you had a plan after all!" she exclaimed, her own relief palatable.

Class' smile faded a little. "I've only bought us some time, that's all. They are still going to come after us, possibly tonight. We need to pick up supplies and get to our laying-up place as quickly as we can. We need to prepare," he said, his tone sombre.

Class followed the line of traffic out of the port and up to the main junction. Left was to Harris and right was to Stornoway and the rest of Lewis. He indicated right and when clear pulled out on to the main road running the length of the island. He estimated that the drive up to Tolsta and the north of the island would take about an hour, depending on the traffic. It would take Rupert and his bunch of cronies at least three hours to sort their transport. Class had toyed with the idea of driving straight to Stornoway and jumping on the ferry back to Ullapool which was on the mainland further up the coast, then disappear into the Northwest Highlands or possibly even head back down into England. He quickly discounted the idea as after some thought reasoned that they would have placed people at all the main land ports by now so he didn't want to take the risk. One good thing on the island and their current situation was at least he had seen all ten faces and would see them coming. Rupert himself had slipped up by saying there was ten of them and Class figured he wasn't lying because he was bragging, inflating his ego and showing off how clever he was. It seemed to be a character trait with these bastards.

Jesse stared out of the window lost in her own thoughts, the surrounding terrain barren and bleak even with the sun shining, the long empty glens and sweeping valleys mesmerising her. If the Jackals wanted primitive then they got their wish, Jesse couldn't think of a more appropriate location. Despite its beauty Jesse wasn't looking forward to staying in a stone hut miles away from anywhere, although she understood the need for getting off the grid. The island was appealing now, but she had a feeling that the weather could turn at the drop of a hat and if it came in bad then they would be stranded. Maybe they could work it to their advantage, she thought.

The trip north truly was desolate yet somewhat beautiful. After leaving the port the road had snaked uphill and through a small mountain range that separated the Isle of Lewis and Harris. The tallest point of which, was a mountain named the Clisham. Snow poles lined the road to warn drivers of the edge. Steep drops and hidden openings could prove fatal if attention was lost even for a second. Luckily it wasn't snowing and Jesse was thankful for small mercies. Jesse couldn't help daydreaming as Class skilfully manoeuvred the Range Rover around tight corners and sharp inclines, all the while keeping an eye out for cars following them. She had been impressed with the DI's sabotage on the Jackal's vehicle and it had gone a long way to give a slight glimmer of hope that they could get out of this alive. She mentally shook her head; she hated this emotional rollercoaster they were on. One minute a glimmer of hope, the next soul-destroying despair, and so it went on. Up and down.

She looked over to Class who was busy concentrating on the road. He smiled when he saw a sign for Stornoway.

"Not far now, a few more miles and we can stop off quickly and pick up some food and a few supplies before heading out," he said, not looking at her.

Jesse grinned. "I presume you can cook? I'm awful so I think it should be your job to feed us," she said mischievously.

Class chuckled. "Baked beans and sausages it is then," he retorted.

Ahead of them the road stretched out in a straight run. They could see for a good few miles. In the distance was the beginnings of a pine forest, its manmade lines equally spaced stretching up the hills on either side of the road. Class took the opportunity and gunned the 4x4. He grinned as the needle nudged 80 mph. He let out a childlike whoop and was smiling broadly. He glanced at Jesse who was holding on tightly to the handle of the door.

"Come on, why not have a little fun!" he shouted, the noise from his open window making it hard to talk. Jesse giggled at his antics, in truth she liked it; it was a slight distraction from what lay ahead. Her head spun with delirium. Was it wrong to be having fun, she asked herself. Class slowed the car as they reached the end of the straight and once again resumed normal driving speed. He let out a sigh.

"Sorry Jesse, just had to blow off some steam, ya know?" Jesse nodded; she didn't need to say anything.

It only took another half an hour and they had

reached Stornoway. Class followed the road down into the town centre. Small shops and houses lined the street. To their right was the sea inlet, beyond which was Lewis Castle and Creed River, the castle grounds a local beauty spot. Class remembered him and his father going for walks and fishing when he was a child. He felt a shiver. It was a strange feeling to be back here after all this time, he mulled to himself.

Jesse gazed out of the window as their vehicle ambled past the small pier and dock. Fishing boats small and large tethered to their moorings, sometimes three abreast, dominated the harbour, the sound of sails and bells echoing in the slight breeze, the smell of sea salt permeating the air. Jesse was surprised with the size of Stornoway. For the capital of the Outer Hebrides she would have thought it to be bigger. There didn't seem to be much in the way of shopping and coming from a sleepy town in rural Somerset that was saying something. Nevertheless, it had a charm to it. It seemed to have its own atmosphere; even its people looked like they belonged here. She glanced at random people, their faces weather-beaten and purposeful.

"The locals have a rich history up here," he said, as if reading her mind. "They are a hardy bunch. The island is a harsh, unforgiving place. Stunning to look at but not a lot of work. Most of the young people up here end up working out on the rigs or deep sea fishing…," he paused as he manoeuvred around a parked car, "…or they just up sticks and leave," he added, once he had passed the obstacle.

Jesse remained silent, content with taking in the surroundings. She relaxed as Class brought the 4x4 to a halt in the carpark of the local supermarket.

"Right then, let's go," he said, his tone once again serious. They jumped out of the vehicle and headed for the store entrance.

The black Shogun quietly pulled into the carpark and switched off its engine. The three occupants sat silently, their attention focused on the store entrance. The driver punched in the encryption number into his Motorola.

"Delta 1 copy, this is Delta 4, receiving."

There was a sharp hiss of static, then the reply, "Delta 1 receiving, go for sit rep Delta 4." The driver waited a few seconds to make sure the airways were clear.

"Delta 4, eyes on targets, one male, one female, location 2, please advise, over." Another sharp hiss.

"Delta 4, green light tracker, repeat, green light tracker, over," came the reply.

The driver turned to one of his companions in the rear seat and nodded. The second man reached into his bag and pulled out a small black box the size of a tobacco tin. He opened the door and made his way between vehicles, heading for the Range Rover. The driver smiled and pressed the call button.

"Delta 1, tracker deployed, repeat, tracker deployed." He patiently waited for the response.

"Delta 4, return to base, repeat, RTB, over and out". The driver started the engine and waited for the return of his man.

Class and Jesse left the shop and briskly made their

way back to their vehicle. Class scanned the carpark for threats. They had been in the store for about twenty minutes and he was eager to make a move. He opened the boot door and quickly emptied the trolley of bags.

Jesse looked to the skies. "Clouds are coming in" she said quietly. The DI looked up.

"Yep, we better make a move," he said and ushered her to get in.

Class started the engine and with a screech of tyre pulled out of the carpark on their last leg of their journey.

"Not far now, only another twenty minutes or so then a short hike to our shieling," he offered.

Jesse tried to smile, her attention drawn to the dark clouds rolling in from the sea. She was eager to get her head down. Her body ached and her mind was fatigued; she needed to rest.

Class followed the road out of town and turned right, heading towards the village of Tolsta. It was starting to get dark, spots of rain bouncing off of the windscreen. It was only just before 4:00 p.m. but the weather was threatening. It was only a matter of time before the real bad stuff hit them and Class wanted to be hunkered down before it struck. He eased the Range Rover around bend after bend, the road dotted with small hamlets and villages. He started to relax a little more the closer they got to their destination.

Finally he saw the end of the road, literally. From here on in it was all on foot. Jesse was a little stunned; it really was a bridge to nowhere. On one side, a road, on the other nothing but a peat track leading off onto the moors following the cliff edge. Class pulled the 4x4 up onto a passing place on the far side of the bridge and switched off the engine.

"Time to get going. We have about an hour's hike ahead of us." Jesse nodded nervously and they exited the car. Jesse felt the Atlantic wind whip 'round her, her hair flapping with the force, the skies getting ever darker.

"Looks like a storm's coming!" she shouted, trying to be heard over the wind. Class nodded and went to the boot and together they hastily transferred their supplies into their rucksack. Satisfied they had gotten everything and zipping up their jackets, Class hefted the pack onto his back, took Jesse by the hand and as one they started to walk onto the peat track.

THIRTY-TWO

Wednesday, 1800 hrs

Class kicked open the half-hanging door and flicked on his torch. He paused, assessing his surroundings, allowing his senses to attune to the murky interior. With his breathing heavy and brow clammy, the DI slowly and deliberately swept the powerful torch around the building. He felt himself recoiling and nearly sneeze as wafts of dust gently danced in the beam, the musky, damp aroma permeating the very structure itself and attacking his nasal passage. Once his eyes had accustomed to the darkness he scanned the interior of the shieling once again. Now was not the time to take any chances, he reminded himself. Its bare floor was aging wood; its walls windowless. On the far side opposite the doorway was a stone fire place, its surround decaying after years of abandonment, a rusting metal griddle perched precariously upon it. To his left was an old wooden cupboard. He reached out and touched it, relived to find it dry and perfectly usable for kindling.

Something caught his eye. He glanced to his right. Bolted to the wall, mounted on a rough-looking plaque rested a large stag head, its horns viciously impressive, its emotionless eyes staring back at him black and glazed. The policeman let out a soft sigh. Apart from that, the room was empty. He smiled wearily, his bones and body aching from the hike. It could be worse, he silently told himself. They had shelter, the ability to make fire and he could use the furniture for fuel. It was a pretty good find he thought, psychologically patting himself on the back. Class smirked. It wasn't five stars but it would have to do.

He turned towards the doorway and signalled Jesse it was safe to enter. Outside the rain was heavy, the weather deteriorating by the minute. It had had proved problematic to say the least. Much to Class and Jesse's annoyance it had severely slowed their progress and it had taken them longer to reach their destination, the undulating and harsh terrain made more treacherous by the unrelenting downpour and whipping wind. Here they now stood at their journey's end. They were soaked, their clothes muddy and sodden and both now eager to get a hot drink inside them and to change into fresh, dry clothes.

Jesse walked in tentatively, she too compelled to wince at the musty fragrance; she shook herself and then peeled off her jacket, tossing it to one side. She cast her gaze around her new abode, her expression unimpressed.

"What do you reckon?" the DI asked as enthusiastically as he could summon. He was grinning as he pushed past her with the rucksack. Jesse turned to face him and frowned.

"I don't know what to say…" The DI chuckled and

flung his gear down onto the floor. "…you bring me to all the best places, dear," she said sarcastically.

Class chuffed softly. "Next time we are being hunted by a social club of sadistic serial killers hell-bent on chopping us up for fish bait I will make sure the accommodation is more to your liking, madam," he sniped, inwardly annoyed by her reaction, but also secretly in agreement with her assessment. It was Jesse's turn to giggle, albeit nervously.

"I'm sorry, didn't mean to snap at you. It's great, I love what you've done to the place," she added, trying to make amends for her unnecessary dig.

Class looked up and grinned, "No harm, no foul," he retorted. "Let's sort a fire then think about getting some food and hot drinks on the go."

Jesse smiled at him warmly. "That sounds like a plan."

It didn't take long for the policeman to demolish the cupboard and have the fire going, the soft orange flames illuminating the dark confines of the small stone hut. Jesse sat back and closed her eyes; strangely she found the sound of the rain bouncing off the tin roof like liquid bullets somehow hypnotic, adding to the atmosphere. She laid out her sleeping bag near the fire and hung her wet clothes on a nail protruding from the wall, then eagerly held her hands up to the heat. She gently rubbed them, enjoying the soft warmth spreading up her body. All things considered she was relatively relieved and despite the coming storm she felt some semblance of peace.

Jesse shivered as her mind suddenly and unexpectedly thought of Damien and once again she was afraid. She squeezed her eyes shut, willing the paranoia and self-doubt to leave her in peace but she could still hear the illness calling to her, the dark corners of her subconscious enticing her to fall ever deeper into her spiral of depression. She casually glanced over at Class hoping he hadn't noticed. He hadn't. He was busy boiling water on a small camping stove for a couple of cups of coffee and to heat up two boil-in-the-bag beef stew meals. She sat there in silence wanting to cry, to fall asleep and never wake again but as quickly as the feeling arose it disappeared again. What would that solve, her subconscious screamed. She had made it this far and she wasn't going to give in now, not when the end was in sight. She started to feel a burning rage welling up deep within. The Jackals had said they would come and there was no doubt in her mind that they were on their way and for all she knew outside right at this moment. It was only a matter of time, she mused. The end game was upon them when the valiant heroes stood their ground and faced down the evil-doers, but this was no Hollywood movie and the good guys rarely win in the real world. Evil seems to prevail and neither she nor Class seemed to have the power to stop them.

"Brews up," Class announced, snapping Jesse back to reality and away from her tumbling and ever-conflicting inner thoughts.

She smiled sedately. "Cheers," she said, accepting a mug from the policeman.

"Penny for your thoughts," he asked quietly. Jesse shrugged.

"You don't want to get in here," she replied, tapping the side of her head.

Class grinned. "Yeah, you're probably right on that score. After all these years I've given up trying to understand what goes on inside a woman's head," he said jokingly.

"How long till dinner?" she asked, wanting to change the subject.

Class shrugged. "About twenty minutes I reckon. I ain't no master chef but I reckon it will taste okay. If it's wet and warm then game on," he quipped, sensing her deliberate evasion. Jesse grinned.

"Then if you don't mind, Sir, one shall take a nap," she joked. The policeman nodded and carried on preparing their evening's meal. After what felt like a few seconds Jesse slowly opened her eyes to see Class gently shaking her arm. She yawned and smiled softly.

"How long was I out?" she asked.

"Twelve hours," the DI replied sombrely. Jesse sat up rubbing her face.

"What?" she exclaimed, her face a picture of confusion. The policeman started to laugh.

"Not really. You've been out for forty minutes but I couldn't resist," he said with childlike amusement. Jesse picked up her pair of discarded soggy socks and threw them at Class; he dodged the attack, his laugh somehow infectious.

"Yeah, yeah, very funny," she quipped. "Where's dinner then, Mr Master Chef?" she added.

The DI reached over and handed Jesse a mess tin and a spoon. She stared at the meal.

"Is that beef stew?" she asked.

Class stopped smiling, his feelings seemingly hurt. "Yeah, why?" he replied, his tone serious. Jesse started to giggle, unable to keep up the pretence. Class also laughed.

"Well done, you had me there," he said.

Despite the banter they both ate their meals in silence. Class thought about making more small talk but there wasn't much to be said. They were on borrowed time and they both knew it. Jesse suddenly broke the silence.

"Pray tell, what is for pudding?" she asked in a mockingly posh accent.

Class smiled. "I'm sure I could rustle up some powdered custard," he retorted.

She stood up and stretched her arms. "In that case I shall retire to the little girl's room before we sit and enjoy the culinary delights that you have prepared for us," she replied, her mood slightly improving. She headed for the door.

"Just go 'round the side of the hut and don't stray too far. It's dark and the moors are littered with peat bogs. If you fall down into one of them its goodnight Vienna," he stated, his tone serious and full of genuine concern. Jesse smiled and feigned a curtsey.

"I appreciate the concern but I'm a big girl now," she retorted smugly, reaching for the latch and pulling the door open. She froze, unable to move or rationalize the scene presented before her. She desperately wanted to scream and warn Class but was unable to move; she felt like a heavy weight was bearing down on top of her. She murmured quietly.

Class took a sip of his coffee and glanced up at her. "What was that? Another smart arse retort, eh Jesse, another pop at my cooking?" he quipped, blissfully unaware of the danger. When she didn't respond Class suddenly felt his heckles go up, his instinct thrust into overdrive. He cautiously rose to his feet all the while watching Jesse in the doorway.

"What is it, Jesse?" he whispered nervously.

"You better take a look for yourself," she croaked, her voice close to breaking.

Class started to sweat, the back of his neck suddenly icy cold. Stealthily he moved forward, glancing around as he did, desperately searching for a weapon. His right foot knocked against something heavy. He looked down at the two-foot lump of wood, remnants of the cupboard. He snatched it up in his right hand gripping it tightly, his knuckles turning white with the strain, his hand and arm muscles pulsing. Once again he moved forward until he was finally level with Jesse in the doorway. He looked out, straining his eyes to focus on what lie beyond, the torrential rain and wind whipping his face and body. At first he couldn't make out anything but then he saw them. Approximately twenty feet directly in front of the shieling were ten figures all kneeling on the ground, their hands tied behind their backs, their mouths taped shut. They were naked, their bodies heavily beaten and bleeding from various wounds.

Jesse and Class stood silently, each of them trying to comprehend what was happening. Jesse started to shake. Class gently touched her arm with his free hand and squeezed it reassuringly.

"Stay here," he whispered and slowly moved forward to get a better look.

Step by step he moved closer, all the while looking around him for signs of attack. He glanced down at his hands; they were shaking uncontrollably. He was scared; in fact he was terrified. Once again he gripped his weapon tighter, the weight of the wood somehow reassuring. He glanced back to check on Jesse but instead of being where he had left her she was two feet behind him. He considered shouting at her but thought better of it; he shot her a scathing and disapproving look before returning his attention to the figures mere meters away. He edged ever closer, every step sending his heart rate soaring. He closed the gap; now only ten feet away the DI suddenly stopped, his heart threatening to explode from his chest.

"Oh my God!" he exclaimed quietly. In front of him the broken and barely alive bodies of Rupert and his nine Jackals cowered in the mud and filth, their heavy breathing and stifled sobs somewhat muffled by thick masking tape wrapped viciously around their heads. Jesse came up to his side and clutched her mouth, suppressing a scream.

"Good evening Mrs Reid, Mr Class," a voice boomed

without warning, emanating from the darkness.

Class frantically strained to locate the source but the weather made it impossible. Suddenly they were engulfed with numerous white lights; they threw their hands to their faces in an attempt to shield their eyes, the little night vision they had now totally eradicated. From behind the kneeling Jackals Class began to make out five figures slowly seep out of the shadows. Jesse also saw them, her whole body trembling with fear. The policeman focused on the five men. All were dressed in black fatigues complete with what looked like tactical assault vests, balaclavas covering their faces with only their eyes visible. Each one carried what looked like a semi-automatic machine gun, the torches on their weapons pointing forward, directly at Jesse and Class. The DI swallowed hard.

"Who the fuck are you? I'm warning you, stay back, I'm a police officer," he rasped, trying to convey a sense of authority. Class instinctively used his left arm to pull Jesse back and shield her from whatever was coming next, his right gripping the piece of wood even tighter.

The five figures stopped moving. There was a soft chuckle from the darkness and then a sixth figure started to emerge. Class stared intently as the figure casually walked towards them. When the newcomer was only a couple of feet away the DI finally spoke.

"You've got to be fucking kidding me," he whispered as Professor Michael Stokes came into full view.

Stokes grinned. "Nice to see you, too," he said cheerfully. Jesse glanced at Class; her confusion was evident.

Class knew what she was thinking.

"Jesse, I want you to meet Professor Michael Stokes, former member of the Order and the last person I thought would turn up here." Jesse stared at Stokes, her hatred evident.

"Are you fucking joking? Former member of the Order? The same Order that wants us dead? Am I the only one who finds this a little too good to be true? What the hell are you doing here? And why have you got your own people tied up?" she asked, her barrage of questions steeped in not only anger but tinged with concern.

Stokes smirked. "Firstly, they are not my people. Secondly, I am an ex-member of the Order—emphasis on the EX bit—and thirdly, I thought you might need a bit of a hand…," he turned to face his hostages, gesturing with his hand, "…and it appears I was correct in that assumption," he added jovially.

Class went to move forward, undecided whether to lash out at the old man or not but Stokes put his hand up. Class paused, his anger continuing to rise.

"Is that supposed to stop me?" he snarled.

Stokes smiled broadly. "No, Mr Class, it was to stop them," he retorted, pointing over his shoulder.

The DI froze at the sight of all five men standing poised, their guns to their shoulders levelling their weapons at the policeman, their fingers hovering on the triggers. Class let out a short breath and slowly backed away a few steps. He dropped the heavy bit of wood then put his hands open and in the air showing he had no weapon and that he understood their message.

"A bit fucking twitchy, aren't they?" he sniped sarcastically, eager to get the last word.

Stokes waved his hand dismissively. "They are just doing their job, Mr Class. You have nothing to fear as long as I am safe and come to no harm, but of course I am perfectly safe, aren't I? After all we come here as friends and allies," the old man retorted. Stokes cleared his throat. "Right then, let's get back to it, shall we?" he said enthusiastically. "Mr Stevens, can you come forward, please."

Class looked on as one of the five men walked forward, his build menacing; even the way he carried himself screamed violence. Stevens walked up next to Stokes. He paused and pulled off his balaclava and stared at Class unflinchingly. Class kept eye contact, not wanting to show any fear. Stevens smirked slightly; he wasn't impressed or intimidated by the policeman in the slightest. Class eyed the newcomer cautiously, definitely ex-military he surmised. The DI secretly hoped he didn't have to fight this man; he didn't fancy his chances.

Stokes leaned in towards Stevens and whispered something in his ear. The mercenary nodded, turned and walked back towards the kneeling Jackals. Stokes smiled at Jesse.

"Keep watching, I think you're going to enjoy this," he said, winking.

Behind him Stevens held up his fist and as one the four remaining mercenaries brought their weapons to bear and aimed their guns at the backs of the Jackals. The ten hostages sensed something was happening and desperately tried to beg for their lives, their pleas obscured by the heavy industrial tape. Stokes glanced at his subordinate and nodded. Stevens smiled.

"Light them up!" he roared.

The sudden explosion of automatic gunfire was immense. The ground around them was illuminated by the muzzled flashes of the heavy weaponry. FMJ rounds slammed into the upper torsos of the Jackals, sending them sprawling to the floor. Blood, brain and fragments of internal organs showered the water-logged ground turning the peat scarlet; the assault lasted mere seconds and then once again fell silent. Class and Jesse looked on in disbelief as Stevens pulled out his pistol then calmly walked amongst the bodies, emptying a round into each of the Jackal's heads, making sure they were dead. He grinned menacingly at the policeman as he holstered his weapon and returned to his employer's side.

Stokes let out an audible sigh. "And suddenly everything is okay in the world..." he quipped. He turned to Class. "Right then, now that the unpleasantness is over and done with why don't we retire to your splendid little cabin for a nice warm brew and a chat, eh?" he suggested.

Class and Jesse looked at each other, neither one truly understanding what was happening nor how to react to such a wanton display of brutality. Jesse could only nod and agree, her bravado somewhat diminishing.

"Yeah, that seems like a good idea," she said as calmly as she could manage.

Jesse's mind was racing; she couldn't believe that ten Jackals had just been wiped out in the space of about four seconds. Was that it? Could it be over now? She found herself asking inside her head. She felt numb to the core. Those bastards had it coming and even though she didn't get to kill them herself she wasn't sorry they were dead. She felt nothing about their deaths; it would appear her morality had found its breaking point. There was something else though, and that was confusion. Who the fuck was this Stokes character and why did he just order the blatant murder of ten people? What kind of man runs around the UK mainland with a heavily armed mercenary force shooting people without regard or fear for the law? Jesse knew there had to be more to this than he was letting on and in truth she suspected that Class knew little more than she did. She was determined to find out his true motives for saving them.

Stokes coughed and gestured with his hand towards the shieling as if hurrying them along.

"After you," he said politely.

All three slowly walked towards the door with Stevens keeping pace five feet behind. The policeman kept glancing back to see what he was doing, un-nerved by the big man's presence yet making no secret of his suspicions nor his resolve to fight if pushed to it.

As they entered the shieling Stokes slipped past Jesse and Class and made his way directly to the fireplace, holding his hands up to embrace the heat.

"Ah, nothing like an open fire to set the tone and to

get you in a conducive frame of mind. Reminds me of my younger days," he stated quietly, his back to his companions.

Jesse positioned herself to the left of the entrance whilst Class edged his way closer to Stokes should the need arise to attack. He didn't fully understand the professor's motives but sure as hell wasn't going to take any chances. He scoped the room searching for possible weapons and cursed under his breath when there wasn't anything obvious. The DI sighed quietly; he didn't envisage the old man being a problem but Stokes' right-hand man was a huge hurdle, not to mention the four heavily armed men keeping watch outside, shrouded in darkness. Class coughed loudly.

"Stokes, just what the hell is going on?" he asked "What is all this about?"

Stokes slowly turned to face him, his face showing no signs of emotion.

"I know this must seem confusing to you both and I wish I could explain more but for now all you need to know is that I am here to help." He waved his hand in the direction of the doorway. "We found those leeches a couple of miles down the peat track, evidently making their way to this location…" He smiled and looked at Jesse. "It's amazing how persuasive my men can be when extracting information but there again it doesn't take a genius to figure out what they had planned for you two."

Jesse remained silent, holding the old man's gaze.

"How did they know we were here? And just how

the hell did you know we were here?" Class enquired, his hostility barely contained.

Stokes grinned. "My dear fellow, my men had you under surveillance the minute you stepped foot on this island. We followed you to the supermarket where one of my men placed a tracker on your car. After that we just kept our distance. Once we knew where you had left your vehicle we tracked you here. My men are professionals, Mr Class. It isn't rocket science, old boy," Stokes replied smugly, his tone patronising.

Class could feel his temper rising again. "Fair enough, kudos to you and your merry band of gun-toting cowboys, but as for those other fucks, I left those bastards stranded on the ferry. How the hell did they get here? They didn't have your hi-tech gizmos to help them out," he asked abruptly.

The professor shrugged. "Apparently they got off the ferry and hijacked a small delivery van then made their way to Stornoway; from there we presume they managed to gain access to the shops CCTV to see which way you headed. It would seem that by a horrific twist of fate a friendly dog walker mentioned she saw a holidaymaking couple hike off up the peat track, which of course she found strange due to the hour and remote location…" he paused for dramatic effect, "…my men found her body an hour ago, her throat severed, dumped in a ditch. Shame really, they even killed her little Shih Tzu dog," he stated, his answer directed to Jesse.

Jesse could feel her emotions rising; another innocent death on her conscious, she mused.

The DI huffed loudly, his patience running out. "Let's just cut the shit old man, what the fuck do you want? No more games, you must have some sort of angle," he spat.

Stokes glared at the policeman. "May I suggest that you not take that tone with me, Mr Class. You are alive because I allowed it, don't forget that," he rasped, spit flying from his curled lips.

"Fuck you old man!" retorted Class, his tone close to full blown rage.

Stokes held his hands up in mock surrender. "What are you going to do, Mr Class, arrest me? For what? Saving your life?" he started to laugh.

Class could feel his body shake with temper; it was taking all of his willpower to stop himself from lunging forward and beating the living shit out of the crazy old bastard. Stokes smiled calmly.

"Back in Bristol I told you about my past dealings with the Order, the way they discarded me, mocked me. They made my life virtually unbearable. They destroyed my reputation and I have waited for this moment for a very long time," he replied, his voice even and tone calm.

Class suddenly started to laugh uncontrollably. Both Jesse and Stokes looked on, puzzled by the policeman's reaction to such an admission.

"What's so funny, Mr Class?" Stokes asked, his tone inquisitive.

The DI cleared his throat. "You stupid old fucker…" he said, still laughing. He looked at Jesse. "This silly old goat used us as bait to draw out the Order but they didn't come. He wanted the ones who dished out the orders so he could get his revenge; instead all he got was ten low level Jackals." Jesse glanced at Stokes whose face was turning scarlet. Class was on to something, she thought.

Class continued, "All of this was for nothing, Stokes. You weren't bothered about us, you just wanted the shot-callers, those who sit at the top of the table. You have achieved nothing professor. When you leave here you are no closer to satisfying your lust for vengeance, they will just replace those you killed. The only thing you have done is tipped your hand. They will know exactly who you are and how many men you have at your disposal. They will be coming for you with everything they've got. They will want to make an example of you. You are the architect of your own demise. You will never destroy them because they have already won." Once again he roared with laughter, amused by the irony of the situation.

Jesse stared at Stokes but this time he wasn't scarlet; in fact he too started to laugh. She glanced back at Class, unsure if he had noticed the turnaround in the old man's demeanour. Class slowly eased his laughing, his amusement giving way to concern. Stokes was clapping his hands together like an excited child, his head bobbing up and down, tears rolling down his cheeks. The DI paused and glanced at Jesse, unsure what was transpiring. Stokes composed himself.

"Mr Stevens, you can come in now!" he shouted.

Class and Jesse turned to the door to see Stevens enter, closely flanked by two of his men. Between them they dragged a body. Jesse looked on in horror as the battered figure of her husband was thrown to the floor.

"Damien!" she screamed as she lunged forward. Class grabbed her by the arm and yanked her back, eager to keep her out of harm's way. Stokes smiled.

"We decided to bring Mr Reid up for a little holiday, hope you don't mind," he said gleefully. "We found poor old Mr Reid in a squalid basement somewhat worse for wear. It would appear the Jackals had been having fun with him. It wouldn't surprise me if they had raped him...," he paused and glared at Class, "...they are a bunch of sickos after all," he added.

The mercenary started to chuckle and gave a short, sharp kick to Damien's ribs. Class glared at Stevens.

"I'm going to fucking tear you apart, you sick fucker!" he rasped, the venom spewing forth, almost tangible.

Without hesitation Stevens pulled out his Springfield XD-9 and pushed the muzzle into the policeman's brow. The DI refused to back down and in a show of absolute defiance pushed his head forward against the cold metal of the barrel.

"I fucking dare you..." he roared.

Stevens smirked and gently squeezed the trigger. The detonation of the 9mm pistol was massive within the small stone hut. The high velocity round tore through the DI's skull, carving a swathe of destruction through tissue and bone, finally eviscerating the back of his head and splashing a gore-filled cocktail of remains across the moss-covered wall. Jesse screamed as the DI's lifeless corpse fell to the ground. Stevens smiled and backed away towards the door should she try to make a run for it. Jesse fell to her knees beside the still-warm body of the former policeman, sobbing.

Stokes walked over to her and delicately stroked her head.

"I'm truly sorry, Mrs Reid, but you have to admit, he was becoming rather tiresome," he quipped. Through bloodshot eyes she gazed up at the professor, her will to fight all but gone. He smiled warmly.

"On the bright side, your husband's still alive," he said with a cheeky grin.

Both he and Stevens started to laugh. Jesse looked across the dirty wooden floor and for a second thought she saw Damien's chest rise slightly. She panicked and in a state of desperation crawled on her hands and knees to him. She flung her arms around his neck and listened to his breathing, checking if he truly was alive. He was, but barely. She stared at Stokes, her confusion evident.

"I thought you wanted revenge? I thought you want to make them suffer for what they did to you, why this? What have we ever done to you?" she screamed through hate-filled, clenched teeth.

Stokes rubbed his chin and sighed. "My dear woman, you misunderstand. I don't want to destroy the Order for what they have done to me. I intend to rule them. I want to terminate all those old fools who have become soft—

those in power who have lived in luxury, forgetting the true meaning of the Jackals. It is my destiny to restore the Order to its rightful glory. Mere carrion like you couldn't possibly comprehend the reasoning of spiritual giants, much like a wolf need not concern itself with the opinions of sheep. Once I am leader, the Order will be elevated and the entire world will hear the calling of the Void. Those of purest heart will join us and embrace the Primitive...," he paused to wipe his brow, "... of course it will take time, but for now...," he stared menacingly at Jesse "...there can be no loose ends."

Jesse just caught sight of the XD-9 out of the corner of her eye as Stevens pressed it against Damien's head and pulled the trigger. Jesse tried to scream but couldn't, her body paralysed in terror. She looked on helplessly as her husband's head vaporised, spraying her face in a crimson mist. Jesse crumpled to the floor, her hands still clinging to her dead husband's neck. She couldn't move, the trauma was too great. Inside her the darkness finally took control and she truly lost the will to live. She started to sob uncontrollably, her face a mixture of water and blood, her black hair hanging down in matted, brain-soaked clumps.

She heard a noise above her and wearily looked up, convinced it was her turn to be killed. For a split second she just wanted to close her eyes and let the bullet take her but her body refused. Jesse stared myopically as Stevens' unconscious body fell to the floor with a sickening thud, a bloody gash visible on the back of his head, a small pool of blood emanating from the wound. Jesse looked on as the XD-9 fell from his grasp and skidded across the dirt-stained wooden floorboards, out of reach. She glanced at Stokes who stood motionless, looking on in disbelief. She swung her head back to the open doorway. She wanted to scream but her lungs felt like they were on fire. From the darkness outside, the rain and blood-soaked figure of Felix stepped over the threshold, clutching a vicious-looking hunting knife and the DI's wooden weapon. Jesse took a massive intake of breath then dug her heels in and propelled herself backwards across the floor pinning herself up against the wall; she frantically searched around her for a weapon. Felix glared at her.

"Good evening Jesse, have you missed me?" he hissed. He then turned his attention to the professor, his hand gripping the hilt of the razor-sharp blade tighter.

Stokes gently smiled at the new arrival. "Hello, Marcus," he said calmly.

Felix stepped forward and grinned, "Hello, Father".

THIRTY-THREE

Wednesday, 2100 hrs

Both men eyed each other, the intensity palpable. Stokes was the first to break the uneasy silence. "It's been a long time, hasn't it?" he said quietly. Felix shrugged his shoulders but held the old man's gaze.

"Who's counting?" he retorted emotionlessly.

Stokes started to smile. "I had heard rumours it was you they had sent after these two, and I had secretly hoped that we would run in to each other. We have a lot of catching up to do. A family reunited, just like old times, eh Son?" Felix grimaced.

"I told you never to call me that, old man, and for the record my name is Felix," he hissed aggressively.

Stokes held his hands up in mock surrender. "Now now, Marcus don't be like that…" he replied confrontationally. He turned to face Jesse but still addressed Felix, "May I ask, was it down to you that she was chosen for the hunt or did one of your team members make that decision for you?"

Felix looked over at his prey, his eyes glazed and unstable; a wry smile touched the corner of his lips.

"She was Rosie's choice. This bitch killed her and massacred my team so I am here to even the score and all in the glorious name of the Primitive," he replied, not taking his eyes off of the battered and blood-soaked figure of Jesse Reid who was huddled against the wall, her legs drawn up to her chest. Felix turned to Stokes once again. "I must admit I am a little surprised to see you, especially after you chose to abandon everything you held dear. How could you turn your back on everything we had worked so hard to achieve? In truth I would have thought you would be hiding under some stone somewhere, terrified that we would find you and cut out your treacherous heart, but then again you never were that clever at playing the game, were you?"

It was Stokes' turn to shrug. "You've got it all wrong as usual and have misinterpreted my guile for weakness. I have not been hiding, my dear boy. I've been preparing, putting all the pieces in play ready to make my final move," he stated confidently.

Felix smirked. "How so...?" The Jackal was intrigued to hear more. Stokes went to put his hand into his inside jacket pocket. Felix took a step closer, tightening his grip on the knife. "Be careful old timer, we wouldn't want anything bad to happen to you would, we?" he asked menacingly.

Stokes grinned and slowly pulled out a cigar and lighter, his moves exaggerated to emphasis his non-threatening action.

"Come now Marcus, what could this ancient and

fragile body do to a magnificent specimen such as yourself?" he jibed as he put the cigar in his mouth and lit it. Felix eyed him cautiously as his father blew out a large plume of smoke, the blue haze drifting harmlessly around them. Stokes grinned.

"They really didn't tell you I was coming, did they? That wasn't very sporting of them, was it?" Felix remained silent but remained aware of any sudden movements. "...I wonder why they wouldn't inform their golden boy, their star pupil, that his father—a traitor to the Order—was after the same carrion as he was. Surely if they wanted me dead so badly they would have instructed you to kill me, yet here we are, father and son shooting the breeze and reminiscing about old times."

Felix began to feel his temper rise. "I'm sure they had their reasons," he replied curtly, not wanting to play into any game the old man had planned. Stokes shrugged and took a large draw of cigar smoke. Stokes nodded his head towards the doorway.

"Am I to presume that you have efficiently dispatched my men stationed outside and disposed of their bodies?" he asked causally.

Felix smirked. "You are," he replied smugly.

Stokes was intrigued. "All six of them?" he enquired.

Felix smiled. "Nice try, traitor but there was only four outside and this one...," he said as he kicked out at the unconscious Stevens. "The other two left after delivering Mrs Reid's husband." He stared unblinkingly at the mercenary sprawled out on the floor. "So this is the big bad Stevens we keep hearing about, eh? Some sort of bogeyman to scare Jackals into submission? He doesn't look that special to me," he added.

Stokes started to chuckle, "If I were you, Marcus, I would kill him now whilst he is out cold, because if he wakes up he is going to hurt you in ways you couldn't possibly imagine."

Felix paused for a second; he didn't want to rise to the bait but on reflection couldn't fault the old man's logic. Inwardly he recognised that Stevens was a formidable opponent and could prove hard to kill should he awake. Why take the chance, he mused. The Jackal knelt down next to Stevens and with one quick, fluid motion embedded his hunting knife into his skull; with two hands he pushed down, forcing the blade deeper. He smiled when he heard the satisfying crunch of the blade exiting and hitting the wooden floorboard. Stokes turned away slightly.

"That's a shame. I actually quite liked the man," he said flippantly.

Felix rose and wiped the blade on his trousers. He sighed and moved in closer, his eyes now back at Stokes.

"I'm trying to decide what to do with you," he stated bluntly. "You are probably not aware of this but I have decided that I should either part ways with the Order or usurp them and as such become their leader but regardless of my choice I am in a quandary regarding whether I should just kill you now. During the course of this glorious hunt one of my team whom I disliked made a valid point. He alerted me to the fact that I should be governing the organisation, not tipping my hat and acting as their little errand boy. He also stated that I had been passed over for too long and no-one was going to give me what I deserved. I have to take what I'm entitled to by force and in the process spill as much blood as necessary to obtain it," he stated, his body straight as if filled with purpose, his conviction overwhelming. Stokes started to giggle. Felix glared at him, his jaw clenching with anger. "You find that funny?" he rasped, annoyed by the professor's lack of respect. Stokes coughed slightly.

"Forgive me but I find it hard to believe that you of all people would ever contemplate leaving the warm embrace of the Order. You have nestled at the teat for so long you are unable to survive without it. As for the other option, you would be wise to forget about it. It is not out of malice I tell you this, Son. Give up and kill yourself now because there is no way in hell you will ever lead it," he replied politely. Felix eyed him malevolently.

"Be very careful what words come out of your mouth, old man. I am starting to lose my patience with you."

Stokes once again shrugged. For a man facing possible death he appeared deceptively calm and composed. The professor turned his attention to Jesse, apparently bored with the pointless exchange.

"I take it you are still with us Mrs Reid; you haven't been selfish and died and neglected to inform us? That really would be impolite of you," he remarked flippantly.

Jesse looked up over her knees, her arms pulling

them tightly to her chest. For a split second Stokes thought he saw a slight spark of defiance still burning.

"Oh my word, how smashing. You appear to be alive and well and very much in good spirits." He jabbed a finger at Felix, "…however I sense that you may be coming to the end of your journey very soon at the hands of Felix here. I'm afraid even though he is my son I have to say that he can be a tad overzealous when it comes to his work." He started to giggle. "In fact I think it's safe to say that he really does enjoy his chosen path in life."

Jesse remained silent, all the while eyeing the XD-9 a few feet to her left. Stokes sighed and turned to face Felix.

"Well then, I suppose you better get on with it. I would say make it quick and painless but we both know that isn't likely to happen," he said jovially, relishing the chance to watch the Jackal in action.

Jesse made her move; she suddenly sprung to her feet and dived head-first at the pistol. Felix reacted first; he leapt forward, his knife raised ready to lash out but he was too late. Jesse got to her weapon first; she felt her hand clasp the grip and in one smooth movement turned and hefted the gun towards the incoming Felix, her face contorted with rage. Her hand tensed as she started to squeeze the trigger but before the hammer slammed down Stokes lashed out with a kick, knocking the gun away from its target. Jesse gasped at the retort of the 9mm pistol exploded inside the small confines of the hut, its deafening roar catching all three of them off guard. With a bright muzzle flash the Springfield spewed forth its deadly load, its trajectory taken two feet to the left of Felix. The bullet whistled past his left shoulder and punched its way through the shieling wall and disappeared into the storm. Jesse let out a scream as she fell to her side from the impact of the kick. She tried to roll but Felix was on her. He slammed his clenched fist down into her face nearly knocking her out but somehow she remained conscious. The Jackal slowly rose and loomed above her, his face sweating, his eyes bulging. Stokes took his place next to his son.

"Well that was exciting, wasn't it? Ten out of ten for effort, Mrs Reid," he said eagerly.

Jesse glared at Felix as he rained down a second blow into her jaw. She laughed and spat out two teeth, her mouth awash with blood and saliva.

"Big tough man hitting a woman!" she bellowed, her defiance growing with every second.

Felix grinned; he loved it when the carrion fought back. He dropped the lump of wood and with his left hand reached down grabbing her by the throat and in a single movement dragged her to her feet. She was on her tip toes, her hands clasped around his hand trying to release some of the pressure. She started to feel faint, her breathing becoming more sporadic, the blood unrelentingly pumping around her head. Felix smiled as he drew the knife blade towards her face. Jesse wasted no time, her survival instinct kicking in. With her last few seconds of consciousness she coughed and spat a mouthful of blood and phlegm into his eyes and at the same time raised her leg, slamming her knee into his testicles. Felix howled in pain, his body doubled, lessening his grip slightly. Jesse frantically gulped at the air, desperately filling her lungs with fresh oxygen. She kept the momentum of the attack going, unwilling to give the edge back to the Jackal. With all her strength Jesse grabbed his right hand and sunk her teeth into the flesh. The Jackal screamed, his fingers convulsed, forcing him to open them and allowing the knife to tumble harmlessly to the floor. Jesse bit down harder, her teeth touching bone. Felix counteracted by throwing a tight left hook aimed at her head. It made contact on Jesse's temple, the shockwave forcing her to release her grip; her head was spinning from the immense trauma, she was on the verge of passing out but something made her keep fighting. Again she pushed forward. Jesse let go of his hand and snaked her arms around the back of his head clasping her hands together, once locked she braced herself then with all of her force drove her head-butt full force into his face while at the same time pulling his head down towards her own, effectively doubling the impact. There was a sickening crack as his nose and cheek fractured; his eyes welled up and started to roll back in their sockets. Jesse stretched her arms out using her forearms and biceps to force his head to roll backwards then launched a second attack. Once again the force of the head-butt was devastating. Jesse screamed as Felix's face was reduced to a bloody pulp. She steadied herself as she felt his legs give way, his weight causing him to topple backwards. Jesse stepped back allowing him to stumble, then watched gleefully as he crashed to the floor. Jesse wasn't finished, her bloodlust was in full flow and needed to be quenched. She ran at him and slammed her heel into his face one last time. Jesse looked down at the Jackal and spat in his face.

"Who's the alpha predator now fucker!" she roared in triumph.

Jesse's victory and euphoria was abruptly cut short when she suddenly remembered the gun and the fact there was a third person in the room; she had to find it, she told herself. She span on her heels just as Stokes landed the heavy wooden lump directly into her face. She was unconscious even before she hit the floor.

From the blackness, shades of grey started to appear. Gradually the grey turned white, swiftly followed by other colours. Shapes started to manifest then finally her vision returned. Jesse blinked heavily in an attempt to brush away her slumber; slowly things came back to her—the fight with Felix, the Jackals and finally being struck by Stokes. She started to panic, unsure if she was alive or dead.

"Ah, you're back amongst the living, I see," said the voice.

Jesse tipped her head to her left to see from where the voice was coming. Her heart sank as the figures of Stokes and the heavily-injured Felix came into focus.

"I must congratulate you, Mrs Reid. You put up one hell of a fight; for a second I honestly thought you might win. You gave Felix here a damn good thrashing…," he paused, "…poor lad will never be a model now," he quipped.

Jesse looked around her. She was on the floor by

the fire, her legs bound with thick industrial masking tape, her hands lashed together with rope. She wriggled trying to loosen her constraints but it was of no use. She was trapped. Stokes slowly walked over to her. He hovered above her, relishing and enjoying the moment. As per normal he was smiling.

"I'm afraid we have come to the end of our cat and mouse game. You really did have us on the edge of our seats. I have to say it has been one of the best hunts I have ever been a part of…" He paused. "Well, there was that hunt in Germany that ended up with a children's hospital being burnt to the ground, but apart from that it has been spectacular." He moved closer and whispered, "I truly hope you don't harbour us any ill will. It's in our nature, you see. We can't help being what we are; all we can do is surrender to the Primitive and let nature take its course. It's not our fault we have been chosen."

Jesse stared at him unflinchingly. "Go fuck yourself…" she hissed, then moved her head so that she was facing Felix. "…and so can you, pretty boy. Bet you're really fucked off that a woman kicked your ass," she added, her contempt evident. She started to laugh, her body shaking with a mixture of fear and adrenaline.

Felix slowly rose and moved quietly towards her, his face heavily bandaged and stained with blood. He glared at her.

"Are you ready to start your journey to the Void?" he asked softly.

Jesse spat at him with as much spit as possible. It

missed him completely. Stokes took a step back, giving the Jackal room to work. Felix grinned.

"I've got something special for you," he said. "Something that I think you will love and find comforting." He held up his hand so she could see what he was carrying. Jesse tried to focus on the object in his hand, its odd shape, the colour. It was then she realised what it was—one of the antlers off of the stag from the wall mount, sharpened to a vicious-looking point, but there was something strange about it. Lashed to the sharp point was another bit of bone, it too transformed into a vicious-looking weapon. Jesse looked on, unsure what was so special about his antler.

Felix smiled. "Do you know what this is, Jesse?"

She remained silent not wanting to engage, her last act of defiance she told herself, don't give the fuckers the satisfaction. Felix chuckled, eager to explain what he had done.

"I made this for you Jesse. Of course you will recognise the stag antler but do you know what this is?" he asked again, gently tapping the foreign-looking object. He smiled softly. "It's one of your husband's ribs."

Jesse felt her whole world fall apart. She started to weep uncontrollably. She turned her head to her right to see Damien's body lying on his back, his chest completely ripped open and his ribcage exposed. Jesse wretched and vomited, her mind tumbling into the maelstrom. She had finally snapped.

Felix grinned and lowered himself on top of her

chest, pinning her to the floor. She felt his hot breath on her face, the stench of his body and the coppery smell of dried blood. She struggled again, one last-ditch effort to free herself.

"Embrace the Primitive," he whispered as he slowly inserted the twin prongs of antler and rib into her stomach.

She arched her back as the bone cut through her. She started to cough, blood bubbling from her mouth. Stokes looked on gleefully as Felix pushed the primitive weapon deeper into her then finally twisted it, yanking it to one side and causing a massive rip horizontally across the width of her stomach. Jesse wretched again as she saw her own entrails slop nosily to the floor next to her. Her body started to go into spasm; her muscles viciously contracted then released. Felix smiled as the slight waft of excrement started to fill his nostrils. He closed his eyes and thanked Jesse for her sacrifice. He would miss her, he mused silently. She exhaled softly one final time. The last thing Jesse Reid saw was Felix bending down and gently kissing her on the forehead, then darkness.

Stokes remained silent, not wanting to encroach on his son's moment. Felix slowly rose to his feet, his eyes still locked to Jesse's deathly hollow gaze.

"I am so proud of you, Marcus," he said quietly. Felix turned to face his father.

"Why are you here?" he asked, still intoxicated with the scent of death. Stokes smiled warmly and moved closer.

"I want us to be together again. It is our destiny—me to rule and you to be at my side."

Felix grinned. "You to rule and me at your side? Why shouldn't I just kill you and rule myself?" he asked, his tone low and deliberate. Stokes took another step towards the Jackal.

"Because I am your father, Marcus and I love you," he implored.

Felix looked on; he suddenly felt a burst of pride deep within, at last some parental recognition from one he secretly held dear. He smiled, basking in the adulation he had always craved.

"Then let us unite and take our rightful place at the head of the table!" he exclaimed in joyous celebration.

Stokes hefted the XD-9 and pulled the trigger; once again the retort was massive as the pistol released its deadly cargo. Felix didn't have time to comprehend fully Stokes' actions; all he saw was the muzzle flash. The professor stood gazing upon the lifeless body of Felix, a fist-sized hole where his forehead used to be. He smiled.

"Or not, as the case may be," he chuckled.

After a couple of minutes Stokes sighed and took in the gravity of the carnage littering the shieling.

"Time to head home," he whispered.

Stokes wasn't bothered about getting rid of DNA or evidence, tidying the scene or even tampering with it in any way. In a few hours he would be crowned the Order's new ruler and the police would be under his full control. From this point hence he was untouchable. The old man headed for the door with a new-found spring in his step and after one last look at the massacre exited the building and disappeared into the relentless storm.

Stokes sat back in the leather seat of the AS355 Twin Squirrel and sipped at his brandy. He stared out of the window, the blackness surrounding him. It had taken him almost three hours to walk back to the bridge and to one of the waiting 4 x 4's. The weather had been whipping in from the North, sending ferocious winds and ice-forged rain. After he had warmed himself and changed clothes he only had to drive a few miles before managing to obtain a phone signal. He had ordered the chopper back to the island and instructed them to pick him up at the airport in approximately one hour. Despite the pilots' reservations regarding the sanity of flying in such weather the lure of large sums of money convinced them that their fears were unfounded.

Stokes was a happy man with the world at his feet. The events of the past few days had been a mere blip in the greater plan. He reached for the mobile phone and punched in a number; the line crackled sharply. Stokes smiled as he was connected.

"It's me. Everything is completed. It's time to engage Operation Tyrant. I want all assets put on standby." He ended the call and tossed the phone to one side. The old man took another gulp of brandy and smiled the broadest smile he had ever produced. The time had come.

EPILOGUE

One Month Later, 0742 hrs, Somerset

The old man stirred the mug of coffee and discarded the spoon on the worktop, then slowly padded through the hallway and into the study. The room was impressive. Large, ornately hand-carved wooden bookcases lined the walls and pieces of Renaissance art hung from every spare foot of real estate, their radiance a visual treat for those special few allowed within the inner sanctuary. He gently pressed the button and took a sip of his coffee, staring blankly at the screen as his computer woke up. It was early in the morning but he wanted to get started. He had plans to make, plans that would take time and precise organisation to put into place. Everything had to be right, he reminded himself.

He drummed his fingers on the desktop, agitated that the computer was taking so long. Behind him the plush curtains had been pinned back, allowing the morning sunlight to flood the room. He turned in his chair, basking in its life-giving rays. He had never been a religious man but at that precise moment he truly believed he was being given the blessings of the Almighty himself.

Once again he turned to his computer, the cursor flashing, requiring a password. He typed out the letters and waited once more. He yawned as he ran his hand through his neatly-trimmed grey hair. To his right the thick cardboard folder remained closed and had been that way since being delivered the night before, a Post-it note stuck to the cover, obscuring the title. He had been tempted to open it but had held off until the time was right. He looked away, fighting the urge to absorb its contents. The old man shook his head. Not yet, he told himself.

The computer burst into life. He selected the required file and as the information flowed he digested every last detail. He started to cry softly but immediately wiped his eyes, not wanting to show weakness. Not now. The old man exited and retrieved another file marked PERSONNEL. He slowly scrolled down until he found the employment record he desired and opened it. A photo appeared showing the upper torso of a well-built, smartly dressed man, his face rugged, his eyes predatory. The old man smiled.

"Hello, Mr Riley," he said softly.

The file was impressive. Four years Pathfinder Platoon followed by five years Special Reconnaissance Regiment, the ultra-secret unit specialising in surveillance and intelligence gathering operations, but more recently deployment with the war on terror. Almost nothing was known about them outside of their unit. The SAS and SBS may have been well-known and publicised but these were the real deal. He read on, eager to see more. It would appear he was now working in the private sector as an Operator. No wife, no children, no ties. The old man smiled once again.

"You are going to prove extremely useful," he whispered as the expressionless photo of the mercenary stared back at him. He turned to face the file. Now was the time, he reasoned. He flicked it open and page by page digested the information. Once he was finished he closed it abruptly and snatched up the phone, dialling the number on the personnel report. He waited as the line was connected.

"Hello," came the voice.

The old man cleared his throat. "Good morning, may I speak to Mr Liam Riley, please?" There was a slight pause.

"Speaking," came the curt reply.

"Good. Sorry to phone so early but I have a job proposal for you…" he paused, awaiting a reply.

"I'm listening," retorted the voice.

The old man continued. "It will be extremely dangerous, highly illegal and in all probability you will die a horrific death, but I can assure you that I am obscenely rich and will make it worth your while. You will never have to work again."

Again there was a brief pause.

"Go on," the voice replied evenly.

"I need Wolves, Mr Riley. Wolves to hunt Jackals. I want you to hunt down a group of men who wield immense power and when you do, I want you to make them suffer, and then kill them. I want you to bring me righteous vindication. I want you to bring me justice, Mr Riley," he hissed.

There was a pause. "I will phone you on this number this evening," the voice stated, then the line went dead.

Sir Rupert DeVine replaced the receiver and smiled. He gently touched the file containing all police reports and the pathologist's report appertaining to Jesse Reid's death.

"It's okay, baby girl. Daddy will make them pay," he said softly.

Made in the USA
Columbia, SC
03 May 2017